DECEIVE
ME NOT

JURA MACLEAN SHERWOOD

To Chick,
Best wishes,

Jura MacLean Sherwood

PublishAmerica
Baltimore

First printing

ISBN: 1-4137-2400-0
PUBLISHED BY PUBLISHAMERICA, LLLP
www.publishamerica.com
Baltimore

Printed in the United States of America

THIS BOOK IS FOR MY CHILDREN:
LINDA SHERWOOD SCHUBERT, PETER SHERWOOD,
JONATHAN SHERWOOD AND LISA SHERWOOD FRANA

ACKNOWLEDGEMENTS

This story was a long time in the making and without the help and encouragement of my loyal friend, Rosalie More, and my faithful critique partners, Cathy Ullrich and Tom Farnsworth, it may still be sitting on the shelf.

I owe thanks to my husband Bill, harsh critic but loyal fan. Thanks also to Marsha Markham for always being a willing "first reader."

DECEIVE ME NOT

PROLOGUE

LONDON, DECEMBER 1940

This bloody war!

Bob settled himself more comfortably in the bed next to Lyn, his wife. He wasn't tired. As usual, making love had left him wide-awake.

In the few hours remaining before he had to return to his ship, he wanted to think of things more pleasant than the war. But everything reminded him of the vast changes he'd seen in his family since his last leave, just months earlier.

Lyn said Barbara's stutter was just a stage that three-year-olds go through. But the way his daughter constantly picked at her fingers didn't seem normal to him. Little Babs was so excited for Father Christmas to come next week and bring her toys and sweeties. But she wouldn't have much of a Christmas this year. She wouldn't even have her daddy here.

The baby appeared the least affected by the constant air-raid sirens, bombings, and being carried back and forth to the air-raid shelter. As Lyn pointed out, "'e don't know the difference, do 'e? It's all 'e's ever known—air raids and bombing and being shoved into that bloody gasmask."

Bob snuggled Lyn closer and she put her head on his shoulder, disturbing the covers. He tucked the blanket around her shoulders and, as he did so, kissed her forehead. She threw her leg across his stomach and wrapped her body around him.

With the blackout curtains securely in place, the room was as dark as a bat cave on a moonless night. Bob could only envision Lyn's hair, the colour of a new copper farthing, cascading across his chest. He stroked her bare thigh and his hand continued to roam over her lithe body as he imprinted every curve of her on to his memory. He sighed with admiration. Bloody marvellous, she was. It was hard to believe she'd borne three children.

He pulled her as close to him as he could, still amazed that this true daughter of London's East End, with her caustic Cockney tongue, was his wife. She used her colourful language to berate everything about the war. She swore at Hitler, the rationing, the air-raid sirens and the bombings that kept her awake day and night. Her world was literally crumbling around her, but as Churchill would have said, she "carried on with fortitude and stamina."

Most of London's population had either moved out of the city or into the underground train tunnels. Lyn had made it clear that she "wouldn't live in a 'ole in the ground like a bloody rat." To her, that was tantamount to admitting the Germans were bombing the British into submission—and *that* she absolutely refused to do. She wouldn't even go to the shelter in her own back garden until an air raid had actually started. Bob suspected that her bravado was her way of dealing with the nightmare, and that she deliberately stayed awake in the shelter to keep watch on her remaining children. She'd already given up one child to the war. Her eldest child, her son by her late husband, had been evacuated and she hadn't yet recovered from the loss. The toll it was taking on her was evident to Bob. Her beautiful blue-green eyes no longer sparkled, and she'd lost weight.

He'd tried to make the most of the time he had at home with his family, but a week was hardly long enough to get to know his children all over again. The baby was a lovely little lad. All chubby and snugly, he was. Bob took every opportunity to change the baby's nappies, feed him and cuddle him to sleep.

Bob moved his shoulders, aware of the ache in muscles unused to throwing a three-year-old up in the air. He didn't really mind. Babs' squeals of laughter were worth it. He smiled at the memory of her giggle when he played hide-and-seek with her.

Babs had been so shy of him the first day he got home. Once she got used to him, she trailed after him wherever he went, like a little shadow. She even tagged along "to help" when he went scrounging through bombed sites for lumber.

The garden of every house in and around London was dominated by an identical corrugated steel structure roughly eight feet long and six feet wide, with a curved roof. The protection against falling bombs was known simply as "the Anderson." Nobody guessed, when the government had provided the bomb shelter fifteen months earlier, that they would be spending half their lives in it. To many people it became a challenge to make it as comfy as possible.

After Bob had sunk the steel shelter into the earth so that only the top half remained above ground, he'd packed earth up the exposed sides and piled it two foot deep on the rounded top. It acted as insulation and further protection. There remained just one problem. Every time an exploding bomb's blast vibrated the ground, dirt filtered down through the joints. He sighed with frustration wishing he'd been able to find enough boards to tack up a ceiling. As it was he'd barely had enough time to stop the water seeping up through the frozen earth. He would have put in a proper floor, but others had plundered the bombsites of discarded rubble before him, and he dared not go into the wrecked houses. Looting was punishable by death.

During a previous leave he'd found enough lumber to build bunks for the kids. Lyn shunned a bunk for herself, but she'd been glad of the wooden lining he'd tacked on the inside walls of the shelter. So, even if it remained cold and damp, it gave the illusion of being warmer. He wished he could have done more. It was difficult to return to his ship leaving Lyn and the children with such primitive protection against the cold and continuous air attacks.

He had little enough time to spend with his family, and so as not to waste a minute of it, he'd tag along every day when Lynn took the children to buy food. He'd push the baby in the pram along the rubble-strewn streets, past what was left of his old local pub, the George and Dragon, to the shops. The shops? That was a laugh. There weren't many shops left, and when they did find one still standing and in business, they'd have to wait for hours in the queue and hope an air raid didn't interrupt before they were served. That had happened two days before when they were waiting for fish. He still smarted at his own embarrassment.

The siren sounded and he'd turned the pram and been ready to run to the nearest public shelter, but nobody in the queue moved, except to stamp their feet against the cold. He'd pulled on his wife's sleeve. "Come on, Lyn, let's get out of here."

She'd given him an incredulous look. "Wha'? And lose me place in the queue? No' on your nelly."

"But it's an air raid." As the planes rumbled closer, the engines vibrated the earth beneath his feet. In the distance great billowing clouds of black smoke roiled in the reddening sky.

"Well of course it's an air raid. But we'll be all right. They're after the docks again." Lyn sounded impatient.

Bob stared at the tired, impassive faces of the women and old men in the queue and felt like a fool. The fishmonger continued his patter as he wrapped slices of cod or whole herring in newspaper, and only occasionally glanced up as a bomber roared low overhead.

Goering's promise to devastate the heart of the British Empire was no empty threat. The *Luftwaffe* had bombarded the capital with incendiaries and land mines, sometimes several times a day, since September. The *blitzkrieg*, the Germans called it.

Bob had more colourful and descriptive names for it.

He dismissed the thoughts with a sigh of resignation and snuggled Lyn closer. She burrowed deeper into his embrace and Bob could tell by her breathing that she was still awake. He kissed the top of her head. "Lyn," he whispered. "I want you to take the little 'uns and get out of London."

"Do wha'?" She raised her head to face him in the darkness. "Where would we go? London's our 'ome." A lot of the neighbours had already gone from the city to beg shelter with relatives in the country, and many older children had been evacuated to farms and country villages.

"I know, pet, but you don't 'ave family 'ere no more. I was thinking maybe you could ask your Auntie Dolly if she could find you a place near her in Littlingham. You'd be safer there, an' I wouldn't worry so much about you."

Lyn put her head back on his shoulder and snuggled closer to him while she caressed the nape of his neck. "Don't worry about us, luv. I don't see 'ow old 'itler can keep this up much longer."

Bob groaned inside. What was the use? It never seemed to occur to her to wonder how much longer London could take the bombardment.

"Well, God help dear old London if he does invade," Bob sighed. "But in any case, you an' the little 'uns would be much better off out of the city." He hugged Lyn to him. "Do you realize this is the first night since I've been home that we've actually spent the night in our own bed instead of that bloody Anderson shelter?"

The words barely left his lips when the all too familiar siren's wail split the cold December night. In the distance the steady beat of powerful engines drove the enemy bombers closer.

"You spoke too soon, luv." In one quick movement Lyn left his arms and threw off the bedclothes.

Bob jumped up and switched on the light. He slipped into his trousers. By force of habit he reached for the dickey, but he threw it aside, and pulled on his uniform jumper.

"I hate that bloody 'itler." Lyn threw a flannel nightie over her head and wrapped a wool dressing gown around her small frame. With well-practiced movements she pulled on heavy socks and shoved her feet into big leather slippers. "Can't even give us one bleedin' night's peace. And they'll be back in the mornin' an' all," she grumbled, furiously tying the dressing gown sash into a knot at her waist.

The coal ration didn't allow them to keep a fire going all night in even one room, and Lyn had learned from her nightly trips to the Anderson to put the children to bed in their one-piece padded siren-suits.

The planes roared overhead, starting their bombing run on the nearby docks along the Thames. The bone-shaking vibrations sent fine white plaster dust cascading from the walls and made the light fixture jerk like a marionette on a string.

Lyn bundled the baby into blankets and Bob wrapped Barbara in a big eiderdown. Switching off the lights, he turned on the shrouded torch to guide them out the back door; showing light was a deadly national sin, indelibly marked in the British consciousness.

He opened the back door and was struck by a blast of frigid air and a searing pain in his foot. "Oh Christ!" In his haste he'd forgotten to put on his shoes and had stepped on the shattered windowpanes strewn across the frozen ground.

How the hell does Lyn do this night after night and day after day?

The night sky glowed crimson through a heavy haze of smoke. Flames from the burning dockyards shot sparks skyward like a Roman candle at a Guy Fawkes commemoration.

A second wave of bombers roared in, bringing another load of incendiaries to add to the inferno. Anti-aircraft shells streaking toward the marauders added their thunderous tumult as London writhed in another night of burning agony.

The bitterly cold ground stung Bob's feet as he picked his way to the steel refuge. He tucked Barbara into the top bunk against one wall of the air-raid shelter, and taking the baby from Lyn bundled him into the lower one. Each night this week they'd played out this scene, and it still amazed him that the children didn't even wake up.

Bob's hands shook and the noise made his ears ring. In the confines of the shelter he was helpless and vulnerable. At least with his gun crew on the deck of his ship he could fight back.

I have to get outside.

He put his mouth close to Lyn's ear and yelled to be heard over the pandemonium. "I'm going back for my shoes and greatcoat, then I'll go and see if I can 'elp the lads on the rescue squad." Lyn nodded without showing surprise. He did the same thing during every air raid.

Lyn snuggled the blankets around the baby and kissed his forehead. By spitballs of light outside, she could see the baby's eyelids flutter as he sucked furiously on the Binky clamped between his rosebud lips. Babs' small brow tightened into a momentary frown as each explosion vibrated through the steel shelter. Lyn tucked the covers more closely around her little daughter and kissed her cheek. The children had escaped into the safety of sleep.

Satisfied that they were as safe and warm as she could make them, Lyn grabbed a thick wool blanket for herself. She pushed aside the heavy canvas curtain covering the entrance to the air-raid shelter and climbed the steps to the outside.

Wrapped in the blanket, she stood momentarily staring out at the blood-red sky. Flames backlit the billowing smoke flecked with red-hot cinders. As often as she had endured this ritual, she could not keep her hands from shaking. Adjusting the blanket she settled into the old deck chair next to the shelter opening.

Above the constant clanging of fire bells, she strained a practiced ear to tell if the engines droning overhead were "ours" or "theirs."

Flames from the burning houses silhouetted her husband emerging from the back door of their home. Lyn watched him race down the alley and join a group of men outlined against the fires. Through voices hoarse with smoke and frustration, they yelled unintelligible instructions to each other, while they dug at the base of a collapsed house

From her vantage point, Lyn watched a probing searchlight catch an enemy bomber in its beam. Another searchlight joined it and together they played and teased their piercing light over the threatening intruder. Gunners on the ground fired shell after screaming shell at the hapless plane. The lumbering craft ploughed on through the flak, miraculously avoiding the guy wires tethering an umbrella of barrage balloons floating like great silver whales.

A nearby ack-ack gunner found his mark. Lyn held her ears against the deafening roar. Her blood raced. Her yell of approval disappeared into the sounds of battle as the aircraft blew apart.

"One, two." Lyn counted the parachutes blossoming into the beam of the searchlight. Only two. The rest of the crew must have perished when the plane exploded. Her heart softened at the realization that she had just watched men die. But she steeled herself thinking of the thousands of Londoners who would die tonight because of those faceless men in the machines above her.

Men who came in waves of bombers night after night and day after day, spewing incendiaries that snapped and crackled like heavy footsteps in a dry forest, as they blanketed everything below in mantle of white-hot cinders.

Like a bursting firework, a brilliant orange flame suddenly stained the sky, followed by the unmistakable deep rumble of an exploding land mine. Lyn thought the horrendous noise had surely woken the little ones. She threw off her blanket and jumped to her feet. In two leaps down the steps she reached her children. But her babies slept on, scowling and sucking. She secured the covers around their shoulders before she crept back up the steps to the outside.

The roar subsided. The surviving bombers, having dropped their deadly cargo, had fled back across England and were by now crossing the English Channel to France. But the fires they left behind would light the sky and keep the night alive for hours with the sudden detonation of delayed action bombs.

A helmeted air-raid warden hurrying down the alley peered over the fence and stopped to call out to Lyn. "All right there, missus?"

"Yea, ta." Lyn's ears rang and her voice sounded peculiar to her, as though she yelled down a tunnel. "Jerry didn't 'alf do a job tonight, didn't 'e? Many casualties?"

"Too true. Albert Square took a direct hit." The ARP Warden peered down at her. "Better stay put. We've got a UXB over the back here." He indicated the street behind him with a jerk of his head.

An unexploded bomb could take hours to defuse. Lyn debated whether to wake the children. It seemed a shame to disturb them now that most of the noise had stopped. She left them in the shelter and returned to the house to pack Bob's kit and prepare his breakfast. An air raid was no excuse for a sailor to miss his ship's sailing, and she knew that Bob would be expected to get there by any means available.

He returned home just before dawn. His smoke-reddened eyes glistened and he didn't appear tired. Lyn knew that look. She'd seen that same adrenalin-induced exhilaration in others who had fought fires all night and dug with their bare hands to rescue the living and retrieve the bodies buried under collapsed buildings.

"Better look lively, luv." She kissed his blackened cheek. "You just 'ave time for a quick wash-up. I'll get your breakfast on."

Ten minutes later he came to the table clean, shaven and dressed in a fresh uniform.

Lyn set his plate in front of him and wiped her hands on her apron, then pulled his collar straight. "Cor blimey! You got a bit too close out there, didn't you?" She indicated his singed eyebrows and blisters forming on his forehead.

"Gawd, Lyn, it was a real basket out there tonight. Albert Square didn't 'alf catch a packet. Took out the whole right side of the street." He grimaced and turned to his breakfast of baked beans on toast.

The one-note wail of the all-clear sounded.

"Thank Gawd for tha'." Lyn splashed milk into Bob's cup and poured in the tea. They'd made it through another night of living hell. "The trains will be running now. You should be able to get back to the ship in plenty of time, luv." Lyn planted a kiss on the top of his head.

She left him finishing a second cup of tea, and went to retrieve her children from the "'ole in the ground."

Half an hour later, standing in the open doorway, Bob held his daughter in one arm while the other encircled his wife. Lyn snuggled their baby son. They'd said their good-byes, now he bent to kiss Lyn.

"Promise me you'll get out of here soon." He tightened his hand on her waist for emphasis.

"I promise. I'll write to Auntie Dolly today and let you know where we are."

Bob hugged his children and slid Barbara to stand on the ground. One last kiss, then he stepped outside and hefted his kit bag onto his shoulder.

The stench of smoke and sulphur clung to the early morning mist. It would hang about for hours stinging eyes and burning throats, never really dissipating before the bombers came again.

Bob picked his way through the still smouldering rubble. The bell-bottoms of his trousers brushed against the piles of bricks and mortar, swirling dust onto his shiny black shoes.

Taking comfort in the sweet smell of her young son nestled in her arms, Lyn fought to hold back the tears burning her eyes.

Beside her, Babs picked at her fingers, softly crying, "D...daddy, d...don't go."

Lyn watched Bob making his way down the road and agreed that he was right. Only her own stubbornness at not wanting to admit defeat kept her in London, putting up with this madness. She had no relatives in the area that she knew of. God alone knew where her father was, or even if he were still alive. *Besides, I wouldn't know 'im if I fell over 'im.* Her mother was dead and so was old Granny Chandler. Auntie Dolly was the only one left and she lived in the country where there were no bombings.

Suddenly the prospect of moving to Littlingham seemed a brilliant idea. An excited shiver ran down Lyn's spine. She hoped she could find something to rent in or near the village, but not too close to that miserable old bugger, Uncle Charlie. He was always moaning about the noise and the mess the kids made. Still Auntie Dolly loved them and they loved her. Maybe Babs could have that cat she was always on about, and the baby could breathe real fresh air. He'd been congested ever since he was born and the doctor said it was the city and the constant smoke and dust from the bombings that affected his tiny lungs.

Bob turned once more and waved before he disappeared around the corner.

Lyn watched her husband until he was out of sight then she sagged against the door jamb. She was tired beyond measure. She settled the baby more comfortably on her hip and took Barbara's hand.

"It's still early. Let's all have forty winks, shall we, Babs? And when we wake up Mummy's going to write a letter to Auntie Dolly."

ONE WEEK LATER

Babs snuggled deeper in her blankets trying to block out a noise more terrible than she had ever heard. The room felt lovely and warm.

The deep growl of the air-raid siren climbed to an ear-splitting wail. Near Barbara's bed, the baby screamed in perfect pitch but stopped for breath long before the siren began its downward spiral

"Come on, get up, Babs." Mummy's voice urged Barbara out of her warm bed.

"Is it time to get up and go visit Auntie Dolly in Littlingham?" Barbara stretched and rubbed her eyes.

"Not yet, luv. In the mornin'." Mummy stripped the covers back. "Hurry, Babs. This one's a bad raid. The house is burning and we have to get out."

Babs opened her eyes. A fire burning through the common wall lighted the room and she could see into the next-door neighbour's.

"Babs, for Gawd's sake, get up. We have to get to the shelter. I can't carry you both."

Mummy used to carry her to the shelter before Bobby came.

"Oh Gawd, here comes another wave of the bastards." Babs had never heard Mummy sound so frightened.

The steady drone of approaching bombers rattled the windows and shook the plaster from the walls and ceiling and covered everything in the room with choking white powder. It filled Barbara's nostrils and made her cough. She covered her ears to shut out the noise of the big guns, but it still hurt. Then above it all, long streaks of sound like one of Mummy's silk petticoats ripping—and the side of the house was sucked out into the flames.

With the biggest noise Babs had ever heard, her whole world blew apart.

Then it was very quiet.

Babs tried to open her eyes, but bits of dirt got in and made them water. Her head hurt so much. Something was heavy on her chest and tummy. Her nose was stuffed but she could still smell the smoke and bad eggs. Mummy's hair was across Babs' face so she couldn't see anything. She wanted to cry and tell Mummy she was squashing her, but the baby's arm was across her throat and when she opened her mouth Mummy's hair got in.

Babs was very cold, and so sleepy.

CHAPTER ONE

USA 1985

Barbara McNab peeled the last potato and dropped it into the pan of water. She dried her hands and began tearing lettuce into the salad bowl.

Tigger, her little dog, let out an excited yip alerting Barbara that John's car had driven into the driveway. Tigger raced through the flap in the kitchen door, and as Barbara watched through the window, he arrived, predictably, before her husband got the car door open.

John came into the kitchen wearing a grin like the proverbial cat that'd swallowed the canary.

"Hi," Barbara glanced over her shoulder at him.

"Hi yourself, beautiful. Hmm…is that my favorite dinner I smell cooking?" Dodging the prancing dog John came up behind Barbara and kissed her neck.

She turned and, holding her wet hands away from him, gave him a quick peck on the cheek. "You're looking very pleased with yourself. What's up?"

Pulling his tie loose he headed for the bedroom. "The new plane is being unveiled at the end of next week," he spoke over his shoulder.

"Next week?" Her voice rose with the question. "Oh, no!"

He stopped, turned and slowly walked back. "What's the matter?" The dog followed him.

"You'll be on vacation."

"Sure. But, we don't have plans to go anywhere." He shrugged. "So we can still go to the ceremony."

"We?"

"You'll come with me, won't you?"

"John...I've made other plans for us. I was going to tell you later this evening."

"What? Tell me what?" He tossed his tie on the kitchen counter.

"I...I've made reservations for us to go to England for two weeks. We leave on Tuesday." She absently wiped her hands on a towel.

He scowled while he vaguely unbuttoned his shirt. "You did what?" The scowl turned to a look of angry disbelief and he yanked his shirt out of the waistband of his pants. "Dammit, Barbara! What were you thinking?"

He hardly ever called her Barbara. In fact, his whole reaction was uncharacteristic.

"It was to be a surprise to celebrate our anniversary." She couldn't hide the disappointment in her voice.

"Yeah. One hell of a surprise! How come you didn't ask me first?"

"It wouldn't have been a surprise then, would it?" She snatched the tie off the counter and tossed it at him. "Don't put your clothes here, where I'm trying to fix dinner."

He snagged the tie. "No, but it would've saved you the trouble of having to cancel."

"Why should we cancel our plans? After all, this is pretty short notice about the plane, and your vacation was scheduled weeks ago."

"Actually, I knew a couple of weeks ago, I just didn't know the date until today."

"So are you suggesting postponing your vacation?"

"No, I'm not suggesting that at all." He turned on his heel and headed back towards the bedroom. "I'm saying cancel the plans. I have no intention of going to England."

"Why?" She'd expected him to balk, at first. It was his nature to need a little coaxing before accepting a disruption to his usual routine. But she hadn't anticipated a flat-out refusal.

He stopped in the bedroom doorway. "Because I have no reason to. Nor do you, Barb. We have no family there anymore."

"What has not having family there got to do with it? I planned this to celebrate our anniversary." She choked back her disappointment, then suddenly brightened. "I could change the reservations and we could go the following week, after the unveiling."

"Dammit!" His tone was pure exasperation. "What part of this don't you understand? I don't care to go back to England—ever!"

"And I don't care about your damn plane." She immediately regretted saying that. He loved his job and had made a very good living for them. She really did care.

On the verge of tears she slam-banged a pot on the stove top and swore under her breath when the noise made her jump.

He turned and narrowed his eyes as he stormed back to her. "You're serious, aren't you? You're so wrapped up in what you want you can't even pretend to be pleased for me."

"Stop it! This has nothing to do with the new plane. It has to do with a subject you've always avoided. The subject is you—and your inability to discuss your parents or your brother or sister. And you think by never going back to England you can continue to avoid dealing with it."

"Oh, for Chri'sake!" he mumbled. Tearing off his shirt he marched back to the bedroom with the dog at his heels.

She followed. "I always told myself it didn't matter to me. I figured I didn't need to know about your family, but I was wrong."

"What's this?" He snorted, spinning to face her. "The infallible Barbara McNab admitting she was wrong about something?"

His controlled sarcasm made her lose what little composure she'd retained. "Don't try to change the subject," she screamed, grabbing a small decorative pillow from the bed and hurling it at him as hard as she could. "I'm not going to let you get away with it."

The pillow plopped at his feet. He calmly picked it up and tossed it back on the bed.

His self-control only frustrated her more. She threw herself down on the bed and buried her face in a pillow, but her mind raced. She had to get control of her emotions—to bring this to a head, now, once and for all. She sat up.

He'd replaced his slacks with jeans and was fastening them while he studied her with a worried frown.

"John." She spoke with all the calm she could muster. "If you can't face your hang-ups by yourself, please think about getting some therapy."

He pulled a tee-shirt over his head. "What?" His face broke through the neckband with a smirk. "Me? See a shrink? You've got to be kidding."

"Just go and get some counseling. Somehow you must come to grips with whatever has bothered you for all these years. You've got to find out what it is."

"I don't know what you're talking about and I doubt you do either. Just because you've had a couple of sessions with a shrink, doesn't make you a Freud."

"How dare you throw that back at me?" Her anger boiled over. "You're the one who encouraged me to go. To find out why I was having those nightmares." She buried her face in her hands and sobbed.

"Oh, geez. Barb. I'm sorry." He sat beside her on the bed and tried wrapping his arms around her. "I was totally out of line."

"Leave me alone!" She pushed him away and stood.

Their love had grown deeper over the years, and in some ways she loved him more than ever. But she could never understand how he could sometimes be so stubborn and irritating. Well, she could be just as stubborn.

Storming out of the bedroom she stuck out her chin and yelled back at him. "To hell with you, John McNab. I'll go to England by myself."

Dinner was a disaster. All her work to make it so special and romantic to soften his reaction when she told him her plans for celebrating their thirty-year wedding anniversary fell in a heap of resentment and unsaid accusations.

Too hurt and stubborn to initiate a truce, she ignored his attempts at casual conversation. After dinner she went to the bedroom to vent her frustration in tears. He followed her.

His deep sigh was audible even over her crying. "I'm sorry I blew my stack. But you understand why I don't want to miss the unveiling ceremony, don't you? I've put my heart into this project."

"Sure." She stood up and wiped the tears from her cheeks. "And I'm willing to compromise, but apparently you're not." She attempted to brush past him.

He reached for her hand and pulled her close, wrapping his arms around her and snuggling his face in her hair. "I'm really sorry to spoil your surprise, Barb. Don't stay mad." He grabbed a tissue from the bedside table and dabbed the tears from her eyes. "Tell you what. I've been thinking. Maybe we can salvage something out of this. You could go ahead as you planned. Then, after the ceremony, I'll join you. I can get the travel people at work to change my ticket."

"Really? That would be great. But I don't know, John. What will I do there all by myself?"

He kissed her forehead. "It's just for a couple of days and it will give you the chance to do that genealogical thing you talked about." He rested his forearms on her shoulders and grinned down at her. "Then we'll walk together along the Embankment and sit and watch the Thames as we did thirty years ago."

His voice had softened as it always did when they spoke of the time they'd spent together in London when they were young.

She smiled through her tears. She couldn't resist him now any more than she could then.

—⚘—

On Sunday the family gathered for a *bon voyage* barbeque. While the grandchildren played on the lawn, the adults sat around the picnic table munching olives and potato chips. The talk was all about the trip to England.

John and Barbara's only daughter, Janet, was a striking, self-assured young woman. She had pale, creamy skin like her mother's, but her eyes were dark blue with thick black lashes, and she'd inherited John's blue-black hair. She was also the most vocal of the three children.

"But, Mom!" Jan handed her baby to her husband and wiped the burp off her shoulder. "What are you going to do in England all by yourself?"

"Oh, didn't Mom tell you? She's taking me to keep her company." Donald, the youngest and the only fair-haired of the three, reached for another potato chip. He had a smirk on his face and his bright blue eyes twinkled at his sister.

"Are you, Mom?"

Barbara chuckled at her daughter's indignant expression. "Janet! Can't you tell when he's pulling your leg? To answer your question, no, I'm showing no favoritism. I'm going alone and I've got plenty to do before your dad joins me. Then I'm afraid we won't have enough time to do and see everything I've got planned for us. We'll probably have to stay longer."

"Hey, wait a minute." John flipped a hamburger on the grill and turned to her. "We agreed to two weeks. That's all."

And he isn't at all happy about even two weeks.

Even the kids picked up on it. The knowing glances they gave each other didn't escape Barbara's notice.

In the distance a fire alarm began to wail and Barbara shuddered. She'd come a long way with the help of a therapist, but she still reacted to loud noises and cringed inside at the sound of sirens. She lifted Laurie, Jan's older child, onto her lap and stroked the tiny girl's bright coppery hair away from her aqua-colored eyes. She kissed the top of the child's head taking comfort in the gesture.

"I don't understand why you want to go anyway," Jack, her firstborn said. "You both left England so long ago, and it's not as if you have family there." He reached for another olive and popped it into his mouth. He was so like John in looks and temperament.

"That's what I've been trying to tell her, Jack." John turned and glanced at his wife.

Barbara took a deep breath and let it out in an exaggerated sigh. "Believe it or not, this started out to be nothing more than a vacation. Your dad isn't able to get away until the end of the week so we decided I should spend a couple of days at the record center to try to find my birth certificate." She wasn't about to let her kids know how heated the argument had become before she and John had reached that decision.

"But, Mom," Jack persisted. He draped his arm around Chris, his blonde, willowy wife. "You know you can do genealogical research without leaving this country, don't you? A guy in the office goes to Salt Lake City and researches in the big library there."

"It's not the same thing at all, Jack. I wrote to England for my birth certificate. Twice, in fact, and they told me they couldn't find it. Since neither Dad nor I know anything about our families, I really need to start from scratch."

"So what you really want is to go dig up the past. The anniversary celebration thing was just an excuse?"

"Of course not. Dad and I will still have plenty of time over there to celebrate our anniversary. Besides, aren't you kids curious about your heritage? Someday your children might want to know who their ancestors were."

"I have to admit I've wondered about our grandparents." Jan, always the more emotional child, was typically the most intuitive.

Barbara smiled at her daughter. "There you are, then. And I think it will be fun for your father to see Littlingham where I was born and raised. And I'll bet some of the old dears who used to come to the bakery where I worked are still around."

"You're kidding! You left there what…thirty two years ago?" Donald chuckled. "That little village where you were born has probably been swallowed up into the nearest city by now. And I'll bet the bakery has been replaced by a parking lot. Don't you think so, Jack?" Donald never missed an opportunity to get a rise out of his older brother.

Jack, the architect, was very sensitive about tearing down buildings and replacing them with high-rise apartments and parking garages. But this time he ignored his impish brother.

Michael, Jack and Chris' little boy, raced around the garden with a balloon on a string with Tigger at his heels.

Suddenly, Michael tripped behind Barbara's chair and, with a loud bang, the balloon burst.

Barbara screamed and her whole body shook uncontrollably.

Startled, Laurie screeched, "Mommy, Mommy," and stretched out her arms to her mother.

Jan plucked the terrified child from Barbara's trembling grasp and comforted her in a hug.

The men scrambled to Barbara's side, but Jack was the first to reach her. "It's okay, I'll take care of her," he spoke over his shoulder to his father and brother. He wrapped his arm around Barbara's shoulders and led her to a wooden bench on the far side of the garden. He sat beside her. "You okay, Mom?"

"Yes, Jack." She was shaking all over. "I feel so stupid when I do that."

"What happened? You haven't done that in a long time. You used to do it a lot when we were kids. You'd scare the hell out of us."

"I know, honey. I'm sorry." She exhaled a sigh of frustration. "I've started having nightmares again, too."

"What are you doing about it?"

"I've had a couple of sessions with a therapist. All she could determine is that I'm suffering a form of post-traumatic stress syndrome. She described it as something like combat soldiers go through. Isn't that the most stupid thing you've ever heard of?"

"But why? I mean, why does it happen?"

"The therapist thinks it's something related to my childhood, but I assured her that couldn't be. I had a perfectly normal, quiet childhood. The only noise I can remember frightening me when I was very young was when my da would whack his cane on the table."

"So, what are you supposed to do about it?"

"Her suggestion is to go back to England where I grew up and try to find the source."

"So that's why you want to go to England?"

"No. I mean…well, partly. But the primary reason was for Dad and me to celebrate our anniversary. The other was an after-thought."

"And he doesn't want to go at all. You know that?"

"Yes, well, we've reached a compromise. I'll go on Tuesday and he'll join me next weekend."

She looked up and smiled at John as he approached and handed her a glass of water.

By the time the aircraft landed at Heathrow very early Wednesday morning, Barbara was already lonely for John. Except for the overnights in the hospital for the birth of her babies, this was the first time they'd been apart. The eight-hour time difference between California and England kept her from phoning him as soon as she arrived in London.

The travel agent had booked her into a small hotel within walking distance of the General Registry Office. So, eager to begin her research, Barbara ate a hearty English breakfast and walked to St. Catherine's House. She had a lot to do before John joined her. Genealogical research would not be his idea of a second honeymoon.

Lifting the huge index books from the shelves and replacing them proved arduous work. After four hours her shoulders ached and it was obvious her birth had not been recorded. With little trouble, she found John's parents' and her own parents' marriages recorded in the indexes. But then came reality. An apologetic young clerk assured Barbara that a three-day wait between applying for the certificates and actually getting them was standard procedure. Until then, her research was at a standstill.

Disappointed and at loose ends, she went to find the London of her youth.

The pale sun held little warmth on the late spring day. She hugged her light jacket around her and wandered along Kingsway.

She made her way eventually to the Embankment. Across Parliament Green, along the Thames, the Gothic spires seemed timeless. Near the House of Commons, Churchill's statue walked out of a block of bronze. Big Ben hadn't changed, nor Westminster Abbey. But the people were different. London seemed to be a city of foreigners. Barbara reminded herself that she was a foreigner now, too—and a homesick one at that.

That night, she phoned John and told him she couldn't pick up the certificates until Monday—after he arrived. "Guess where else I went today."

"Where?"

"Along the Embankment. Remember it?"

"How could I forget…?"

His voice drifted and she knew his visions mirrored hers…wandering the familiar area as young lovers. She changed the subject before she burst into tears. "Are you finding enough to eat?"

He chortled. "You're kidding! You left me enough food in the freezer to feed an army." His voice suddenly softened. "Barb, I miss you so much. I didn't realize how lonely it would be without you." His gentle voice was still filled with love for her after all these years. "Hey, listen, sweetheart. Instead of hanging about for four days, why don't you have the certificates mailed and come on home?"

She laughed. "You're transparent, John, my love. I miss you too, but I want to see this through."

"Well, okay. Have a good weekend."

"What do you mean? You're coming on Saturday, aren't you?"

"That was the plan. But now I can't come until early next week."

"What? Why?"

"Don't be mad, sweetheart. There's a problem with the intake on one of the plane's engines. It should be worked out in a day or two."

"And just exactly when did you plan to tell me this?"

"I just told you." He exhaled in a grunt. "Barb, the Navy's waiting for this plane. I'll join you just as soon as I can."

"Well, okay." She knew she sounded as disappointed as she felt, but it was impossible to stay mad at him when she loved him so much. "As long as you're still coming."

"Yeah. No problem. Next week for sure." His response sounded flippant.

She detected a joy in his voice as though he were glad for an excuse to postpone the trip. She'd never understand his reluctance to even talk about England, or what secret he was hiding about his childhood. She wasn't even sure he knew, but if he did, she'd never forgive him for not being honest with her.

The prospect of spending a weekend alone in London held no appeal for her. If she was going to learn anything about the past and what had happened during her early days to create such violent nightmares, she was going to have to return to her childhood home. The empty weekend seemed made for a visit to the village of Littlingham.

CHAPTER TWO

—❦—

LITTLINGHAM 1985

The bus crossed the cobblestone square and trundled away. Belching rudely, it disappeared between the high hedges lining the road to Stanton.

Barbara wrinkled her nose at the lingering diesel fumes and set her suitcase beside her on the uneven cobbles. Shading her eyes against the shattering sunlight, she glanced about. She could almost have stepped back in time to a late spring morning more than thirty years before. Inexplicably a mood came over her. Not of melancholy exactly, but tinged with a feeling of something…incomplete.

The village was precisely as she remembered it, but strangely diminished. Seen through a child's eyes, Littlingham had been spacious, but now, the same array of little shops surrounding the village square appeared narrow and crowded.

The sudden backfire from a delivery lorry crossing the square startled Barbara and left her momentarily shaking.

She picked up her suitcase and turned to the ancient Black Swan Inn, so familiar in her youth. It stood resplendent in a coat of fresh whitewash. Spring flowers filled the boxes below each window.

Outside the public house, a couple of old men sat on a bench in the sun, as old men had done for generations past, drawing down on pints of dark-brown beer.

Barbara forced a quick little smile at the pair.

"Mornin'. Lovely weather," said one, touching gnarled fingers to the bill of his flat cap.

The other wiped foam from his upper lip with the back of his hand and acknowledged Barbara with a silent nod as she passed on her way to the inn door.

Inside the gloomy interior of the Black Swan Inn, she blinked several times to adjust her eyes to the bar room, lit only by shafts of sunlight from the small windows. The reek of stale beer and long discarded cigarettes stung her throat. Conversation, punctuated by bursts of laughter, hummed through the swirling haze of smoke.

The barman, talking with a customer, stopped polishing the glass in his hand and looked up as she approached. "What can I do for you, love?" His bushy eyebrows rose with the question.

"I'd like to rent a room for the weekend, please," Barbara said.

"Right you are," he smiled and looked past Barbara. "Annie!" he bellowed.

A woman serving a couple at a nearby table responded. "Just a mo'."

"My missus'll be right with you, love." The barman resumed scrutinizing the glass against the light and gave it a further vigorous buffing.

A few minutes later Barbara had signed the guest register and was lugging her suitcase up the well-worn stairs in the landlady's wake. She couldn't recall having ever been in this part of the inn as a child, but she remembered its smell. A familiar mix of age and furniture polish, it reminded her of wet wool socks drying near a heater.

At the end of the dark hall, Annie opened a door and the landing was suddenly flooded with sunlight. "Here we are, then." The landlady's pink cheeks bunched up in a smile as proud as if she were showing off the Royal Suite at the Savoy, instead of the neat little bedroom.

The sunlight streamed through a single dormer tucked beneath the sloped ceiling. A plump bed and a small dresser filled most of the room. Hefty exposed beams and stout wall supports attested to the great age of the structure.

"Will this be all right then, dear?"

"Yes, thank you. It's fine."

"The loo's just down the hall." The woman nodded in the direction of the bathroom. "Let me know if you need anything." At the door she turned. "We'll be serving lunch until two." She closed the door behind her.

Barbara bounced once on the edge of the bed and, flinging her arms over her head, threw herself back on the soft eiderdown cover. If only she could fling her loneliness away as easily.

Yesterday, when she realized she was at loose ends for the weekend, revisiting Littlingham had seemed like a brilliant idea. At this moment she wasn't so sure. The people she'd once known here would surely have moved away, or died by now.

But, this is where my roots are and here is where I must look for my childhood. The question was, where to begin?

She stood, and walked to the open window, catching her reflection in the dresser mirror. Large grey eyes stared back at her, fine crows feet at the corners. At forty-nine, her English complexion still glowed on pale-pink skin and, thanks to Duke, her hairdresser back home in California, her dark auburn hair showed no hint of the white invading at her temples.

At the window, a long unexpected sigh escaped her. If only John were here.

Below the window, Littlingham dozed under a clear sky but clouds gathering on the horizon threatened rain. The view of the village square from above re-emphasized the Lilliputian reality compared to her memories.

Turning from the window, she peeled off her cowl-neck sweater and replaced it with a striped shirt matching her tan slacks and navy-blue blazer. She touched-up her lipstick and wiggled her toes inside navy low-heeled pumps. She decided they'd be comfortable enough for roaming around the village. With a last glance in the mirror she made a mental note to halt the further spread of her hips just as soon as she returned home to the United States.

Downstairs in the pub she ordered a Ploughman's lunch.

"How about a table in the garden?" the landlord suggested. "It's such a lovely day."

The garden was beautiful, but Barbara was not in the mood to appreciate the scented purple hyacinth or blossom-laden apple tree. Bees fumbled among the golden forsythia and birds flitted through the shrubs, but it was the mourning dove that echoed her melancholy.

Annie brought Barbara's lunch. "There you are, m'dear. I'll just charge it to your room. Enjoy."

The fresh crusty roll gave off a tantalizing aroma. Barbara bit the hard shell and sank her teeth into the soft middle. Only one bakery made a roll like it—Nelson's, nestled between Le Coiffure Hair Salon and June's sweetshop-cum-post office on the village square. The knob of creamy yellow cheese had a remembered local flavour, as did the sweet-tart Branston pickle.

Eager to stroll out into the village to rekindle old memories, she drank the last of the cold hard cider and brushed the crumbs from her lap.

She checked her watch and calculated the eight-hour time difference between England and California. She'd call John later when he was getting up for work, and tell him where she was.

Crossing the cobbled street to buy flowers for her parents' graves, she saw her reflection approaching in a shop window. *More memories*. It was here, as a twelve-year-old, that she'd first noticed the rounding of her hips and the hint of breasts beneath the bodice of her cotton frock. She had been too thin then and her thick curls had made her head seem large for her body. These days, Duke kept her hair thinned and styled so that the curls framed her face instead of covering her eyes. "You have such lovely eyes, Mrs. McNab, let's not hide them," Duke had said while he fussed over her.

Passing the chemist shop and the newsagent, she stopped in front of the greengrocer's where colourful plastic buckets jammed full of spring flowers stole half the walkway.

She bought two bouquets of bright red tulips, yellow jonquils and early-blooming irises and dawdled to the far end of the village square. Tucked in a corner, almost hidden behind a barrier of shrubbery, stood the twelfth century grey stone church. Its stained glass windows were dark in the shadows. Its weathered spire contrasted against the blue sky.

The wrought-iron gate leading to the graveyard squeaked open under Barbara's touch. Threading her way between mossy tombstones dappled with shadow, she stopped near a large oak tree. Two handsome granite stones marking her parents' graves stood beneath its branches.

Surprised and puzzled, she studied the markers replete with facts she'd never known about her Mum and Da. Who could have provided the information that Mum was born in Lambeth, and that Da's birthplace was Llangareth? She'd only known he was from Wales. In her mind's eye she could still see him wearing his flat chequered cap, sitting in the big shabby armchair by the fire, dour, staring into the flames.

She placed the flowers on the graves and smiled, imagining Da yelling in his singsong Welsh accent, "Flowers! Flowers cost money, don't you know?"

Yes, Da. But let me enjoy this extravagance.

She sat on a nearby bench and rekindled memories of her parents. Remembering her kind, patient mother who always intervened with Da on her behalf, Barbara's eyes brimmed with tears.

When Barbara was very young Da used to scare her with his bellowing, emphasized with a crash of his heavy oak cane on the table. But as she grew older she came to know that his anger was not directed at her, but with the frustration of agonizing pain and constant poverty.

The sound of gravel crunching beneath someone's feet roused Barbara from her reverie. A young woman in her early twenties searched among the tombstones as she strolled the gravel path. She suddenly halted in front of one grave and peered at the headstone. The woman was too far away for Barbara to get a good look at her, but there was something vaguely familiar about her.

Since she had left Littlingham long before this woman would have been born, Barbara dismissed the thought that she might know her.

Barbara left the churchyard through the lynch gate, and turning away from the village square, ambled up a familiar narrow lane. Wild primroses smothered the banks and mingled their fragrance with the heady scent of a large purple lilac, hanging over a hedge. She stopped and breathed the scents that evoked indelible memories from her childhood.

At the top of the lane a row of stone cottages stood, unaltered in a hundred and fifty years. Barbara paused at the gate of one cottage. Except for a shiny new pram parked outside the cottage door, her childhood home had not changed. She fought the silly urge to peek over the hedge where so often she'd seen the top of Mum's steel grey hair as she worked down among the roses.

She strode to the bright red door of the next cottage and lifted the brass knocker. Memories flooded back.

It had been in this house that she had found comfort in Mrs. Hilton's arms when Mum died. A sudden pang of remembered shock and sorrow enveloped her. Coming home from school one blustery afternoon in early January when she was eleven, she had found Da morose and angry—his usually brooding dark eyes, red and moist. Mum had been ill for over two years, but Barbara had never contemplated a life without her.

In this same house she had sobbed in Mrs. Hilton's arms when Da died six years later. Barbara bit her lower lip. That was thirty-two years ago, and she could still recall how bewildered and terrified she had been at the realization that she was alone in the world.

Before the echo of the rapping doorknocker had faded, a small, rotund woman with white hair and eyes like two ripe blackberries opened the door as if she had been watching Barbara approach. Barbara knew her at once.

"Hi, Mrs. Hilton."

The old woman's brow knitted.

"I'm Barbara McNab. You don't recognize me, do you? I used to live next door, here." Barbara gestured towards the cottage that had been her home.

The woman's mouth formed a surprised "O," and her twinkling black eyes disappeared into folds of wrinkles as she broke into an enormous smile. "Oh! Oh, yes. It's Barbara Thomas, isn't it?"

"Yes, that's right." Of course, Mrs. Hilton knew her only by her maiden name. "You do remember me then?"

"Oh, yes, I do. Come in, please. What a surprise." She stepped back inviting Barbara into the neat little parlour.

Some of the furniture had been replaced since Barbara's youth, but the smell of fresh polish hadn't changed. She had obviously arrived in the midst of the annual spring cleaning. Freshly laundered white lace curtains hung at the sparkling windows and the brass martingales around the fireplace shone. The pillow covers on the couch were clean and crisp and the rugs looked as if they'd had a thorough beating.

"I hope I'm not intruding. I stopped on an impulse, really. I wasn't even sure you still lived here." Barbara felt she should explain.

"No, no. Of course you're not intruding. How nice to see you again. I've often thought of you and wondered what became of you." Mrs. Hilton chuckled. "By your accent, I think you must have lived in America for some time now."

It had never occurred to Barbara that anyone in the village would care about her after she left Littlingham. She hadn't ever thought to write, even to her next-door neighbour, who had always been so kind.

Mrs. Hilton showed her to a comfortable chair, and sat down opposite. "Do tell me what you've been doing all these years. The last I heard of you was when you left to join the air force."

Barbara opened her mouth to speak, but Mrs. Hilton suddenly popped up out of her chair and started out of the room, saying over her shoulder. "Just a tick. I'll put the kettle on and we'll have a cuppa, shall we?"

"I'd like that, thank you."

The old woman came back and sat down. "It will only be a minute. Now. What have you been up to?"

"Well, I only stayed in the WRAF for two years then I got married and went to live in the United States. My husband, John, and I have three children. And," she laughed, preening with exaggerated pride, "I'm a grandmother three times over, too."

"How lovely!" A shrill whistle interrupted. "There's the kettle. Shan't be a minute." Mrs. Hilton scurried out of the room.

The clink of china sounded from the kitchen. Barbara looked about the small room that had been a cozy haven when she was a child and a fairy castle when she and Mrs. Hilton's daughter, Mary, had played at being princesses.

On the mantle piece were the treasures of the old woman's life—a Toby jug with a sprig of white heather for luck protruding from the top. Beside it was a photograph of an attractive woman whom Barbara recognized immediately as her little playmate Mary, now all grown up.

She stood up to inspect other photographs more closely. One picture was of Mary, a man and two children, all laughing. Another was of Mary's two brothers in a snapshot with what could only be their families, grinning for the camera. The last photo Barbara remembered from long ago—the portrait of a young, dark-haired Peggy Hilton, her chin tipped proudly, holding the arm of a fair young man whose laughing eyes belied his solemn posture. This was George Hilton who had gone to serve his country at the first call. He'd survived Dunkirk only to be captured when Singapore fell. George did not survive the harshness of the Japanese prisoner-of-war camp. Beside the treasured photograph, Peggy Hilton proudly displayed George's medals.

A slight movement caught Barbara's eye. A very large black and white cat lay curled up in a sagging armchair in the far corner of the room. She gently touched his head. "Hello, big fella."

He gave a loud "purr-ump," and unwrapped his tail from across his nose to look up at her with big amber eyes.

Mrs. Hilton bustled into the room carrying a tray holding a cozy-covered teapot, two delicately patterned china cups and saucers with matching milk jug and sugar basin. "I see you've met Reginald," she nodded indicating the cat. She set the tray on a small polished table between the two chairs, and left the room, returning with a plate of biscuits.

Barbara scratched Reginald under the chin before she resumed her seat.

Mrs. Hilton poured tea into both cups and offered Barbara milk and sugar. She settled back comfortably into the chair. "Help yourself to a biscuit."

"Thank you. I noticed your photographs. Mary is a pretty woman. How is she?" Barbara said and sipped her tea.

Sadness crossed the old woman's face and her black eyes glistened with unexpected moisture. "She died last year. Cancer."

Barbara's insides lurched. "Oh, I'm so sorry." *Damn! I didn't mean to upset the old woman. Maybe coming here wasn't such a good idea after all.*

Mrs. Hilton lowered her head. "Thank you," she whispered. She shook her head as if dismissing a painful thought and smiled at Barbara. "Now, tell me what are you doing back in Littlingham?"

"Well, I arrived in England a couple of days ago to do some genealogical research at Saint Catherine's House." She was glad to change the subject. "I didn't know there would be a three-day wait before I could pick up the certificates I needed. I can't get them until Monday." She shrugged. "London is an unfriendly place when you're alone, so I thought I'd come and see if the village of my birth had changed since I left. Thought I might get a bonus and find someone here who remembers my parents. Lucky me, I found you." Barbara sipped her tea savouring the rich flavour.

"Your parents?" A puzzled expression spread across the old woman's face. "Do you mean Dolly and Charlie Thomas?"

"Yes, my mum and da."

The old woman shifted in her chair. She took another sip of tea and eyed Barbara over the top of her cup. She blinked several times and swallowed. Seconds became a full minute before she finally spoke again. "But they weren't your birth parents, my dear." Her voice was barely above a whisper.

Barbara's spine stiffened. The cup in her hand clattered on the saucer. "What do you mean?"

"I remember the day Dolly brought you here from London. During the war, it was."

"Brought me here?" Barbara gave a short uneasy laugh. "I was born in the house next door…Wasn't I?"

"I'm sorry," Mrs. Hilton said. "I assumed you knew." Her cheeks had turned bright pink.

Barbara stared at the old woman's troubled black eyes and shook her head in silent disbelief. Her brain spun with the tangle of thoughts falling all over each other as she tried to make some sense of Mrs. Hilton's inference. *Can it be true? Peggy is getting on in years. Maybe she has me mixed up with someone else. Perhaps she's a little senile.*

Mrs. Hilton's lip quivered and her eyes filled with tears. "I'm so sorry, Barbara, my dear. I had no idea you didn't know the Thomases had adopted you. Dolly always intended to tell you, I know. I…I just don't know what to say." She leaned forward and poured them each another cup of tea and handed Barbara her cup.

Barbara sipped the steaming liquid, but had trouble swallowing it. She fought the bile rising into her throat, determined to take control of herself. She carefully placed the cup and saucer on the table, sat back in the chair and folded her arms. "Perhaps you could start at the beginning, Mrs. Hilton. And tell me all you know, please."

CHAPTER THREE

The ragged clouds gathered, blotting out the blue sky and hiding the late afternoon sun. The impending rain matched Barbara's gloomy mood, and she shivered. She uncrossed her arms and settled more comfortably into her chair. "How did the Thomases come to adopt me?"

Peggy Hilton's cup and saucer clattered and it took both her hands to set it firmly on the table. "It's just not on, you know," she said. "It's most annoying." She waggled her shoulders with indignation. "I'm not blaming you, mind. Dolly should have told you."

Barbara bit her lip. "I'm so sorry you've been put in this position, Mrs. Hilton, but I'd really appreciate you telling me anything you can. If I wasn't born here, how old was I when I came from London? I must have been really young, or I would have remembered."

"Oh, dear." The old woman stroked her cheek and seemed to be gathering her memories. "It was such a long time ago. So much has happened since then. I don't know if I even can recall all the details."

"Please, Mrs. Hilton, try. I really need to know."

The woman nodded. "And you deserve to know." She shivered and pulled her cardigan tightly around her.

"It was just a few days before Christmas, nineteen-forty. The Battle of Britain was over and the blitz was in full swing…"

—8—

LITTLINGHAM, 1940

Peggy leaned her folded arms on the kitchen windowsill and stared out at the pale wintry sun in a crystal blue sky. The naked branches of the old apple tree whipped back and forth as if tormented by an unseen hand, while the voice on the wireless droned the usual gruesome news, *"...London again last night. Incendiaries scattered over a wide area set the city on fire. The flames, visible from as far away as southeast London, lit the way for wave upon wave of enemy bombers. The Prime Minister, speaking from number ten Downing Street, said..."*

Snapping off the radio, she silenced the dispassionate report. She had a rule; if you can't mend it, don't dwell on it. She could do absolutely nothing to stop the war or to prevent the destruction of London, and saw no reason to torture herself by listening to the reports. She pulled off her slippers, jammed her feet into rubber Wellingtons, and buttoned her old wool coat over her pinafore. She hoisted a basket of wet laundry onto her hip and opened the door. An icy blast struck her and almost wrenched the door from its hinges. Adjusting the heavy load, she yanked the door shut and struggled against the wind to the clothesline.

"Hello, Peg." Dolly Thomas peered around her bed sheets billowing on the clothesline like galleon sails.

"G' morning, Dolly. You sound bright this morning. Gawd, isn't it cold? I almost wish it would snow, just so it would warm up a bit." Peggy rubbed her freezing hands together and reached into the wash basket pulling out her sons' socks to peg on the line. "All ready for Christmas, then?"

"Nah. You know we don't never do much. There's 'ardly anything in the shops anyway. But I've got lovely news." Dolly peeked from behind her flapping pillowcases. "My niece Lyn, you know my sister's gew? Well she an' her little 'uns are coming on Saturday."

"Ooh, I'll tell my Mary. She'll be so happy to have young Babs to play with. I expect the kiddies will enjoy a day away from London." Peggy flicked a pair of wet, wind-driven knickers away from her cheek.

"Yes, that's what Lyn said in her letter. She's fed up with the bombing day and night, and tired of practically living in the air-raid shelter. It must be awful, mustn't it? She wants to move down here, near me. Coo! I'm that excited!" Her voice trembled. "I think Lyn must be lonely too. Her husband's gone back to sea again. Only had a short leave, 'e did."

"Let's hope it's a bit warmer by Saturday, eh?" Peggy blew on her ice-cold fingers before plunging them once more into the basket of wet washing. "What's Charlie think about it?"

"Dolly," called a gruff voice from inside the cottage. "How about a cuppa tea, then?"

"Speak of the devil. Must go, Peggy," Dolly mouthed confidentially, then raised her voice. "Coming, Charlie."

Peggy nodded. She knew Charlie. A miserable old bugger, if ever there was one. Wracked with pain, he was always grumbling and complaining, especially when Dolly's niece brought the children to visit. Peggy was sure he wasn't nearly as excited as Dolly at the prospect of having his Saturday routine disrupted.

As it turned out, more than his routine was disrupted. His whole life would change.

Saturday dawned gloomy and bitterly cold. Mary sat on the window seat and watched for Barbara to arrive. As the morning dragged on with no sign of her little friend, she ran outside to wait. When she got cold, she came crying to Peggy.

"Mummy, I'm frightened. The Thomases' house is all dark. What's wrong with it?" Mary pulled Peggy by the hand outside to see the cold, forlorn-looking little cottage, with tightly drawn curtains.

Peggy was as puzzled as the child. "I don't know, love. They don't look as if they got up this morning." That made little sense to Peggy knowing how eager, on this day of all days, Dolly would be. She would certainly have got up extra early.

Peggy wiped the tears from her daughter's eyes. "Never mind, my pet, I'll make you a nice cup of hot cocoa to cheer you up." She kissed Mary's cold cheek and led her back into the house. "Perhaps Babs is just late. You know how the trains get delayed when London's had an air raid."

Later that morning, Peggy hurried to the village before the shops closed for the weekend. Several of her neighbours had gathered outside the butcher's shop. Stamping their feet against the frozen pavement, they talked earnestly to one another. As Peggy approached the gossiping knot of women, one called out to her.

"Peg, did you hear about Dolly Thomas' niece?"

"What about her?" Peggy clutched her coat across her chest and buried her chin in her collar against the biting wind.

"Killed last night in an air raid, she was. Her and her kiddies."

"Oh, my God!" Peggy grabbed her mouth and swallowed the lump rising in her throat. "So that's why the curtains are still drawn at their house. How did you hear about her niece?"

"Old Bert Pushkin delivered the telegram to Dolly this morning. He told Mabel Frost."

"Oh, poor Dolly. I must go to her." Peggy left the gossiping women to the freezing wind, and hurried to comfort her friend.

She found Dolly huddled on her bed with her arms wrapped around herself as if to keep her shaking body from flying apart.

Charlie was his usual disagreeable self, showing no compassion for his wife. "Don't carry on so, woman. Death comes to all of us eventually, and we're in the middle of a war, don't you know? What do you expect? Not getting my dinner ain't going to bring 'em back."

Peggy jammed her hands on her hips and shouted, "Charlie, you're a callous old sod. Give some consideration to Dolly for a change. All you ever think about is yourself."

"You shut yer gob, woman," he growled.

"Oh, Charlie, you'll never change." They'd been neighbours long enough to banter without either taking offence. "Don't worry, you won't starve. I'll make sure you get your meal." She turned and put her arm around Dolly's shoulder, easing her off the bed. "Meantime, come to my house, Dolly. We'll have a cuppa and a natter."

Dolly meekly allowed Peggy to lead her to the cottage next door, and seat her at the kitchen table. Silent, she stared through the window at something far distant, while Peggy bustled around making tea.

Peggy set the cups of tea on the table and sat facing Dolly. "Now, my dear, tell me all about it."

Dolly wrapped her hands around the teacup and stared over the rim. "You know Peggy, Lyn and her family were my whole life. I can't believe they're really gone." She set her cup and saucer on the table in front of her and covered her unattractive face with her large, square hands. Her anguish exploded in piteous sobs that shook Peggy's kitchen table.

Later that day, Dolly received another telegram, one that would alter her life. It was true that Lyn and the baby were dead, but Barbara had been found alive, buried in the rubble that had once been her home. She had severe head injuries and was in a deep coma. Convinced that the little girl would recover, Dolly was over the moon with joy.

Despite Charlie's loud objections and complaints about the money Dolly was spending on train tickets, she made regular visits to the hospital. For four

long months Barbara remained in a coma, and before she came out of it, a
further tragedy struck. The ship bringing her father home to England to make
arrangements for her was torpedoed and sunk with all hands.

CHAPTER FOUR

LITTLINGHAM 1985

From behind her freshly washed lace curtains, Peggy watched Barbara descend Primrose Lane. When the younger woman reached the bottom of the hill and rounded the corner disappearing from her view, Peggy turned away from the window and let out a disheartened sigh.

She turned on the television and shuffled slowly to the kitchen, returning with a bowl of rabbit stew. She set her dinner on the table beside her chair and sat in front of the television. Absently buttering a piece of bread, the idea of eating suddenly made her queasy and she pushed her meal aside. Feeling as spent as the elastic in a pair of old knickers she exhaled noisily and abandoned her attempt to watch *Coronation Street.* She snapped off the telly even though it meant missing an episode of her favourite show.

Reggie, apparently thinking the gesture was an invitation, jumped up on her lap. Peggy found comfort in stroking the cat's head.

"Oh, Reggie. I feel so sorry for that poor woman. Imagine finding out at her age that you were adopted. That would take some getting used to. What is she now, almost fifty years old? But you know, Reg, I don't remember her actually being adopted. Officially I mean."

The cat arched his back, taking full advantage of Peggy's fingertips running vaguely back and forth along his spine.

"I answered all her questions and told her all I could remember, but I still have the oddest feeling that I've forgotten to tell her something. I wonder what it could be?"

Reacting to Peggy's mutterings, Reggie leaned into her hand and, kneading her thigh, closed his eyes and purred.

"Still, it was funny that," Peggy mumbled. "Barbara never remembering anything about when she first came to Littlingham. She must have been at least three. Maybe even four."

Peggy's hand slipped below the cat's chin and she idly scratched his jaw. Lulled by Reggie's rhythmic purring, her thoughts drifted back to a time more than forty-five years before.

"I remember the day Dolly Thomas found out Barbara was coming. It was about four months after Barbara was injured, so it must have been in the springtime... Yes, that was it. I remember now. A lovely warm day in April."

LITTLINGHAM, 1941

The village of Littlingham quietly basked in the spring sunshine. Peggy took advantage of the beautiful weather to tend her herb garden and admire her spring flowers.

The four identical little cottages strung together at the top of Primrose Lane shared the same walls, but the layout of the rooms was reversed, so that Peggy's kitchen door was right next to the Thomases'. A fence separating the gardens had long since disappeared under a thick laurel hedge giving each of them privacy of sight, if not of sound. On this sunny day, when everyone had their doors open to the fresh air, Peggy heard the hum of conversation between Dolly and her husband in their house. Suddenly there was a clatter in the kitchen and Charlie's voice rose in anger, accentuating his Welsh dialect.

"This is my *youse* and I say who lives *yere* and what goes on *yere*. And don't you forget it, Dorothy Thomas."

"Well, for once I'm going to have my say. And I say Barbara will come and live here."

"We'll see about that," Charlie bellowed.

"Well, I've already told the hospital I'll have her, so there's nothing you can do about it."

Peggy stood transfixed, uncomfortable eavesdropping, but she couldn't announce herself now without embarrassing them. She pressed her body against the trunk of the gnarled old apple tree.

"I don't want a child around the *youse*, making noise. And what's more—"

"Oh," Dolly interrupted him. "It's not the noise that worries you, it's that it might cost you an extra couple o' bob to keep her. I know that's why you denied me a child of my own. It's the money. It's always the money."

Peggy heard the sobs in Dolly's voice as she continued venting her frustration at Charlie.

"Well, old clever clogs. Let me tell you. This little girl means more to me than anything in the world. She's been through hell, and either you accept her with good grace or I'll take her somewhere else. Then just you see if you can find yourself another woman who'll work as hard and as cheap as I do!"

Dolly must have stormed out of the kitchen and back into the parlour, because her last words faded.

Peggy continued to hear raised voices, but could not make out what they were saying. She bolted across the garden into her own kitchen and quietly closed the door.

Later that day, a beaming Dolly told Peggy over the garden fence, "Barbara's finally recovered. She's come out of the coma and she's coming to live with Charlie and me."

"Oh, Dolly, I'm so pleased for you." Peggy really meant it.

"Yes, the only thing is, she doesn't remember anything from before the bombing. Not even her Mummy or Daddy. Nothing. Doctor said it's just as well though, if she forgets what happened."

"The doctor is probably right," Peggy reassured her friend. "She'll bounce back all the quicker and have a happier life without the memories."

Dolly enjoyed few pleasures. One was her victory garden where she grew all the family's vegetables for both winter and summer. Her hollyhocks were the envy of the village and her roses usually won prizes at the annual church fete. The other was Barbara.

Barbara arrived in the village shy and bewildered. She was small for her age and frail after being hospitalized for almost four months. Her translucent skin emphasized her large, wary eyes peering from under thick auburn curls. She took immediately to Dolly and clung to her as if she knew instinctively that she could trust Dolly to care for her. Having the child to love had transformed Dolly's life, too. Homely, she had remained gentle and unassuming to everyone, until it came to defending Barbara.

Peggy often heard arguments next door. Charlie would yell, making more noise than Barbara and Dolly put together.

"No, you can't have no bleedin' cat," he'd bellowed. "A cat costs money to feed, don't you know?"

"Oh, Charlie. Let her have a kitten. It wouldn't cost that much." Dolly's soft voice had cajoled and eventually persuaded him. Barbara got her kitten.

When Barbara pretended she was a ballerina, the old misery had yelled at her, "Stop acting like a bloody whirling dervish." The sound of Charlie's heavy cane crashing onto the table as he emphasized his point, and the short scream from the child, echoed through the thin, common walls of the cottages.

Dolly could be heard calming Barbara and venting her anger at her husband. "Leave the child alone. She's just happy. But that's something you wouldn't know about."

Peggy remembered the terrible row Charlie had put up when Dolly wanted a little celebration for Barbara's fifth birthday, the first one she would spend as their daughter. Dolly asked Peggy to come over while she put it to Charlie, thinking he wouldn't throw a tantrum if the neighbour were there. She was wrong.

"What the *yell* do she need cake for?" he'd bawled.

"I just thought it would be nice to have a little party for her." Dolly wrung her large square hands.

"Party! Party! Where the bloody *yell* do you think I'd get money for a party?" His face turned purple with rage. With his usual scowl, he'd resumed his hooded stare into the fire.

After all the intervening years Peggy still recalled, in vivid detail, how she and Dolly had pulled a good one over on Charlie. She chuckled to herself.

Peggy had plucked at Dolly's sleeve and silently encouraged her out of Charlie's hearing.

"You have all the ingredients for a cake?"

"Yes," Dolly nodded. "I didn't eat my egg this week and I've kept back a bit of marg." She checked off the items against her big red fingers. "I saved points for the extra flour and I traded my sweet ration coupons for eight ounces of sugar. I've got everything to make a cake but I wouldn't be able to put icing on it." She shrugged her shoulders and turned her hands palms up.

"That's all right," Peggy patted Dolly's arm. "I've got a bit of marzipan for the top. It can be my birthday present to her."

"Ooh ta, Peg. I'm ever so grateful." Dolly's thin lips curved up in a smile.

"Come on then," Peggy said. "What are we waiting for?"

They made the cake and immediately had the party right there in Peggy's kitchen. They had no candles for the cake, but when little Mary and her two brothers sang "Happy Birthday," Barbara's smile lit her whole face. She was bashful, but obviously thrilled to be the center of attention.

Dolly had given her a new blue frock with gold-color buttons. Barbara beamed and hugged her Mum, raining kisses her all over face.

Dolly rarely laughed aloud, but embarrassed, she'd giggled and called Barbara "a soppy girl." Their mutual affection for once broke through Dolly's reserve and Barbara's shyness.

"How did you manage the frock?" Peggy was continually impressed with Dolly's ingenuity.

Dolly confided that she'd sold her clothing ration coupons for the money, and used Charlie's clothing ration for the fabric. In another nearby town, she'd found a shady scrap-metal dealer who traded her the brass buttons for some fresh vegetables from her garden. She was very chuffed with herself for having pulled the whole thing off without Charlie's knowledge, and secretly made the dress right under his nose.

Peggy wasn't really surprised. Dolly was amazingly resourceful and the best barterer and coupon trader in the area, with sources as far away as Stanton. Many of her best customers were the "girls" who plied their trade on the streets there and were always in need of clothing coupons. Of course, what Dolly had done was quite illegal, but in those war-ravaged times, even the most law-abiding Britons found it necessary to bend the rules a little.

By the time Barbara was eight years old everyone seemed to have forgotten that she hadn't been born in Littlingham.

She became a familiar sight flying down Primrose Lane with Charlie's voice echoing behind her. "Don't slam that bloody door!" But it was usually too late, and the thud of it slamming shut would cut Charlie off in mid-sentence.

Barbara's thin face seemed dwarfed by large grey eyes, topped off by a mop of unruly auburn curls. Her skinny, bird-like legs pumped her along, while the tail of her tatty coat spread out behind her like wings as she ran. She'd bound up to the gossiping women with a collective, "Hello," then hurry from pram to pushchair talking to each baby and toddler. "How is young David today then, Mrs. Martin?" Without waiting for an answer, she'd speak to the toddlers who knew her freckled face. Chucking a baby under the chin, she'd say, "Hello, Jill, how is your cold today?" The little ones responded to her with coos and gurgles.

By 1944 the war seemed as though it had always been with them. Littlingham wasn't bombed or bothered by air raids like London or Coventry, but they still had to make sure the blackout curtains were in place each night, and their food and clothing rations were just as meager. It became common practice, as clothes were outgrown, to pass them to a smaller child. Some like Barbara seldom had a new piece of clothing, except for some new knickers or a pair of socks from Father Christmas, and fortunately never knew the difference.

Charlie's only pleasure seemed to be his pint down at the Black Swan. As regularly as clockwork every Saturday night at seven o'clock, after his weekly bath and shave, he'd put on a clean shirt, his same heavy wool pants, seedy old tweed jacket, polished black boots, and the chequered cap he wore winter and summer, indoors and out. Leaning heavily on his stout cane, he'd limp off down the lane.

At ten o'clock, when the pub closed, Dolly waited outside to bring him home. A couple of pints were enough to deaden Charlie's pain. He'd become almost happy and he'd sing and laugh on the way home. More than two pints and he'd fall asleep somewhere along the way. He'd become lost on more than one occasion. So Dolly began meeting him and seeing him safely the few hundred yards to their door.

When Peggy was younger she'd occasionally go to the pub for a bit of company. She was there the first night Barbara came to get Charlie.

The door inched open and Barbara peered tentatively around the unfamiliar bar, searching the faces of the men playing a lively game of darts. Finally spotting her da sitting at the far side of the room, laughing and talking with a hand from Billy's farm, the little girl clenched her lower lip in her teeth and tiptoed up to him. She plucked at his sleeve. "Da, it's time to go home now."

Startled, he'd turned to look at her, his heavy brows rising into his forehead. "Where's yer Mum?"

"Mum isn't feeling well. She sent me to get you."

"A'right then." He swallowed the last of the thick brown liquid and got painfully to his feet. "Give us a *yand* then." Barbara steadied him and handed him his cane. She pulled his arm around her skinny neck and led him to the door.

"G'night, Charlie," called the bartender, and Charlie lifted his cane in acknowledgement. The door shut behind them.

It was the beginning of a Saturday night ritual...

LITTLINGHAM 1985

Peggy roused herself from her memories, suddenly aware that it was dark and rain beat against the window.

She prodded the cat awake. "Go on and do your business, Reggie. Then we'll go to bed." The cat stretched and yawned then, encouraged by a further nudge from his mistress, padded out of the room.

The flap in the kitchen door banged and Peggy nodded with satisfaction. He'd waste no time out in the rain.

Grunting at the pain in her arthritic joints, Peggy levered herself out of the chair, picked up the dish of cold stew, and carried it to the kitchen. She scraped the congealed lump into the bin and had just begun her nightly ritual of closing up the house when the cat flap thudded, signaling the cat's return.

"Good boy, Reggie. Let's go to bed now." She gripped the banister ready to pull herself up the stairs, and then stopped. There it was again! Just for an instant the thing she wanted to tell Barbara teased her brain. Panic gripped her. She'd admit she was getting old, but until now she'd always had a good memory and she was afraid of losing it.

She waited in the darkness until her fear subsided, then she concentrated—and was rewarded. A photograph belonging to Barbara. Someone had given it to Peggy after Barbara left for the air force. But what was it a photograph of? And more important, what had she done with it?

CHAPTER FIVE

LITTLINGHAM 1985

Barbara's head throbbed and her eyes ached. She thumped her pillow into a ball and buried her face into it. If only she could sleep. She was sure everything would seem better after she had rested. She straightened her pillow and threw herself onto her back once more, staring up at the ceiling. Tears dribbled from the corners of her eyes and into her hair.

The rain had stopped during the night and a glimmer of moonlight, playing hide and seek around the clouds, created deep shadows in the corners of her little room at the top of the Black Swan Inn.

She'd been so engrossed in her afternoon with Peggy Hilton that she'd forgotten to call John until it was too late. She never liked disturbing him at the office and what she had to tell him was something he needed to hear away from the office gossips. By the time he would have been home for the evening, she'd been too upset to talk.

Her eyes brimmed again, and irritated with the state of her emotions she climbed out of bed. In the predawn chill she rubbed the gooseflesh prickling her upper arms. Pulling on her robe she wrapped it around her and curled up on the window seat hugging her knees to her chest.

She cursed the time difference between California and England. She really missed John and desperately needed to talk to him.

The hint of daylight turned the landscape purple but had not yet reached the cracks and crevices of the village square below the window. Under a single streetlight a patch of wet cobblestone glistened. A light twinkled in the distant hills. Then another. The farmers' day had begun.

The first rays of sun to penetrate the receding clouds held no warmth. Barbara shivered and turned back to the bed. Telling herself she'd call John in an hour, she snuggled under the eiderdown—and slept for several hours.

USA 1985

From the depths of sleep, John heard the sharp trilling. The phone rang for the third time before he fumbled the receiver to his ear.

"Hello?" He yawned, still half-asleep and barely conscious of the long-distance hum.

"Hi, honey," Barbara's voice lacked its usual exuberance. "Sorry about the time. I meant to call you before you went to bed, but I overslept."

Her voice sounded different somehow, as if distorted by the overseas connection. No. After thirty years, John could tell when something was amiss. He sat up, immediately alert. "How you doing, Barb? You okay?"

"Yes, I'm fine, just drained." Her voice cracked. "No, damn it. I'm not okay. I'm forty-nine years old and I've just found out my parents weren't my parents!"

"Honey, what are you talking about?" He gripped the receiver between his jaw and shoulder and scoured the sleep from both eyes with his knuckles. So far she wasn't making much sense.

"I was adopted." She sniffled then spoke in quick little bursts. "I lost my whole family in the war. Just like you."

"What? What do you mean?"

"You know. Your mother died in an air raid. So did mine. My baby brother died, too. But I was rescued. I must have lost my memory. Then my mother's aunt and uncle adopted me."

He squinted at the bedside clock. Midnight. He'd only been a sleep about an hour. "Slow down. How'd you find out all this stuff?"

"I'm in Littlingham. My old next-door neighbour told me."

She rattled on recounting her whole conversation with Peggy Hilton. He tried to concentrate, but she was wound up and spoke so quickly he lost the thread a couple of times.

"John, do you realize this must be the reason for my nightmares? Peggy Hilton said I went through lots of air raids, so I guess my sub-conscious remembers all the noise and the sirens and all. But I'm really ticked at my mum and da. I wonder why they never told me." She seemed to choke then cleared her throat. "Old Mrs. Hilton couldn't remember anything about my father. Or rather, she never met him."

John tensed. "What about your father? What happened to him?"

"He was in the navy and his ship was torpedoed."

In the ensuing silence, John's heartbeat resonated like thunder. What Barb was telling him sounded terrifyingly familiar.

"John? You still there?"

He swallowed. "Yeah." He took a deep breath. "Yeah. I'm here. You okay, Barb?"

"I guess so. It's been such a shock. It still hasn't sunk in. Oh God, John. I wish you were here. I really need you." There was pleading in her voice. "How soon will you get here?"

He wanted to wrap her in a hug—to comfort her and be comforted by her. They'd always prided themselves on being there for each other, and now when she really needed him, he was thousands of miles away.

"Barb, this is no time for you to be alone. You need to be with me, and the kids, not all by yourself in a hotel. Why don't you forget the research thing for now and come home?"

Her quick intake of breath was audible. "You aren't coming, are you?" Her voice held a note of resignation, but he could tell she was on the verge of tears.

"It doesn't look as if I can get away right now. I'm sorry, Barb." He was feeling like a traitor deserting her when she needed him the most. "Come home and maybe we could go back together again, sometime."

"No. I don't think that will ever happen." She drew in a deep breath. "I came looking for answers. Instead I've got a whole new set of questions. I think I should stay and try to find out who I really am."

When she'd stormed off to England without him, he'd thought he could handle it, but he could not have imagined how much he'd miss her. "Geez, Barb, you can't mean that. It could take one hell of a long time."

"I realize that. But knowing what I do now, about being born in London, and having been adopted, I think it's important to dig deeper. If the therapist is right, I could be free of my nightmares and anxieties forever. That would be so wonderful."

He heard the yearning in her voice. "That would sure make me happy, sweetheart." She was a different woman without the anxieties and at that moment, he hated himself for not being there to support her. "I wish I could be there with you, but I can't right now. Still, I hate for you to be there all by yourself."

"John, I don't want to be here alone, and I don't want to do this by myself, but it looks as if I'll have to." Her voice took on an edge. "And I hope when I'm through, I won't have any hang-ups over *my* family."

Damn, she was back to that subject again. He knew he'd really screwed up about the England thing, and he really regretted the way he'd acted before she left. Hell, even he didn't know what made him lose his temper. Maybe it was her determination to dig up skeletons.

"I'm sorry, John. Forget I ever said that. Okay? I guess I'm just disappointed that you aren't coming."

"Sure. That's the way things go sometimes. The best laid plans and all that."

"Well, you don't have to sound so damn happy about it."

He ran his fingers through his hair and let out a frustrated sigh. An awkward silence stretched between them.

"Barb? You still there?"

"Yes."

"I love you, honey."

"I know you do." She sniffled. "And I love you, too. I'll call you again when I'm less emotional."

The phone clicked in his ear.

He held the receiver at arm's length, staring at it, not quite comprehending that she'd actually hung up on him. "Damn!" he mumbled. She hadn't even told him where she was staying, let alone said goodbye. Slowly, reluctantly, he replaced the receiver.

He clasped his hands under his head and lay back on the pillow staring into the darkness. Was Barb right after all? She was pretty astute. Did he really need professional help to understand his hang-ups about England and his dead family?

He remembered when she had first suggested it, how emasculated it had made him feel. He'd damn near fallen over backwards at the time, but he'd quickly dismissed it. He figured she'd been so mad at him, she'd said the first thing that came into her head. Now he wasn't so sure. She was right about something else, too. He had been happy he had an excuse not to go to England, but he wished it hadn't been so obvious.

He stretched his arm to where her familiar head of red hair should be resting, and found her pillow cold. He re-clasped his hands under his head. Sleep evaded him, and although he tried to suppress it, his thoughts returned again and again to the conversation. Dozens of times during the restless night he wished he could take back the stupid things he'd said. There were so many things he'd wished he'd said instead. He recalled the tone of her voice—the anger—the disappointment and finally the resignation that he was abandoning her to her own resources.

He tried to ignore the other part of the conversation, but his thoughts finally settled on her parents having died so similarly to his own. The old, childish anxieties began to gnaw at him. What was the matter with him? He was a grown man—a grandfather, for God's sake!

It took no great effort on his part for his thoughts to fly back through the years to that bright Sunday morning—the day his world had started to disintegrate…

LONDON 1939

John ate his breakfast with gusto. But his little sister pushed her food around the plate with a fork encased in her fat, baby hand.

Mrs. Cooper hovered over them. "Babs, don't play with your nice eggy bread. Do you want some tomato sauce on it?"

Babs shook her head and pushed her mop of curls out of her eyes with a greasy hand, leaving remnants of her meal across her forehead.

John laughed, pretending to choke on the last mouthful of his breakfast. "Eggy bread? We don't say eggy bread. That's what babies say."

The door flew open and Dad bounded in, his face flushed and his eyes shining. "It's a boy, Mrs. Cooper. A big, healthy baby boy."

He rushed to John and Babs, threw an arm around each of them and hugged them together. "You have a baby brother, a lovely baby brother." He sang it to a little tune and lifting Babs into his arms, twirled her around. "A baby brother. A lovely baby brother. Wahoo!"

His sailor hat flew off his head and skittered across the floor. Babs gripped her egg-coated fork and squealed with pleasure, as she sprayed droplets of her breakfast around the tiny kitchen.

John giggled and skipped around the spinning pair.

Mrs. Cooper's face crinkled into a wide smile. "Oh, lovely. I'm right glad everything went well." She pulled up the corner of her apron and dabbed away the tears threatening to spill onto her apple-red cheeks. "How about a nice cuppa tea?" She busied herself clearing away the dirty dishes.

Dad put Babs down. "Ooh ta, Mrs. Cooper. I'd love a cup."

The old woman poured the tea and moved the cup towards Dad. "I'll take Babs home with me, if you like," she said, relieving Babs of the slippery fork and wiping her greasy face.

"Thanks, Mrs. Cooper. That would be a big help." Dad drained his cup of tea and turned to John. "Come on, lad. We've got work to do."

John followed him into the garden. The early September morning glowed under a clear blue sky. Autumn leaves shone transparent as stained glass against the deep golden shafts of sunlight.

A half buried air-raid shelter now filled the space where Mum's summer vegetables had grown. Dad picked up a shovel and began throwing dirt on the rounded top. The steady chunk, chunk, of earth hitting steel echoed from other gardens as the neighbors finished installing their own air-raid shelters.

Around the city, church bells tolled a mournful roundelay. Down the alley, solemn music played on a radio someone had placed in an open upstairs window.

The music stopped, and Big Ben struck the quarter hour. The sounds of shoveling ceased. The air stilled, expectant, as if the whole world held its breath until the last boom of the great clock faded.

A solemn voice began: "I am speaking to you from the cabinet rooms of number ten Downing Street…"

John followed Dad's troubled gaze. Dad stared intently up at the window, as if he expected to see the speaker. Nobody stirred until the announcement ended.

The neighborhood sounds resumed. People called to each other over the garden fences. Little knots of worried old men and crying women gathered in the street.

"What's it mean, Dad?" John said.

"It means we'd better get this bloody Anderson shelter finished." He reached for the shovel.

"But why, Dad? Does it mean there's going to be a war after all?"

A year later, people had settled into a routine of living with rationing, gas masks and the sounds of air-raid warnings while the RAF fought the *Luftwaffe* in the skies over Britain. Then, having failed to defeat Britain by those means, the Germans began what they called *blitzkrieg*.

The indiscriminate bombings closed the schools, much to the delight of the children. When the death toll in the cities climbed, trainloads of children were sent off to the crofts of Scotland and the sheep farms of Wales.

Mum had resisted sending John away, until the government offered a unique opportunity to escape the terror. The plan was to evacuate children out of Great Britain altogether and John's aunt and uncle, who lived in South Africa, had agreed to take John for the duration of the war, however long that would be.

Great sobs shuddered John's body and he made no attempt to stem his running nose. "But why do I have to go?"

Mum knelt in front of him, tears coursing down her cheeks. A small half-packed suitcase lay open on the floor beside her. "Please, John. Don't cry. I can't bear it." She wiped his face with her handkerchief. "Blow," she ordered, blinking back her own tears as he snorted into the little cotton square. "Think of the wonderful adventure you'll have. And perhaps you'll see lions and elephants. You could write and tell me all about it." She smiled, then put her arms around him and drew him close to her. "And, John, it won't be for long, truly. We've got old Hitler on the run already." She wiped her eyes and smiled a big smile as she released him.

He wasn't convinced. "I don't want to go. Please don't make me."

"It isn't a matter of making you go, darling. You'll be safe there. Besides, all the arrangements have been made now."

"Why can't you go, and Babs and the baby?"

"Because mums have to stay and take care of babies and little girls who are too young to go. You can go because you're seven, and a very big boy."

"Will the ship be like Dad's?"

"Yes, I believe it is."

He puckered his lips and thought for a moment. "Well, perhaps I'll go then. And maybe I'll see Dad."

Mum checked the list of clothing he had to take with him. "I don't see how we're going to fit all of this into the tiny suitcase you're allowed." Several of his favorite model cars and an airplane lay beside a photograph of his father waiting to be packed. His mother had always insisted that the photo sit on the nightstand, beside his bed, so that he would never forget what his birth father looked like. John never knew the man who died in an accident at sea when John was only a year old.

Now Mum tried to cram the photograph into the suitcase. "It's no use, John. You'll have to leave Daddy's picture. It just won't fit. And I'm afraid your plane and cars will break if we try and force them." She shook her head at the suitcase and punched at the pile of clothing. "Still, not to worry. You'll have lots of lovely toys in South Africa, and I'll keep Daddy's picture safe for you, until you come home." She kissed his cheek and tousled his hair.

He went resigned but unconvinced, wearing a large nametag pinned to his school blazer and his gasmask bumping against his bottom as he walked. He lugged his small suitcase full of new clothes, but none of his favorite toys.

One last time, at the train station he asked, "Mum, did I do something bad? Is that why I have to go away?"

Mum threw her arms around him and cried harder than he had ever seen anyone cry before, but she didn't answer him.

That's it then. I'm being sent away not because I did something wrong, but because she wants to be rid of me. She likes Babs and the baby better. This thought remained to haunt him.

A very nice lady, called Mrs. Green, herded John and three older boys and two older girls onto the train. A great empty ache settled in John's stomach and although he tried to stop the sobs, they bubbled out of him. He knelt on the seat and pressed his face against the window for one last look at Mum, Babs his half-sister, and his baby half-brother. The train pulled away and gathered speed until all he could see in the distance was a white handkerchief waving back and forth. He had been abandoned.

Why?

Under the disapproving scowls of the older boys, John bit his lip and controlled his crying, but his body still jerked in silent sobs. He sat with his legs dangling over the edge of the seat and stared out of the window.

The youngest girl in the group cried the whole time and her brother kept repeating to her, "Be brave, be British." Mrs. Green patted the girl's shoulder and wiped at her tears. John watched and wished he could be allowed to cry too.

Confined to the compartment, the children soon became bored. "'Ere, where we goin', then?" asked the Cockney kid called Simon.

Mrs. Green tried to ignore him, but he continued the constant questioning. "Do you know where we're going, Mrs. Green?

"Yes, Simon."

"Ow, come on. Tell us, we're not going to let on. Tell us where we're going, please," he wheedled and pleaded.

John was more interested in where they were, but all the railway station signs had been taken down. Supposedly, when the Germans invaded they wouldn't be able to tell where they were.

"That's stupid, 'innet," said Simon. "They'll have maps." He tried every imaginable trick on the escort. "'Ere, if we guess right, will you tell us, Mrs. Green? We won't tell the Germans, honest." He grinned at her.

Mrs. Green joined in the laughter, but she refused to give him a clue as to their secret destination. There were no other passengers in the compartment, so the escort allowed the other children to join in the guessing game.

"Southampton?" asked Tom, the eldest.

"Plymouth, then?" said another child.

But when they changed trains and Simon saw their luggage tags, he yelled, "Liverpool. We're going to Liverpool."

Mrs. Green spun around with a look of fear and horror on her face. "Shh, Simon! This is no longer a game. Be quiet."

Later at Liverpool, wearing only his underpants, John stood in the queue to see the doctor for his medical examination. Simon stood behind him and noted that some children were being sent back home.

"I hope I get sent home," John said.

"Naw. You don't wannna wish that. It'll mean there is something wrong wif yer. Besides this is goin' to be a lark." Simon grinned and slapped him on the shoulder. "You'll be all righ'. You stick wif me. I'll keep me eyes on yer."

They waited two weeks in Liverpool for the ship to take them to South Africa. Every night there were three or four air raids so that by day the children walked around in an exhausted stupor. Simon declared "it was stupid to have left London for this." John agreed. After all, Simon was ten and knew everything. It was good to have an older friend who was never afraid, especially when the ship sailed and the land disappeared. The ocean was very, very big.

Simon could distinguish a tanker from a troopship, and he and John counted the convoy of camouflaged vessels that surrounded the evacuee ship. "Fifty. I make it fifty," Simon had said. "What 'bout you? How many did you count, John?"

He told Simon he counted fifty also, but in truth, he'd got mixed-up somewhere about thirty-two.

John loved trailing around after the sailors, even if his dad wasn't one of them. They were jolly good company for a homesick little boy. When the ship neared the equator, the sailors rigged up a canvas swimming pool on deck and held a King Neptune ceremony. It marked the occasion for those crossing the equator for the first time, including several young sailors, some not much older than the oldest evacuees.

John didn't know how to swim, and the canvas pool was deep, so he couldn't take part, but later, when he had a bath in hot seawater, he pretended he was celebrating his first crossing of the equator.

It had been a year since the war began and everything in Britain had been rationed, especially food. On the ship there was no limit to wonderful fresh meat, bread and fruit.

The old ship had a very pronounced list, so John ate with one hand, while his other arm rested next to his plate to prevent it from slipping off the table, as the ship rolled. The dining room steward often teased and played with the children, telling them there were no bananas because the banana boat had been sunk. Then he would produce something better than bananas—ice cream—lots and lots of ice cream.

Several times each day the alarm bells sounded for life-boat drills, and once John sat in a life boat while the sailors practiced lowering it over the side. Simon had been envious.

Some of the escorts were teachers so they taught the evacuees lessons, but it wasn't like real school. John liked the singing best of all and they learned to sing a South African folk song in Afrikaans.

The children had been warned not to climb up and stand on the railing of the ship, but John would forget when someone spotted a pod of whales, or he saw flying fish for the first time. Then the officer known only as Feet on the Deck would come up behind him and slap his bare legs with a little switch and shout, "Feet on the deck."

During the daylight hours, the children were not allowed to take off their lifejackets and at night they slept with them placed ready at the foot of their bunk. But for three nights, while a U-boat stalked the convoy, they had to sleep fully dressed and with their lifejackets on. John followed Simon as he ran around the deck trying to spot a periscope.

Then, one morning when they went on deck, John and Simon found the sea bare of other ships. No destroyers darting around the merchantmen. No frigates or tankers. The convoy had left the old ship to make her way alone to the African coast.

The evacuees were suddenly all talking about another ship full of evacuees that had been torpedoed. John listened to an older girl spreading the terrible news. "They were tipped out of the lifeboats, at night, in a storm and they've all died."

John was frightened that something like that might happen to them. He didn't know how to swim! He went to find Simon to ask if they were in any danger.

"Naw," said Simon. "U-boats can't reach this far. We're almost a' Souf Africa now, anyway. You'll see, in a couple a' days we'll be in Cape Town."

Still, at Sunday Service when they sang "Eternal Father, Strong to Save," it had particular effect on John and he paid special attention to his prayers.

The weather turned very hot and humid, and a few days later the ship dropped anchor just off Freetown. Soon little boats laden with fresh fruit and rowed by the first black people John had ever seen came alongside. The men wore just a skirt of coloured cloth, but one wore a top hat.

The children were forbidden to buy or eat the fruit in case it carried diseases. But the sailors bought it and threw coins in payment. Most of the money fell into the sea and the black men dived after it. The children squealed and laughed. The evacuees had no money so Simon threw a shiny metal bottle cap and the man took off his top hat and dived into the sparkling sea. This was so much fun that soon others began throwing bottle caps. It made the black men very angry. Still they dove after them. Simon reckoned they did that just in case one might be a coin.

After two days, the ship sailed on toward Cape Town.

Then, very early one morning, John awoke to find the ship's engines had stopped. He jumped up and peered through the porthole at land. "Simon, we've stopped. We're here. We're at Cape Town." He shook his friend.

Simon opened his eyes and sat up all at once. "Wha' did yer say? We've stopped!"

"Yes. Come on, there's land out there." He pointed out the porthole. "Let's go on deck."

John pulled on his trousers, shoved his feet into his shoes, and raced after Simon. Other excited children were already lining the railing staring at the towering cloud-topped mountain.

The deck steward was explaining that the "giant puts on his table cloth for breakfast every morning and again in the evening for his meal." As the sun climbed higher, the cloud lifted, revealing the flat top of Table Mountain.

Back on deck after breakfast the children sang the Afrikaans song they'd learned and the people waiting on the dock waved and cheered.

Simon and John parted, promising to stay in touch. Simon was to live with a family in Cape Town, and John was put on a train with other children who were making the three-day journey on to Natal. He really missed Simon.

At Durban Station Aunt Kat and Uncle Walt were waiting to take him home with them.

Aunt Kat was born Katherine McNab. Her younger brother was John's birth father who had died when John was just a baby. She had left her native Scotland as the bride of a young Englishman seeking to escape the memories of World War I, to find a new life in the lush South African province of Natal.

John soon settled in quite comfortably with Aunt Kat and Uncle Walt, although he was disappointed that his cousins were much older than he. He made new friends who taught him to swim. He loved the warm Indian Ocean and the white sandy beaches. He gorged himself on the fresh and exotic fruits, and as the weeks turned into months, he forgot about England and the images of his family faded

On his way home from school, John squirmed in his seat. Excitement made him fidget as he silently urged the bus on toward home. He had an afternoon of adventure planned.

The Umbilo River had receded after the winter flood, and frogs would have spawned in the remaining puddles. If the deluge hadn't washed out too many snakes, John and his friends would catch tadpoles. Or if the mangoes were ripe, the afternoon promised good scrumping. The children of Umbilo thought it fair game to steal the fruit, if they could outwit the guards.

From his favorite seat, upstairs at the very front of the bus, he had an unobstructed view into the old witch's orchards. He was the only one of his gang who came home past the orchards on a double-decker, so it was his job to reconnoiter—he'd learned that word from the war reports. As the bus slowed to make a sharp curve, John had a clear view of the golden fruit hanging in the trees. He also noted the kafir guard armed with a knob-kerry. It didn't make sense to anyone who lived in Umbilo that the old woman who owned the orchards of mango, guava and avocado trees would pay natives to guard the fruit while it rotted in great stinking heaps under the trees.

Nearing his stop he ran to the back of the bus and down the stairs. On the platform he grasped the pole and waited, poised to jump as the bus slowed to make the corner. The conductor spotted him.

"Hey, boy. You wait till the bus stops completely, you hear?"

John nodded his head then jumped off the still moving vehicle and ran in the direction of his home. Behind him, the conductor yelled.

John grinned. The afternoon of adventure had already begun. Despite the oppressive humidity, he ran the rest of the way home.

Aunt Kat rocked in her chair on the veranda where she read most afternoons. But today the book lay closed on her lap

John bounded up the front steps two at a time calling out to her as he ran, "*Goeienaand, Tante* Kat. *Hoe gaan dit met jou, vandag?*" It was a game they often played. She didn't speak Afrikaans and in response to his teasing she'd pretend to be angry and indignant. "I'll not have that Jarpie tongue spoken in my house, John McNab." But she spoke Zulu like an African. Sometimes, when she and Mariah, the kafir woman who helped her in the house, talked and laughed together, John couldn't tell which of them was the native. He spoke only a few words of Zulu, being unable to master the clicks, but he had learned a few swear words from his friends. He had become fluent in Afrikaans, for which Aunt Kat praised him. "You'll be a real *springboek* yet," she told him.

She stood up from her chair and came towards him, her usually sparkling blue eyes were dull and red-rimmed.

He tried the game again, asking what was going on. "*Wat is hier gaande?*"

But she shook her head. "Not now, laddie," she said and wrapped her arm around his shoulder. "John, bide a wee while, I have something to tell ye."

He gaped at her—his suspicions aroused by the flavour of the West Highlands in her speech. It usually meant she was angry or upset. And she didn't seem angry right now.

She gently pushed him into the chair beside her rocker and sat next to him. Tears brimmed in her eyes as she gazed at him. "I'm so sorry…your mum and Babs and wee brother are dead."

"Dead?" He repeated the word, without fully comprehending it. Death had never touched him personally. He'd seen a dead snake and a dead bird and he'd killed *hundreds* of insects. With people it seemed to be different. In the pictures people died, but the next week at the bioscope, the same actor would play in another picture. He couldn't imagine a real dead person. "How?" His gaze locked onto his aunt's anguished face.

"In an air raid." The words came in a sob. She put her arm around him and rested her head against his.

Her tears tickled his neck and he struggled to free himself from her embrace. He stood up and turned to stare at her. Why was she crying? She'd never even met his family. His family! He hardly ever thought of them anymore. Mum had sent him away without even telling him why. Now she was dead and he'd never know what he had done wrong. A surge of anger washed over him as he tried to imagine his mother and to recall the sound of her voice, but he couldn't hear it. He still visualized his little brother as a baby with no hair, and he thought of Babs as just a mop of red curls. People often remarked on her beautiful eyes. What color were they? He couldn't remember. It had been too long, and his efforts to forget them had been too successful. Tightness grabbed at his throat, but he couldn't cry.

I don't care. I'm glad they're dead. Mum sent me away because she liked Babs and that stupid baby better than me. Now they're all dead.

Aunt Kat always came to listen to his prayers before she tucked him in. That night, when he got to the part where he always asked God to take care of Mum, Dad and his little sister and brother, he choked on the words. And though he clenched his jaw he could not stop it. A sob bubbled out.

"Ah, John," Aunt Kat said as if relieved about something. She leaned forward and, wrapping her arms around him, pulled him close to her. "My poor bairn."

He fought the urge to snap at her that he wasn't a baby. She knew he'd be eleven on his next birthday. He was a big boy

"Cry, my dear laddie. Cry," Aunt Kat said.

And while he wept, she silently held him. It was a long time before he could control his quivering gasps and Aunt Kat tucked him into bed. She stroked his hair and kissed his forehead.

John remembered his father only from his photograph. Aunt Kat had the same smile and laughing eyes.

He had come to love her and think of her as his mother, in place of Mum who had rejected him and sent him away, while she kept Babs and the baby. He wondered if his aunt knew. "Aunt Kat, I love you." He put his arms around her neck and hugged her. The pressure of her arms around him made him feel all funny inside.

In the darkness with no distractions, he tried again to give his mother's memory a face. Vivian Leigh, the movie star he'd seen the previous Saturday at the bioscope, kept popping into focus.

It was all Mum's fault—if she hadn't sent him away.

Frustrated and angry, he gathered all the rags and snatches of memories of his life before he came to South Africa, and shoved them far back in his mind.

In the morning Aunt Kat said he didn't have to go to school if he felt too upset. He didn't feel upset at all, but he welcomed the excuse to stay in his bedroom and check on his lizard eggs and silkworm collection. The cocoons weren't quite ready to unravel. By afternoon he was so bored he could hardly wait until his friends came home from school and they could go scrumping. He tried not to think too much about his family again.

A few weeks later when he came home from school, Aunt Kat and Uncle Walt met him on the veranda. Uncle Walt worked odd hours and took lots of business trips so John had never got really close to him. But it was Uncle Walt who sat John down and in a kind, quiet voice, told him that Dad's ship had been torpedoed. "I'm sorry to have to tell you this, old man. Your step-father is dead. There were no survivors."

John had stared at him, unsure of how he should respond. His memories of Dad were even more vague than those of the rest of the family. Even before the war, Dad was at sea for many months at a time, and when he had come home, he always seemed like a stranger for the first few days.

"That means I don't have anyone at all now. My mum and sister and brother and both my dads are dead. What will happen to me?" His length of stay with his aunt and uncle had always seemed to hinge on "after the war." Now he wasn't sure what that would mean to his future.

"You still have Aunt Kat and me, John. We'll always love you and be here for as long as you need us." He rumpled John's hair. "We'll talk about this again, old man, but in the meantime, you mustn't worry. You'll stay here with us."

That night, as Aunt Kat tucked him into bed she reassured him that she and Uncle Walt would take care of him.

He lay curled on his side listening to the night insects while a soft frangipani-scented breeze fanned him, and it felt good. But he still couldn't help worrying. Not about himself, but about his family and where they were. Would they ever hear the night sounds again or smell the blossoms? Aunt Kat said they were all in heaven with God now. He wasn't convinced. People died when they got old and then they went to heaven to be with God. He imagined his dad being trapped in the sunken ship, and wondered how he could get out to get to heaven. And he couldn't reconcile his baby brother and little sister dying when they weren't even old yet.

He turned onto his stomach and buried his face in his pillow with his eyes squeezed shut.

It was all Mum's fault. She should not have sent me away.

CHAPTER SIX

LITTLINGHAM 1985

Barbara and the woman she'd seen examining tombstones in the graveyard appeared to be the only two guests of the Black Swan Inn. Earlier she'd seen the young woman heading out across the village square so Barbara figured she had the bathroom to herself and saw no reason to hurry.

Waiting for the tub to fill, she wondered again why, if the other guest was a visitor to Littlingham, she looked familiar.

Barbara lowered herself into the steaming tub and her thoughts turned to John. Her phone conversation with him had not gone at all as she'd planned. She'd roused him from a sound sleep then given him a hard time. Poor guy. It wasn't his fault her mum and da had deceived her. She owed John an apology for hanging up so abruptly.

Relaxing in the bathtub she mulled over what she now knew about herself. She still had difficulty accepting it, and yet she knew it was true. The question was how could she use that information to find her true identity?

Back in her room she opened the window to the bright spring morning and looked out on the distant hills, but her thoughts were far removed from the purple horizon. She was considering John's suggestion that she go home, but she was still a bit annoyed with him.

He hadn't shown any inclination toward resolving his problems. In fact, he'd ignored everything except getting her to come home, so she was reluctant to just give up her plans. She knew it was her vindictive streak that wanted to punish him. Besides, she would never forgive herself if she left England without even trying to find out more about her birth parents. She also knew she might never have the opportunity to get back to England again.

As she applied her make-up, she became aware of a tantalizing aroma wafting from the bakery on the opposite side of the village square. The smell of yeast and baking bread had once been part of her daily life. Her thoughts shifted and memories flooded back to the last she had worked in Nelson's Bakery...

LITTLINGHAM 1953

She cleaned the crumbs out of the empty bread display cases and carried the trays to the sink at the back of the bakeshop.

The front door bell jingled, signalling a customer. Wiping her hands on her sugar-sticky apron, she returned to the shop. What would anyone expect to buy this late in the afternoon?

The village constable stood in the doorway cradling his helmet in the crook of his arm.

"Hello, Mr. Wapham," Barbara said. "I'm afraid we've pretty well sold out today."

"That's all right, miss. It was you I came to see." He chewed the corner of his ginger moustache and fidgeted from one large-booted foot to the other. His bright-blue eyes darted around the shop, avoiding her stare.

"Oh?" Barbara said. He wasn't his usual jovial self and his uncharacteristic behavior confused her.

"Yes, miss. Ah...You're needed at home."

"At home?" An uneasy sensation settled over her. Her heart thudded. She waited for him to explain, but wondered if she really wanted to know. "I can't leave, Mr. Wapham. I can't close the shop. I haven't finished my work yet."

The policeman bent his huge frame until his eyes met hers. "I'll take care of things here, miss. Mrs. Nelson is on her way to close up. You get along home now." Even his gentle voice and slow speech couldn't calm the panic rising in her.

She tore off her apron, raced out the door and across the village square with her heart pounding so hard it made her ears ring. She flew up Primrose Lane, stopping to gulp air only when she reached the front doorstep. She grabbed the handle and barged into the tiny entry, sending Mrs. Hilton staggering against bulky Doctor Sunderland.

"What is it? What's wrong with Da? Has he had an accident? Is he ill?"

She gaped first at Mrs. Hilton who was trying to recover from falling into the doctor's beefy arms, then at the doctor.

The physician reached out and patted Barbara's arm. "I'm sorry, my dear," he said. "He was already dead when I got here. He had a stroke." Dr. Sunderland shook his shaggy head as though he didn't believe it either.

Barbara bit her quivering lip. Her entire body was numb. *This can't be happening. It is some sort of terrible mistake.* She wanted to go and see for herself if it was true and Da really was dead, but her feet felt like lead weights anchored to the floor.

The doctor put his arm around Barbara and gave her a reassuring hug. "I've sent to Stanton for the undertaker." He picked his black leather bag off the hallstand and squeezed between Barbara and Mrs. Hilton. At the doorway he paused and turned. "Keep an eye on her, Peggy. I'll check back later."

Mrs. Hilton wrapped a protective arm around Barbara's shoulders. "You come home with me, love." She opened the door and nudged Barbara outside. "Don't you worry, they'll take care of everything."

Dazed, Barbara meekly allowed her neighbour to lead her next door. She sat on the chintz-covered sofa and contemplated her future.

Mrs. Hilton had said they'd take care of everything. *But who'll take care of me?* The full realization of what Da's death would mean to her suddenly had its impact and she gave vent to her emotions. Great wracking sobs shook her body.

Da was buried three days later next to Mum, and the neighbours gathered afterwards at Peggy's house.

Good manners kept Barbara until the last of the mourners had left. "Thank you for all you've done with the funeral and everything, Mrs. Hilton, but I must go home now. Reverend Morris is going to help me find Da's will."

The vicar accompanied her next door and together they pawed through the assortment of papers strewn across the rickety kitchen table. Barbara quickly found the insurance policy, whose funds would just cover the costs of the coffin and hearse. A rent book confirmed that Mum and Da had never owned the cottage, but that the rent was paid until the end of the month.

"Oh, dear," said the vicar, leafing through the pile of papers for the third time. "Are you quite sure this is everything?"

"Quite sure, Reverend Morris." She sighed and studied the piece of paper torn from one of her school exercise books. "It seems this handwritten note is Da's will." The scrawled message merely said, *Whatever is left after my death goes to Barbara.* He'd signed and dated it six years before, on January

28, 1947, just two weeks after Mum had died.

Barbara looked at the scarred table and mended chairs, the age-worn sideboard and wardrobes. As long as she could remember, the tarnished brass bedsteads held the same lumpy mattresses. *Whatever is left goes to Barbara.* She wasn't sure whether to laugh or cry.

"Oh, dear. Oh, my," the vicar tutted to himself. The wattle above his reversed collar swayed back and forth with each shake of his old white head. Even he, a man who saw hope in all things, understood the hopelessness of searching any further.

Barbara watched him totter down Primrose Lane. She reached for the photographs she'd found with Da's papers, and idly browsed through them. They meant no more to her than all the old letters beside them.

Propping her chin on her fist, she sat looking about her, and realized that if the contribution of half her wages since she began work in the bakeshop, when she was fifteen, made no more difference in their lives than what she saw here in the little weaver's cottage, then all her wages couldn't support her. Her mind was far from her task as she stacked the photographs and papers together and put them back in the sideboard. Acutely aware of the black band tied around her left arm, fear gripped her. She was seventeen and alone in the world. What was to become of her?

Within days she had her answer in the form of a red-faced man in a wrinkled tweed suit and run-down shoes. He introduced himself as coming from the "The Council."

"Something must be done about you, young lady. I understand you have no living relatives who can take you in?" A cigarette dangled from his lips and he squinted through a cloud of smoke as he talked.

"That's right." Fear gnawed at Barbara's belly. "Can't I just stay here?"

"Oh, my. No. We have families waiting for Council housing, and you're too young to live alone anyway."

"What will happen to me then?"

He shrugged. "Unless we can come up with some other alternative, we'll have to find you a live-in job, somewhere." He blew out a stream of smoke. Dark bags hung under his red-rimmed, pale eyes, and combined with the rumpled suit, he reminded Barbara of an exhausted basset hound. He took one last drag on the cigarette, lit another from it and stamped the fag end out on the clean doorstep.

"A live-in job? You mean be somebody's maid?"

He sucked smoke deep into his lungs and spoke from the new cigarette dangling from his lips. "Not necessarily. Do you like children? I'm sure we could find you a position as a nanny."

"Nanny?" Barbara groaned.

Smoke curled from the side of his mouth as he spoke. "We'd find you a nice home with a good family."

She stiffened her back. "The alternative you mentioned?"

He nodded. "Yes?"

"I think I have one." The idea had been hovering at the back of her mind for the past few months. The tiny village stifled her but Da needed her so she couldn't leave Littlingham. She'd considered looking for a job in Stanton. She even thought of going to London after she turned eighteen but she wasn't trained for anything that would pay enough to support her and Da. Then she'd seen a half-page newspaper advertisement and knew what she wanted to do. His death had given her the opportunity. "I want to join the forces." She had finally put it into words.

The Councilman's head jerked up, disturbing the inch-long ash on the cigarette still clamped between his lips. Ash and sparks fell onto his greasy Royal Air Force Association tie, but he didn't seem to notice.

"Oh, jolly good idea, what! Which branch?" He smiled showing uneven, dark tobacco-stained teeth.

"The air force."

"Oh, bang-on!"

"There is a problem though."

"A problem?" The smile slipped off his hound-like face and the cigarette drooped.

"I need permission to join before I'm eighteen. Without parents, I need someone to sign for me."

The official straightened his shoulders. "Of course." He smiled and ruffled through the papers in his briefcase with nicotine-stained fingers. "You're seventeen, is that right?"

"Yes. I'll be eighteen in six months." She held her breath.

"Wonderful. That's settled then. I'm sure your vicar or the village doctor can sign for you. I'll make the arrangements, shall I?"

The Councilman kept his word and, within a week, she was no longer his responsibility. Hectic days followed. Barbara bundled Da's few items of clothing and gave them to the vicar's wife for the next church jumble sale. She found it hard to believe that her life was changing so rapidly. She tried not to dwell too much on Da's death, but quite often she found herself expecting to see him sitting in front of the fire, wearing his old cloth cap, staring into the flames. And if she listened, she could hear the echo of his bellowing voice and the crash of his cane against the table.

Mr. Hotchkiss, the second-hand man, came with his ancient lorry and carted away the worn-out furniture, lumpy mattresses and miscellaneous remnants of the Thomas household. Barbara was so relieved and happy to be starting her new life, she didn't even argue over the pitifully few pounds she received in return.

Of the papers she'd stowed in the sideboard, she decided to keep only the message that King George had sent in 1946, to all the boys and girls at school, to celebrate victory by the Allied Nations. The king had died in 1952 and his message made Barbara feel very noble and patriotic. The letters, along with the photographs, she had tossed into the fire, wondering as she did so, who the smiling young woman holding a baby could be, or the fair-haired sailor, or the little laughing boy with dark tousled hair, wearing short pants and a crooked school tie.

CHAPTER SEVEN

USA 1985

John came in the front door juggling house keys, car key, his briefcase and a stack of mail he'd picked up from the post office box on his way home. He hooked his foot around the door and pushed it shut behind him. The winking red light on the message machine across the room seemed especially bright in the darkened entryway. He flicked the light on just as Tigger bounded out of nowhere.

"You been sleeping on the bed again, mutt?" John untangled his legs from the excited dog and dropped his keys on the hall table. He set down his briefcase and thumbed through the mail as he crossed the room. He hit the play button on the message machine.

"Hi, John." Her voice startled him and he looked at the machine. "I know you're at work right now. I wanted to apologize for hanging up on you. I didn't even tell you where I'm staying in Littlingham." She told him the phone number of the Black Swan Inn. "Call if you can, otherwise I'll try and coordinate with the time difference and call you. I love you, honey. Bye for now."

He stood looking at the phone for another few seconds hoping there was more to her message. The call made him very lonely for her. He still didn't want to go back to England, but he sure wished he were there with her now. Thirty years of marriage hadn't diminished the love he'd felt for her since the first time they'd met.

He'd first seen her with her head thrown back, laughing as his buddy twirled her in a jitterbug. Her auburn curls bounced with each frenzied step.

John watched from the shadows on the edge of the brightly lit dance floor and admired her shapely legs, exposed each time her skirt flared.

Her stocky young partner, with his tie pulled loose and the jacket of his United States Air Force uniform unbuttoned and flying, exuded confidence as he swung her up and over his hip. John envied his friend's self-assurance.

The trumpets wailed and a drum roll brought the music to a crashing finale. She landed lightly on her feet and came to rest right in front of John. Her partner gave her waist a squeeze. "Thanks," he said, breathing hard from the exertion of the dance.

Excitement sparkled in her eyes and she gasped with exhilarated laughter. "Yeah, thanks. Smashing band!"

"Can I get you something to drink?" Budd seemed reluctant to let her go.

"Yes, please. A shandy would be fine."

"A shandy? What's that?" Budd drew back, his eyes widening with feigned horror.

"It isn't poison," she said, laughing at him. "It's fizzy lemonade with a dash of beer."

Budd rolled his eyes. "Oh, geez," he said, "What a God-awful thing to do to good beer. Say, while you're waiting, meet my buddy." He pointed to John, inconspicuous in the shadows, sprawled on a folding chair with his long legs stretched out in front of him.

She turned, obviously seeing him for the first time. "Oh! Another Yank," she laughed.

He and Budd stood out like a pair of sore thumbs in their US Air Force uniforms among all the Limeys.

"Hey, McNab, keep an eye on this gorgeous thing for me, will ya? This is—uh...what's your name, sweetheart?"

She giggled. "Barbara. My name is Barbara Thomas." She turned to John, "Hello."

"Hi." He slid his arms from the backs of the chairs on either side of him, and stood. "I'm John," he added as an afterthought.

Budd left them and swaggered towards the bar. "Don't mind, Budd," John inclined his head after his friend. "He's always like that. He's a heck of a nice guy, really." Secretly John envied his friend's cavalier mannerisms.

"He's a smashing dancer." Barbara collapsed onto a metal chair and fanned her face with both hands. "What about you? I haven't seen you out on the dance floor."

"No. I can't dance." He sat down and fumbled in his shirt pocket, pulling out a pack of cigarettes. "Smoke?"

She shook her head. "Can't dance or have never learned? There is a difference you know." She ran her fingers through her hair, releasing the damp curls clinging to her neck and forehead. The gesture fascinated him. He was watching her when she suddenly turned and scrutinized him. "You should learn. You've got the build of a dancer."

He lit a cigarette and inhaled. "Yeah." He didn't really enjoy smoking, but it was something to do with his hands. He never knew what do with his damn hands.

Ill at ease, he averted his face. Blue smoke drifted from his lips as he gazed out at the bandstand, pretending that the musicians lounging there were the most absorbing sight in the world. He wracked his brain for something to say to break the awkward silence.

"I've been wondering," she said. "Are you really an American?"

He glanced at her, and then quickly looked away again, concentrating on the musicians. Of all the things she could have said! "Why do you ask that?" It came out like an accusation, which he sure didn't mean. He sounded like blithering idiot.

"Well, don't get your knickers in a twist! I've only heard Americans speaking in the pictures and none of them sounded like you."

He leaned forward resting his elbows on his knees and took another drag on the cigarette. *You're really blowing this, McNab!* "I'm sorry. I didn't mean to sound so rude. I'm not American. I'm British." He was naturally shy, but for some reason, this girl had his tongue tied in knots.

"Hey, McNab," Budd interrupted, yelling as he approached with their drinks. "This beer is warm. These people don't know about ice, I guess." He handed Barbara her drink and gave John a beer. "I tried to get something to eat too, but there's not much up there, and what they have looks *b-a-a-a-d*." He dragged out the last word wrinkling his nose in a gesture of disgust.

Barbara stiffened and threw dagger looks at Budd. "Bloody cheek! Who are you to criticize the food? You look pretty well-fed to me, Yank."

"Geez! I didn't mean to upset you." Chagrined, Budd pretended to hide behind his glass of beer.

She was not amused. "Don't you know that Britain has only just come off ration? Nine years we were rationed! Consider yourself lucky there's anything to eat here."

"Okay, okay. Geez, I'm sorry."

John stifled his laughter. He'd never before seen Budd at a loss for words.

A small dark-haired man in bebop shoes and a wide-lapelled suit hurried over to her. "Hey, Babs. I wondered where you'd got to. Do you want something from the bar?"

"No thanks, Mike." She flashed a smile at the interloper and held up her glass. "I have a drink."

"Right, I'll see you after the interval." Eyeing the two Americans, he turned and walked towards the bar.

John's gaze followed him. "Who's that, your boyfriend?" The uncharacteristic jealousy surprised him.

"No. Not in that sense. He's just a very good friend."

Budd raised his eyebrows. "A friend! That's all? What's wrong with him?"

"Nothing's wrong with him," she said. "He's engaged to a girl back home in London. He loves to jitterbug and so do I, so we usually dance together a lot. That's all there is to it." She dismissed it and ran her hands through her damp hair.

Budd exploded into raucous, taunting laughter.

To hide his embarrassment at his friend's malice, John reached for another cigarette.

Barbara's grey eyes turned the color of slate. She set down her drink and stood.

John watched in dismay as she angrily tossed her auburn curls and stormed out of the dancehall. "You jerk, Budd."

He watched the door, eager for her return. He could hardly believe it when Budd brought her to meet him. Then he'd blown it. Damn his shyness. He'd tried to cover his introversion with bravado and come across as a complete ass.

She'd embarrassed him talking about learning to dance. And why the hell did she have to mention his accent? He'd been trying to lose his South African speech patterns and develop a real American drawl.

She strolled into the dancehall just as the band struck up a slow foxtrot number. A very tall, gangly boy with a shock of carrot-red hair, and a bad complexion, grabbed her by the arm and spoke to her. Barbara looked startled. Then he crushed her to his shirtfront, burying her head somewhere around his midsection. She wrinkled her nose as though he smelled.

He steered her onto the dance floor, and gave a triumphant buck-toothed grin to his friends, who cheered and shouted encouragement at him. He didn't dance, but rather loped, and not altogether in time to the music. His open jacket flopped against Barbara's face and she looked as though she might throw up.

Watching her misery, John's stomach muscles tensed with empathy. "Hey, Budd, go rescue the poor girl," he said.

Budd threw back his head and laughed. "You've gotta be kiddin'. This is the best show in town." He held his stomach and roared with laugher.

"You bastard," John mumbled through clenched teeth.

Barbara, her cheek held fast against the sweating shirt front, a grim determined scowl across her face, gave Budd a blazing glare as she was dragged past.

John stood rooted to the floor. Finally, unable to stand by and watch her discomfort any longer, he ran after them and tapped the carrot-top on the shoulder.

Barbara raised her head, a look of surprised pleasure on her face. "Oh, thank you. I thought I was going to die."

He held her in his arms and smiled down at her but made no attempt to speak.

"I thought you couldn't dance."

He grinned. "Shh, two, three," then gave her a big wink and pressed her close to him.

"You're joking, of course?" She squeezed his hand and grinned back at him. "You're not? You're actually counting in time to the music! Well, all right if that's what it takes. I'll help you."

What he did was more of a shuffle, but he didn't care. He held her in his arms. The fresh smell of her aroused within him a sense of familiarity, a belonging. He never wanted to let her go, but the guy in the bebop suit cut in and John reluctantly gave her up.

The band struck up the national anthem and brought the whole room to a standstill. The last notes of "God Save the Queen" had hardly faded before the crowd rushed the exit door. John watched Barbara being swept along in the sea of pushing bodies. He grabbed his coat and hurried outside, afraid she'd leave and he'd never see her again.

Cold air struck his face. A soft mist swirled, driven by icy wind that brought tears to his eyes. He pulled his greatcoat collar up around his ears and stamped his feet. He alternately blew hot breath on his hands and rubbed them together while he scanned the exit.

She came through the door and ran down the steps tying a scarf around her head. She'd changed into slacks and a heavy coat, and had a small bundle tucked under her arm.

He pushed through the crowd and stepped in front of her. "Can I see you home, Barbara?"

She reacted with surprise. "Oh, it's you. No thanks. The last bus for Manby leaves in a few minutes. It will get us back just in time for the one o'clock check-in."

"What?" He had no idea what she was talking about.

"I've got to catch a bus." She stood on her tiptoes peering over the crowd. "Where is Jean?" The question wasn't meant for him.

"What's a Manby?"

"The RAF station. It's about five miles from here. That's where I'm posted. Now do you understand?" She didn't seem to care whether he understood or not, but fidgeted, looking this way and that around the heads blocking her view.

"Oh, you're in the military?" It took him so much by surprise that the question came out like an accusation. "You didn't tell me that."

She gave him a sidelong glance before returning to her search among those milling around the dancehall entrance. "Well it never came up, did it?"

"No, I guess not. Uh…what did you mean about checking in by one o'clock?"

"We had to get special passes from the CO to stay out past eleven o'clock."

Craning to see over the heads of the crowd, and sounding more exasperated with each word she pulled back the top of her glove, and glanced at her watch. "And if we miss that bus we'll be late and end up on charges."

A young blonde woman pushed through the crowd. "Ready, Babs?"

"Yes. Where have you been?" Barbara pulled the bundle from under her arm and stowed what seemed to be her skirt in the tote on her friend's shoulder.

"Wait a minute," pleaded John. "Can I see you again? How can I get in touch with you?"

She bristled. "Are you sure you want to? I'm in the air force, remember?" She used the same accusing tone he had used to her.

"I'm sorry." He grinned at her. "You just took me by surprise, that's all." If his courage failed him now, he knew she would be gone forever. "I've never met a woman in the military before." He bent to look directly into her eyes and grinned. "Forgive me?"

She shrugged. "That's all right. I've never met a Yank before." She gave a little laugh. "I'm sorry. I'm not usually like that. I'm just concerned with catching that bus." She fumbled in the depths of her purse and brought out a pen and a piece of crumpled paper. "Just a minute." She balanced her bag on her raised knee, and smoothed the paper across it. By the light of the open door above them, she wrote.

Laughing, jostling dancers still poured out of the building onto the street. Nearby, Budd chatted up a group of giggling local girls. They wore no coats over their party dresses and must have been freezing. They wrapped their arms around themselves, rubbing their bare skin against the cold. The mist had left limp rat tails of their curls.

Barbara straightened up and handed the paper to John. "Here's my address. Either write to me or telephone that number in the evenings. Cheerio."

She waved then ran after her friend and disappeared into the darkness.

CHAPTER EIGHT

MANBY 1955

"Picture this," Barbara said to the young women clustered around her. "Tall. I'd say about six feet—maybe six-one. Dark hair tumbling over his forehead, just like Gregory Peck, and black eyes so deep you could drown in them." She hugged herself and grinned. "A lop-sided smile that sends shivers up your spine, and..."

"Sounds like he could do more for me than send shivers up my spine."

"Shut up, Faye. We all know where your mind is." Lorna leaned closer to Barbara. "Come on, tell us more about this American."

"Well, to top it off he has an accent. Not an American accent like you hear in the pictures, but a really different way of saying his words." Barbara pirouetted. "Oh, Lord, he's *abso...bally...lutely* smashing."

"I wish I'd gone to the dance," Lorna wrinkled her nose.

"Oh, stop your whinnying, Lorna," Jean said. "You could have gone."

"No, I couldn't. I was broke."

"Yeah, as always."

"Put a sock in it, you two. Babs, tell us what happened next." Faye leaned expectantly towards Barbara.

"Well, nothing. I gave him my address and phone number." Barbara shrugged.

"We almost missed the bus over it, too." Jean chimed in. "We had to really scarper, didn't we, Babs?"

"Ooh! How romantic. You ran off and left him standing in the moonlight. It sounds like a modern version of Cinderella." Junie, the youngest member of the billet, took a deep breath and let it out in a long sigh.

"Nark it, Junie," Faye snapped. "It's winter and it was piddling rain, for God's sake. Go on, Babs."

Junie's face crumpled and tears glistened in her eyes.

Beryl, the oldest member of the billet, joined the circle of chattering airwomen. "Leave Junie alone, Faye." Beryl rarely involved herself in what the younger girls found entertaining, but because she was older and had served in the air force longer than any of them, they respected her and listened to her advice. She put her arm around Junie's shoulder. "Listen, all of you. I'll give you a word of warning about the Yanks. During the war, when they first came to Britain, there was a common saying about them—They're overpaid, oversexed and over here. That still applies. In other words, they have plenty of money and think that will buy them anything. Don't be taken in by their smooth talk and generosity. All they really want is to get into your knickers."

"Yeah." Faye snickered.

Barbara gaped, her cheeks suddenly hot as if they were on fire. "Oh, no, Beryl. John isn't like that. Honestly, he's smashing!"

"All men are like that. Take my word for it." Faye guffawed and sauntered away.

Barbara expected a phone call the next evening and when it didn't come she thought perhaps he didn't have access to a phone on a Sunday evening. Monday's post brought no letter for her. Throughout the week she waited anxiously for the daily mail delivery. Each evening she hung around the billet in hopes that the next time the phone in the duty NCO's office rang the call would be for her. There had to be a reason why he hadn't phoned or written— Sunday or Monday or any other day of the week. She started to wonder if she'd imagined his interest in her. Perhaps he didn't have access to a phone. Was a member of the American forces allowed to phone or write letters to a WRAF?

A week passed—then two. In memory, their meeting at the dance grew more vivid and she went over and over their conversation outside the dancehall. She hadn't imagined it, he'd seemed really keen. He must be busy—or perhaps he'd been transferred or gone back to America!

In the end she decided it was her own fault. She hadn't given him any real encouragement. In fact, she'd acted rather blasé about their meeting and nonchalant about whether he phoned or not. Secretly she prayed she would still hear from him.

Her friends stopped asking if she'd heard from "her Yank." She was glad for that. She was not only crushed but also embarrassed after the big scene she'd painted of him and their meeting. At night, alone in the dark, she embellished the remembered sensation of his arms around her as they had danced. She imagined the scent of his aftershave imbedded in her pillow and burrowed her head, inhaling the memory.

After three weeks without hearing from him she had almost succeeded in banishing him from her consciousness. She was ready to move on, and as she and her friends wandered back to the billet from the mess hall, they were making plans for the following weekend.

"Well, we can't waste a forty-eight-hour pass, here." Jean indicated the surroundings with a flick of her hand.

"Too right. I could do with a change of scenery. Let's go to London." Barbara began to warm to the possibility. "We could stay at the Union Jack Club and it wouldn't cost very much to eat."

"Sounds good." Lorna pursed her lips. "The problem is, I'm broke."

Jean gave an exasperated sigh. "Lorna, why are you always broke? What do you spend your money on that Babs and I don't?"

"I dunno." Lorna shrugged, dismissing the subject.

Lorna was highly intelligent, but she was so effervescent and compulsive, that she often appeared scatter-brained. Her dark brown hair bobbed when she walked and her flashing brown eyes and wide smile endeared her to everyone.

"Tell you the truth, Babs," Jean said, "I don't really want to go to London this weekend."

"Why?" Barbara couldn't keep the disappointment from her voice. She really wanted to get away from Lincolnshire, away from the memory of John.

In contrast to Barbara's curly, dark-red mop, Jean wore her blonde hair in a smooth page boy. She was heavier than either Barbara, who was small, or Lorna, who was the tallest of the three. Quieter than her friends and not as bright as either of them Jean was, nevertheless, the steadying force among them and her blue eyes observed all that went on around her.

"My mum wants me to come home. Besides, I can take my dirty laundry and Mum will do it for me." Jean grinned.

"You lazy lump." Barbara laughed at her friend.

"Hey, why don't you two come home with me?" Jean seemed pleased with her idea. "You can't bring your washing though, my mum'll balk at that."

"No thanks," Barbara chortled. "Your mum is going to get fed up with me turning up every time we get a forty-eight, even without my laundry."

"Yeah, me too," Lorna said.

Ahead, the billet door opened. Mavis Cross peered out and beckoned.

A puzzled frown creased Jean's forehead. "What's the matter with her?"

"I dunno," Lorna said. "She's Duty NCO. What's she doing out here?"

Mavis waved her arms wildly. "Babs!" she yelled. "There's a long-distance phone call for you."

"For me. Who is it?"

"A man with a peculiar accent."

Barbara pressed her hands against the wild flutter in her chest and turned to her friends. "It's him!" She took the billet steps two at a time. Gulping air into her starved lungs, she picked up the phone. "SACW Thomas," she gasped.

"Hi, it's John McNab. Remember me from the dance the other night?"

Her heart beat wildly at the sound of his voice. "Oh, yes, hello." She wanted to remind him that "the other night" had been three weeks earlier. Instead she meekly said, "How are you?"

"I'm just great. Say, er...when can I see you again? Can you get a pass or something this weekend?"

"Well, yes," she hesitated. She didn't want to sound overeager, but on the other hand, she was not going to let this opportunity slip by. "I have a forty-eight-hour pass for this weekend."

"Great. Where can we meet?"

"What? I don't believe this." She was disappointed in him. He hadn't even apologized. "I don't hear from you for three weeks..."

"Yeah. I'm sorry about that, but I can explain..."

"Where are you? You didn't tell me where you're stationed or what you were doing in Louth that night."

"Oh, Budd was looking for girls and a dance, and somebody told us that some big band was going to be playing at the Louth Town Hall. We took the train there from Peterborough."

"How did you get back? The last train must have gone by midnight."

"Yeah, well, we had to take a cab."

"A cab! You mean you took a taxi all the way from Louth to Peterborough? That must have cost a bomb." Beryl's words rang in her ears.

"Yeah, well, we'd just been paid so it was okay. Anyway, where can we meet? Where do you usually go?"

"My friends and I were thinking of going to London."

"Oh." The disappointment dripped like treacle off a suet pudding. "I'd hoped we could meet in London."

"Well…" Nothing had been decided, but it didn't seem as though Jean and Lorna wanted to go. "I don't know." She'd waited three weeks for this and now she was feeling hurt and resentful.

"Please. I know I should have called before. If you'll give me another chance, I'll explain." He sounded contrite and really pathetic.

"All right. Meet me under the clock at Victoria Station at nine o'clock, Friday night."

"I'll be there." His excitement was palpable.

She cradled the phone receiver and immediately regretted agreeing to meet him. It seemed a bit daring for a nineteen-year-old from a tiny English village to be meeting a man in London.

John's long strides carried him through Victoria Station. The hotel bellhop had given him the wrong directions and he'd got lost. Now he was already five minutes late and frantic that Barbara wouldn't wait.

He rounded a corner of W. H. Smith's bookstore and found the clock, but she wasn't among the crowd beneath it. Disappointment churned his stomach.

Suddenly, she was beside him. "Hello, John." Her voice was quiet and shy. He hadn't thought of her as shy.

"Oh, hi. I thought I must be in the wrong place. I didn't know you in uniform."

She shrugged. "I always travel in uniform. Get half-fare on the train. It's safer too."

"Well, where to?" He picked up her small suitcase.

"Waterloo. I'm staying at the Union Jack Club." She looked at her watch. "I have to check in by ten o'clock."

They rode the tube train to Waterloo and walked to the Women's Union Jack Club. She checked in and left her suitcase.

She soon lost her shyness and began to chatter as she had at the dance when they'd first met. "Do you know where you are?" she said.

"Crossing a bridge in London."

"Not just *any* bridge. Waterloo Bridge! Did you ever see the picture *Waterloo Bridge?* It was smashing, but sad."

Wow, she's a real romantic. He reached for her gloved hand and would have liked to kiss her, but was still too shy. Instead he gently squeezed her fingers and was rewarded by her lovely smile.

Icy winds blowing off the river stung his face and made his eyes water. He kept hold of her hand as they dodged the traffic, and left the Embankment for the bright lights of the West End. He put his arm around her waist to guide her through the theatre crowds at Leicester Square and, enjoying the sensation, kept it there.

At Piccadilly Circus she pointed out Eros and he did his best to be enthusiastic and hide how cold he was. He marveled that she just kept talking, pointing out interesting statues and throwing out bits of history.

He lowered his chin into the upturned collar of his overcoat, but he was still so cold he was sure his face had cracked. He wore a wool sweater under his shirt, but still the raw night air penetrated the layers of clothing. Twelve years of living in a humid South African coastal city, a year in hot dry Texas and the last couple of years in California had thinned his blood and dulled his memory of just how miserable an English winter could be. Still, this was the country of his birth and it surprised him that he felt such a stranger. He shivered and hunched deeper into the collar of his overcoat.

Finally he stopped and wrapped his arms around her. She looked surprised but didn't object. He smiled down at her. "Your history lessons are great, but I'm freezing. Let's find someplace warm."

She stared at him and grinned. "Oh, I'm sorry. I do tend to rattle on, don't I?"

"Don't apologize." His arms slipped from around her waist and he brushed his lips across hers. Her grey eyes widened and she smiled as he took her hand. "Come on. We'll look for a pub with a fire."

A noisy, laughing crowd lined the counter of the brightly lit public house where a frenzied barman washed and polished glasses as soon as they emptied. John swore under his breath. He'd hoped for a little quieter place than this, but it was warmer than the streets of London. He eased through the mob and ordered drinks from a frazzled barmaid who pumped dark beer with lightening speed. There was nowhere to sit or even put their drinks in the large public room.

John took Barbara's hand and pulled her after him into a small lounge warmed by a roaring fire. It was empty of people. He closed the door behind them shutting out the noise.

Barbara took off her hat and fluffed her hair. He watched her holding her hands before the flames. Firelight glowed off her face and burnished her hair.

Her long eyelashes made shadows on her cheeks. She wasn't beautiful in the classic sense, he decided, but she was pretty. She had an open honesty, or perhaps it was innocence, about her.

Turning from the fire, a half-smile tugged at the corners of her mouth. "You know," she said in a whisper, "I feel really stupid. I've rattled on and on about Lord Nelson and The Battle of Trafalgar, and I've just remembered you said you were British. You've probably been laughing at me." She giggled and covered her face with her hands. "I'm so embarrassed."

"Hey, no, don't feel like that. I left England when I was just a little kid. Besides, you make it much more interesting than my old history teacher."

She sat down at the table opposite him and sipped the glass of tart scrumpy. "Where were you born then?"

He bit his lip, then chuckled and looked into the fire. "Right here in London."

"Really? Why did you leave?"

"I was evacuated to South Africa during the war."

She slapped her hand on the table. "So that's the accent," she said. "Is your family still there?"

He reached for a cigarette and lit it before he answered. "No. They never went. My brother and sister were too young to go, so they stayed here with my mother." It had been a long time since he'd dragged up those memories.

"That's incredible! Where did you live? Who did you live with in South Africa?"

"Geez, so many questions."

"I know." She laughed, wrinkling her nose so that the freckles danced across it. "But I'm interested, so tell me anyway."

"With my aunt and uncle—my dad's sister and her husband, actually."

"How did you end up in America?" She was obviously not going to quit asking questions.

"After my aunt and uncle died I had no reason to stay in South Africa. I didn't have any family left in England either. So, I decided to try someplace new."

"Why? What happened to your parents and your brother and sister?"

He took a deep drag on the cigarette and gulped some beer while he tried to gather his thoughts.

A puzzled frown wrinkled her forehead. "What's the matter with you? What are you hiding?"

He chuckled. "I'm not hiding anything. I just never talk about it."

"Why? Are you a fugitive from the law or something?"

"Of course not. Look, if it means that much to you, I'll tell you. What do you want to know?"

"No. It's okay. I don't have the right to pry." She flicked her hand as if to dismiss that subject and readjusted herself in the chair. "So, finish telling me how you got to America."

"I wanted to do something different so I signed on to work my passage on a small cargo ship heading for America. I liked San Francisco, so I just stayed."

"How did you end up in the American Air Force?"

"The Korean War had started and guys were getting called up. I wasn't an American citizen so they couldn't draft me into the army, but I had nothing better to do, so I volunteered for the Air Force."

"So it's true that you have absolutely no relatives in the world?"

He fidgeted, drumming his fingers on the arm of the chair and chuckled at her persistence. "That's right, I'm an orphan. But you could adopt me."

"Not today, thank you." She laughed shaking her head. "How do you know you don't have cousins or something here in England? Maybe you have relatives you don't know about."

"I don't. Okay? But now tell me about you."

She gave him a rueful grin and flicked the tip of her nose with her finger. "I'm British, and proud of it." She glanced sideways at him and smiled. "I was born in a tiny village called Littlingham. My parents are dead, and I have no brothers or sisters. There you have it." She sounded emphatic and final.

"Where's your home now, then?"

"Wherever the air force sends me. Right now, Manby."

"Where do you go when you have leave?"

"Oh, sometimes one of my friends invites me home with them. How about you?"

He often felt lonely with no home or family. "Same thing." He shrugged his shoulders and they both laughed.

"Two orphans in the storm," she said, chuckling.

"Do you like the military?" He wondered why he really cared and why he felt so relaxed with her, as though he had known her all his life.

"Well, I like my job, the pay is terrible, but I have three meals a day, such as they are, and I have a roof over my head. But best of all, I have some really great friends. They are my family." She turned to stare back into the fire.

John studied her, wondering if she'd ever experienced the depths of loneliness he'd known. And if he ever had another opportunity, would he really be able to tell her about his family without the guilt that tore him to pieces whenever he dared to let them into his thoughts. He'd make sure the opportunity didn't come up at least for the rest of that weekend.

She'd suddenly looked at her watch. "Oh, I almost forgot. I have to get back to the Union Jack Club or they'll lock me out."

At the door to the Union Jack Club he'd finally found the courage to kiss her and had been surprised. He'd surmised she'd had boyfriends, but if she did, they either hadn't kissed her, or didn't know how. He'd kissed her again until her lips were pliable and she relaxed into his arms, returning his kisses with a passion that he wished would never stop.

The next morning he'd arrived earlier than they'd planned to meet. The anticipation of spending another day with her was too exciting. They'd had breakfast while planning a day seeing the sights of London.

Barbara loved the pageantry and history of London. She'd insisted on them seeing all the touristy sites and he didn't complain just as long as he could be with her. He kept his arm around her waist while they watched the Changing of the Guard at Whitehall. He didn't even mind having to stand in line to see the Crown Jewels at the Tower of London. She'd stood close beside him and he enjoyed the sensation of her body next to his.

They'd found a quiet little pub with a cozy room all to themselves and had eaten dinner in front of the roaring fire. When she'd returned his kisses, she'd lit a fire in him such as he'd never known.

He was in love.

The weekend came to an end too soon. John returned to his base slumped in a corner seat of the train and stared at his reflection in the frost-covered window. Beneath the visor of his cap pulled low over his forehead, his features were hidden in shadow. Beyond his image through the dark glass, distant lights flickered, distorted by the late winter drizzle pattering against the window.

The gentle rocking of the train and the rhythmic clackety-clack of the wheels on the rails lulled him. He closed his eyes and the years receded to a time when his feet didn't even reach the floor of the train, and he'd said goodbye to another red-haired girl named Barbara—his little sister.

Not wanting to go there, he roused himself from his reverie.

CHAPTER NINE

LITTLINGHAM 1985

Wisps of white cloud streaked the bright blue sky and a warm breeze carried the scent of lilac through the ancient churchyard. The sun shone through the branches of the gnarled old oaks, playing shadows across the tombstones.

Barbara stopped in front of the stones marking her parents' graves and took a pen and little notebook from her bag. She carefully copied her mother's name, Dorothy Gladys Thomas, and her birth date, which Barbara hadn't known before. She remembered Dolly's death date only too well and Barbara knew she had been born in Lambeth, London.

The tombstone recorded only the year of Charles Rhys Thomas' birth and the place, Llangarren, Wales. But the full date of his death date was chiseled in the stone marker. Each grave bore a verse from the Old Testament.

Barbara still hadn't figured out who could have known so much about her parents. Her mum and da had been very private people.

She'd felt guilty about abandoning her parents here in the graveyard when she joined the Women's Royal Air Force, but before she left, she gave Reverend Morris her last few pounds for markers for their graves. The old vicar would surely be dead by now, she thought, but perhaps Peggy Hilton could tell her who knew the details of her parents' birth dates and places. Peggy had invited her for lunch, so she would ask her then. Barbara closed her notebook and idly dropped it and her pen back in her bag.

"Excuse me."

Startled, Barbara spun around and sucked in a sharp breath. "Good grief!

Where did you come from?" The young woman she'd seen here in the cemetery the previous afternoon smiled at her.

The woman laughed softly. "I'm sorry. I didn't mean to scare you. Guess you didn't hear me because I walked on the grass. I just wanted to know if you've always lived in this village." Her accent was definitely not British.

"Well, no. I was born here…no, I mean I grew up here, but I left a long time ago. I'm just visiting now."

"Me too. From Toronto, Canada. My dad was born in Littlingham." She extended her hand. "Hi. I'm Lilianne Paddington."

Barbara shook the young woman's hand. "My name is Barbara McNab." She studied the familiar face. "I feel as if I know you…Paddington. Yes, there was a family by that name living here when I was a little girl."

"Oh, really." Excitement suddenly animated Lilianne. "Then you probably know my dad. Ben Paddington."

"Of course. Ben and I went to school together. Your father would know me as Barbara Thomas. What brings you to Littlingham?"

"Research. I'm gathering information about my aunt's death. Do you remember Lily Ann Paddington?"

"Ah, yes. I see. Lily Paddington was your aunt. That's why you look so familiar. You look so much like her." Her smile was very like her aunt's.

"That's what Dad says."

"We called her Lilypad," said Barbara.

"Yes, I know. That's my nickname too. So you were living here when she was murdered?"

"Yes, I lived here at the time." The recollection of the horrific murder and the effect it had on the village flooded Barbara's thoughts. Every Littlingham male was under suspicion and the event pitted neighbour against neighbour.

"I'd love to talk to you about her. Could we have lunch together?"

"I'm sorry, I can't today. An old friend has invited me to her home for lunch."

"You're staying at the Swan, aren't you?"

Barbara nodded.

"How about getting together for dinner? Tonight?"

"Fine, but I'm not sure I can help you. I was just a child at the time your aunt died." She couldn't bring herself to say murdered. "Did they ever catch her killer?"

"No. That's one of the reasons I'm writing about it." She looked quickly at her watch. "I think I'll run into Stanton and look up their old newspapers in the library. See you about six-thirty at the Swan, okay?"

"Sure. I look forward to it."

Lilianne turned and with a quick wave, hurried out of the churchyard.

Drawn by the ancient grey spire piercing the brilliant blue sky, Barbara crunched along the gravel path leading to the door of the old church. In no particular hurry she stopped in front of Lilly Ann Paddington's grave and read the inscription before continuing. Lily Ann had been only fifteen when she was murdered.

Barbara stepped through the heavy oak door to the interior of the church. Chilled, musty-smelling air trapped by the stout stonewalls sent a shiver through her. She took off her sunglasses, blinking to adjust her eyes to the gloom. Familiarity enveloped her, and a whispered "Oh," escaped her lips.

Her slow footsteps echoed against the stone floor, worn uneven by the feet of countless worshippers. Running her hand along the rough-hewn wall, she sensed the warmth of history in her fingertips. She slid into a well-polished pew and studied the stained-glass windows portraying the life of Christ. One, a large sun-backed transparency above the alter depicting Jesus surrounded by little children, cast shafts of blues and reds across the age-worn pews and faded kneeling cushions. She'd learned the Bible stories from these scenes, just as illiterate serfs who had worshipped here centuries ago had done.

The last time she'd been in this church was for her da's funeral, more than thirty-two years before. She'd been so frightened then, not knowing what was to become of her. Tears for the frightened girl she had been flooded her eyes. Had she truly been alone in the world? Would it have made a difference if Mum and Da had told her they had adopted her? Peggy Hilton said she was sure Mum had intended to tell her. Perhaps she would have when Barbara was older, but Mum had died before that time came.

She remembered sitting in the front pew at Mum's funeral when she was eleven, wearing a navy blue dress with a white collar. It was too big and too long, so that when she sat down the skirt almost covered her scuffed, brown school shoes. Peggy Hilton had sewn a black mourning band around her sleeve and she remembered being very conscious of it as she wiped her nose and her eyes with the back of her hand. Da sat beside her and used his big handkerchief to noisily blow his nose. Peggy Hilton had handed Barbara a little hanky to mop up her endless tears.

Mum had been ill for some time, but the prospect of her mother dying had been unthinkable. After all the years that had passed, Barbara remembered the love she had felt for the large, rather shy, soft-spoken Londoner who never completely lost her Cockney intonations.

"You can do those sums. A clever girl like you." Mum always called her a clever girl when they worked together on her arithmetic homework, and praised her when Barbara mastered an embroidery stitch, or read a knitting pattern correctly. She loved helping Mum in the garden or around the house, and was often rewarded with extra sweet ration coupons and a couple of coppers to buy sweeties. When money was scarce and food was rationed, Mum would make sure that Barbara got plenty to eat. "Growing girls need a bit more nourishment than greedy old men," she'd whisper as she slipped an extra bit of meat on Barbara's plate. "Da's 'ad mor'n 'is share of the ration this week."

Although Barbara seldom had any new clothes, Mum always saw that the hand-me-downs were in good repair, so that she'd never been embarrassed among her friends. Shoes were a problem for everyone during the war. Leather went for army or flying boots and the children's shoes wore out quickly. When Barbara's shoes developed holes, Mum usually managed to find a stout piece of cardboard to put inside them.

As a little girl, she tried to show her mother how much she loved her by a hug, or a kiss on the cheek. But Mum would blush to the roots of her silvering, curly hair and she'd call Barbara "a soppy thing." But sometimes, when they sat quietly together beside the fire, Mum would fondle Barbara's curls, and that became her sign of affection for her little daughter.

Reticent and completely dominated by Da, Mum had nevertheless managed to keep her independence in some respects. And she must have been strong to persuade Da to adopt a four-year old. Barbara always thought of Da as old, and now, as an adult herself, the image of him as little boy seemed ludicrous.

She was nine when Mum first fell ill and she and Da began their Saturday night walks home from the Black Swan Inn. At first he'd been so heavy, leaning on her shoulder, but she grew and got stronger so that by the time he died, she hardly noticed his weight. On those short, plodding walks home up Primrose Lane, she'd learned what made him so cynical and complaining.

One night, after Mum had died, Barbara asked Da about his own mother.

"I left home when I was twelve and never saw her again."

"Why didn't you write to her?"

"Ach! She couldn't read. Besides she only spoke Welsh."

"What about your father?"

"He died when I was just a lad, don't you know."

"How did he die?"

"Down the mines. In a cave-in."

"Did you have any brothers and sisters?"

"I had two brothers, both older, mind. The younger one had a wonderful singing voice and should have gone to be trained. Instead they sent him down the mines. I vowed I'd not work in a dark, wet hole in the ground to make other men rich, so I left."

"Wasn't your mother upset when you left? You were so young."

"Humph," he grunted. "Not nearly as upset as my oldest brother. He wanted to get married, and said I was selfish because I wouldn't stay and be a miner to help support my mother."

Instead Da had gone to work for the railroad. Elevated to porter at fourteen, he'd worked his way up to conductor, a prestigious position. It came to a sudden end in a train crash, and his pension, hardly adequate to begin with, didn't increase with the rising costs of living. So life became one of endless pain and poverty.

During another Saturday night walk home from the pub, he'd told Barbara that he'd served, briefly, in the army during the First World War, and hated it. But listening to the wireless during the Second World War, he was full of opinion. He swore at the "bleedin' Germans, the gutless French and the bloody Italians, who can't make up their bloody minds which side of the bloody fence to sit on." He alternately swore at and sided with Churchill's decisions and had he, Charles Rhys Thomas, been leading the army, he could have done a far better job than "that stupid, bloody fool Montgomery." The tirade invariably climaxed with a crash of his cane on the hearth, for emphasis.

The memory of his blustering made her smile.

A sudden shaft of sunlight flooded the church and Barbara turned to the door. A young cleric peered at her through the gloom. "I didn't realize anyone was in here. I hope I'm not disturbing you."

"No, not at all. I just felt the urge to see this beautiful church again." She indicated the interior of the tiny building with a gesture.

"Again? You've been here before, then?" He walked toward her.

"Oh, yes. Many times. Years ago I lived in Littlingham and have some very fond memories of this church and Reverend Morris."

"Ah, you knew my predecessor. He retired about fifteen years ago. A very old gentleman." He sat down beside her and held out his hand. "I'm Dennis Hartley, vicar here at All Saints."

She shook his hand and introduced herself. "Reverend, do you think I might examine the church's burial registers?"

He turned a quizzical expression on her. "Yes, of course."

Barbara felt obliged to explain that she wanted to see if there were any notes written with the entries of her mum and da's funerals. "You see, my adoptive parents are buried outside, and there is so much more information on their gravestones than I ever knew. I'm curious as to where it was obtained."

She followed him to the vestry and he indicated a heavy leather-bound volume. "Here is the modern burial register for All Saints. It begins 1812."

"Modern?"

"Oh, yes." He chuckled. "Our old registers begin in 1532, during the first Queen Elizabeth's reign. Of course, they've long since been transferred to London."

Barbara laughed. "I don't need to go back that far. Just to 1947 for the record of my mother's burial, and 1953 for my father's."

"What do you think you'll find?"

"I'm not sure. But perhaps Reverend Morris or the church clerk made a notation beside the entries."

An hour later she thanked the Reverend Hartley for his interest and time and left the church. At least now she knew there were no hidden clues concerning her mum and da in the parish burial register entries.

The vicar had become so involved in the search and had been so eager to help, that he insisted they search the baptismal register for a record of her own christening. Of course it wasn't there.

"Reverend Hartley," she explained, "I came to Littlingham at the age of four. And I feel quite certain I would have been christened in London, where I was born."

Barbara thanked the cleric for his help and wandered out of the churchyard, retracing the steps she taken the previous day up Primrose Lane.

Peggy Hilton greeted Barbara with a smile and a hug. "I'm glad you came." She led the way to her tidy kitchen where the table was laid for two. "Lunch is ready. It's just cold ham and salad but we'll have a nice cup of tea first, shall we?" The kettle began to scream, but the sound died as soon as Peggy poured the boiling water on the tealeaves. The little kitchen filled with the smell of the aromatic brew.

"Peggy, do you remember the Paddington family?"

"Yes. Their daughter was murdered here in the village. The mother never got over it, and the family moved to Canada." Peggy's brow furrowed.

"Whatever made you think of them?"

"Do you remember their son, Ben?"

"Yes, I do."

"Well, Ben's daughter is here in Littlingham. I met her in the churchyard looking at Lily's grave. The girl's name is Lilianne and she looks the image of Lily. I'm having dinner with her tonight at the Black Swan. Why don't you come too? I'm sure she'd love to talk to you about her grandparents."

"I can't tonight, dear. This is bingo night at the British Legion Hall. I go every week."

"Some other time then."

Over lunch, Barbara told Peggy about the young vicar and how he had helped her.

"He's such an intense young man, isn't he?" She chuckled at the memory of him rummaging through the pages of the baptismal register, trying to find something that would make her visit worth the while. "I told him I had been adopted, but he insisted we search from 1940 onward. I stopped him at 1945. My memories are very good of that time, and I would have remembered if I'd been christened then.

"I feel just awful that I never wrote to Reverend Morris to ask about the gravestones, though. And to thank him." She sighed. "But I'm puzzled. I only got a few pounds from that second-hand man who bought the furniture—such as it was. I can't remember now how much I gave to Reverend Morris when I asked him to have the markers put on the graves. But it certainly wasn't enough for those gravestones. They are really beautiful." She looked up at Peggy in time to see a pleased smile on the old woman's wrinkled face.

"What is it?" Barbara tilted her head and smiled. "You know something about it, don't you? Where did the money come from?"

"We had a whip-round." Peggy poured tea and avoided Barbara's gaze.

"Who did?"

"Well, it was the village, you see. Everyone liked your mum and after you left and it came out that there wasn't much money for markers, we passed the hat."

"Oh, God. What a thoughtless kid I must have been." She ran her hands through her hair. "I never gave the people of this village a second thought." A tense knot formed in the pit of her stomach.

"You mustn't let it trouble you. That was a long time ago and you were just a child."

But the guilt did trouble her, and she had another question. "Peggy, do you know who provided the information about where and when my mum and da were born?"

"No, but I suppose it was the Reverend Morris. Your mum used to talk to him."

"I guess I'll always regret that I didn't keep in touch with him and I could have asked those questions."

"Well, you could ask him now," Peggy sipped her tea.

Barbara gaped at her. "Ask him? You mean he's still alive?"

"Oh, yes. He lives over Piggen way with his son. Do you remember Gordon Morris?"

The vision of a sturdy, sandy-haired boy a few years older than she, kicking a soccer ball, filled her mind.

"I haven't seen the old vicar in years but I hear he's a bit frail these days," Peggy said. "Well, he would be, wouldn't he? He's got to be well into his nineties, if he's a day. Mind you," she continued in a confidential tone, "they say he's three ha'pence short of a shilling these days. Funny, isn't it? He married Agatha who was so much younger, but she died first."

"I'd love to go and see him." Barbara found it hard to contain her excitement. "How can I get in touch with Gordon?"

"I'll give him a jingle on the telephone." Peggy left the room and a few minutes later dashed back into the kitchen. Her faced glowed. "Gordon isn't there, but the old vicar is in rare good form this afternoon, according to Lizzie—Oh, excuse me." Peggy tittered and pursed her lips. "I mean Elizabeth. She doesn't like being called Lizzie since she went up to London and married a Harley Street specialist with a double-barreled name. Do you remember the daughter? About your age, she is. She's very posh these days, you know." Peggy raised her eyebrows and looked disdainfully down her nose.

Barbara laughed hard, enjoying a wonderful release of her pent-up emotions.

CHAPTER TEN

LITTLINGHAM 1985

The Reverend Mr. Bartholomew Morris had been the vicar of All Saints Church in Littlingham for twenty years before he shocked the community by marrying a woman young enough to be his daughter. His bride settled quickly into the village life, and soon produced a son and then a daughter for the surprised old man.

Barbara remembered the vicar's daughter as a cherub-faced little girl with large brown eyes and long dark hair. The woman who greeted Barbara and Peggy at the door looked nothing like that.

Elizabeth Morris Smythe-Bickerton's large matronly form filled the doorway. Now in her mid-forties and dressed in country tweeds, she appeared every bit the city doctor's wife who had condescended to spread her bounty among the less fortunate workers of the land.

"Good afternoon, Mrs. Hilton." She sounded as if she had a whole plum in her mouth.

"Hello, Elizabeth." Peggy indicated Barbara. "Do you remember Barbara Thomas? Barbara McNab she is now."

"How very *nace* to see you again, Barbara." The vicar's daughter extended a fat, ring-laden hand. Several gold bangles clanged together with each movement of her arm. Her well-endowed bosom rose and fell with every laboured breath, and several chins fought for space at the neck of her blouse. Her once expressive eyes were mere shining dots in her chubby face. She wore her dark hair in a style suited to a much younger woman. "Do come in." She stepped back to allow them to pass. "Would you care to take tea?"

93

Barbara stifled a giggle when she caught Peggy's wink. "No, thank you, Elizabeth. We've just finished lunch."

"Peggy, you said you thought my father could provide some information for Barbara for a tombstone. Is that correct?"

Peggy corrected her and explained what Barbara was trying to find out.

"My father has his moments, but don't expect too much. He's rather frail now, you know. Do come through."

Elizabeth led her guests into the sitting room where a shriveled old man sat, engulfed by an overstuffed chair. His lined face was clean-shaven and his sparse white hair neatly combed. Although the day was warm, he wore a heavy cardigan over a white shirt. The knot of his striped tie lay almost hidden behind his wattle, which swayed as he breathed. His gnarled hands, resting in his lap, shook involuntarily. He stared vacantly out of the window at the wildly blooming flowers and the birds flitting around his garden. He gave no indication that he knew anyone had entered the room.

More than thirty years ago he had been old, but he had been spry and tireless in his efforts for his Littlingham flock. He regularly visited the old and infirm, coached the soccer team and played on the village cricket team. He helped his wife and her committees prepare for the annual church fete and jumble sales, organized youth activities several nights a week, and reveled in playing Father Christmas at the annual village party. Amid his busy life and schedule, he always found time to talk to anyone who needed his advice or guidance.

Barbara studied him, remembering when he was ageless. Now he just seemed ancient.

"Now, Father," Elizabeth said, "This is Barbara Thomas." She gave Barbara an odd little smile. "Do you remember her? She used to live up Primrose Lane, behind All Saints?"

Reverend Morris first scowled at his daughter then looked about him, as if trying to make out his surroundings. His dull gaze settled on the visitors. He smiled, and a transformation took place before them. He suddenly seemed younger, more erect, and his periwinkle-blue eyes twinkled. "Hello, Barbara. How's your mother?"

Barbara's heart lurched then sank, but she smiled back at the old man. "Hello, Reverend Morris. I'm so very pleased to see you."

"No! No, Father." Elizabeth said in a commanding voice. "We talked about this. Dorothy Thomas is dead. Don't you remember?"

"Dead?" His quavering voice faded, and he gazed about the room again.

94

"Agatha's dead."

"Yes, Father, but we're not talking about Mother now, we're talking about Dolly Thomas." Elizabeth grabbed onto the chair and lowered herself to kneel beside her father. She looked directly into his eyes, demanding, "Father, listen to me. You had Dorothy and Charles Thomas' names put on their tombstones. How did you know where and when they were born?"

His gazed looked past his daughter and settled on Peggy. "Oh, hello. Have we met? I'm Bartholomew Morris." He tried to rise out of the chair.

Peggy reached to him and patted his shoulder. "Yes, Reverend. You're looking well."

Before he regained his seat the old man shifted his gaze to look straight at Barbara. "Hello, Lyn." He fell back heavily into his chair. "Oh dear," he said. "You'll have to forgive an old man for his bad manners."

Elizabeth blew a quick breath and heaved herself up onto her feet. She straightened her skirt, smoothing it over her round hips.

Barbara pulled a nearby chair next to the old man and sat. "Reverend, I'm not Lyn. I'm Barbara, Lyn's daughter." It was the first time she had thought of herself like that and it seemed very strange to actually say it.

He hesitated. "She's dead too, isn't she?"

Barbara nodded thinking she needed to work fast while his mind was on her mother. "Do you remember Lyn's surname?"

"Yes. I remember now. She died in the war with her baby son."

As quickly as recognition appeared, it vanished again and the dullness settled into his rheumy eyes. He raised his head and asked, "Is it time for lunch yet?"

"Father," Elizabeth spluttered, "you had lunch an hour ago. Do try to concentrate. Barbara wants to know her surname. Do you remember Lyn's married name?"

Bartholomew Morris leaned back in his chair and glared at Elizabeth. "You're very disagreeable. Who are you? Do I know you?"

"Oh, for goodness sake," Elizabeth's voice reflected her exasperation and she expelled a noisy breath.

The old man straightened in his chair "Don't you scold me, young woman. I'll tell Matron." Yanking the cardigan closer around him he set his shoulders. "Humph." He clamped his lips together and rested his trembling hands in his lap.

Barbara reached over and took one of the old man's cold blue-veined hands in hers. "Thank you for seeing me today, Vicar. I'll try not to tire you, but I do want to know more about my parents. Did you ever meet my father? He was a sailor."

He slowly turned to look into Barbara's eyes. "Oh, you mean Bob? Yes, such a nice lad. I never met the other one." The bright blue eyes twinkled, and just as suddenly, he gave a raucous cackle, and the vacant stare settled once more into dull eyes. A soft moan replaced the hollow laugh, and he began to cry and then a ghastly wail filled the room.

"Oh, please, Reverend Morris. What was my father's surname?" Barbara searched the lined, contorted face. "What other one?" But all recognition had vanished.

"I'm sorry," Elizabeth said in her haughty voice. "He's left us again. I think that's all he can help you with today."

Tears welled in Barbara's eyes. She stood and released the frail hand. "Thank you," she said and leaned over to kiss the wrinkled cheek before she left him.

She thanked Elizabeth and, with even more questions to contemplate, she and Peggy walked in silence to catch the bus back to Littlingham.

His daughter left and the old man closed his eyes and slept briefly. He awoke alone, still facing the garden, his memory as sharp as when he was sixty years younger.

He folded one shaking hand inside the other. Something had triggered a memory of Dorothy Thomas. He couldn't recall what that was, but he clearly remembered her. A rather unattractive woman with a heart so pure one tended to forget her physical appearance.

Charles, her husband, was another matter altogether. Reverend Morris shook his head dismissing the image of the old Welsh curmudgeon.

When Dorothy and Charles had first come to Littlingham, Dorothy had been the proverbial fish out of water. She'd lived all her life in London and village life was very difficult for her. She'd planted a garden and grew magnificent flowers, which she shyly offered for the church altar. Each week she decorated the church with something from her garden. In the summer she brought huge bouquets of her prize-winning roses or dahlias. In the autumn she decorated the church with chrysanthemums and colourful leaves. In winter she brought bunches of red-berried holly.

Reverend Morris invited her many times to share a pot of tea with him, before she finally accepted. Then they had become friends, and over time she'd shared her memories of her family with him. Through her, he'd come to know her pretty sister Clarice and their mother Gladys. Dorothy's love for her niece was evident and she idolized Lyn's children, especially the little red-haired Barbara.

Dorothy Thomas' lot had not been an easy one, but the old cleric never once heard her complain.

LONDON 1930

Dolly's mother, Gladys, craned her neck around the window, and peered in the direction of the train station watching for her daughter.

Arthritis had stiffened the old woman's hips and knees so that she could no longer go down the stairs to the street for a daily natter with her neighbours. Grimacing at the pain in her swollen knuckles, she dropped her knitting into her lap and massaged her fingers.

Confined to the tiny flat she shared with her daughter, she relied increasingly on Dolly for company. But recently Dolly seemed preoccupied, and Gladys watched with increasing interest the small changes in her daughter.

Though Dolly remained unattractive, and nothing could alter her small eyes, square jaw, and large nose, lately there was a glow in her cheeks. Her thin lips still covered uneven teeth, but a spring had developed in her long stride. Her one good feature, curly dark auburn hair, remained hidden in an unruly bun at the back of her head.

Gladys checked the time on the mantelpiece clock and glanced out of the window again. Dolly's tall figure swung into view. From months of practice, Gladys' timing was perfect. Wincing, she rose to her feet and shuffled to the stove. She lifted the simmering kettle and poured a little water into the teapot, swirling it around the inside before dumping the water into the sink. She measured tealeaves into the pot, and covered them with boiling water. Nestled under a brightly colored hand-knitted cozy, the tea steeped so that by the time Dolly reached the flat, it was ready to drink.

"Hello, Mum." Dolly dropped her umbrella and bag in the entry. "How was your day, then?"

Gladys splashed milk into two cups, and filled them with tea. "Ow, can't complain. It wasn't a bad day," she said and stirred a spoonful of sugar into the cups. "Old Shirl was 'ere for a cuppa this a'ernoon."

Dolly sat down at the table and picked up her cup and saucer. "Mum, I've invited a friend for tea on Sunday. You don't mind, do you?" She took a sip of tea and peered over the rim of the cup at her mother.

Gladys squinted at her. She could tell Dolly was gauging her reaction. "Naw, I don't mind but it is someone from yer work? Someone I know?"

"No, you don't know him. I met him on the train. He's the conductor."

"Cor blimey! You met the conductor and invited him for Sunday tea?"

Dolly's cheeks flushed. "Oh, Mum, it's not like that. I met him weeks ago and we've become friends."

As four o'clock approached on Sunday afternoon, Dolly bustled about slicing tomatoes and making fish-paste sandwiches. At ten minutes to four she tested the strawberry blanc-mange with a light touch of her fingertip.

"That's ready then. Now I'll make the tea. He should be here any minute." She pulled off her apron and glanced in the mirror. She ran her hands over her wiry hair, and patted the bun. Her face glowed with excitement.

Charlie Thomas arrived at precisely four o'clock.

Gladys shook his extended hand and looked him up and down. His tall, portly figure almost filled the little sitting room and he spoke in a gruff, sing-song Welsh accent. Hooded by heavy brows, his dark eyes flickered acquisitively about the small flat.

Gladys made note of his flaccid jowls and fringe of white hair on his otherwise bald head, and concluded that he was closer to her own age than to Dolly's thirty-odd years.

"Bloody cheap-skate that one," Gladys said after he'd left. "I'll bet 'es got the first tanner 'e ever earned."

"Don't be so critical, Mum. You hardly know him."

"I don't have to know him to recognize the signs. Asking how much rent we pay. Bloody cheek of the man!" She gave Dolly a sidelong glance. "An' wanting to know if we owned the furniture. All 'e did was talk about money and what things cost. An' another thing, Dol, I know times are 'ard, but his clothes were downright old fashioned."

As the weeks grew into months and Charlie continued his Sunday visits, he began coming earlier and earlier, until he arrived in time for Sunday dinner and stayed through teatime, bringing nothing with him but his hearty appetite.

Gladys complained to her friends. "'Es going to ea' us out of 'ouse and 'ome, and he don't never bring a bite towards the meal, nor even a little somethin' for our Dolly. An' 'er only lucky to have a job at all. We can't afford to be feedin' the likes of 'im."

"I do wish you'd stop complaining about Charlie to the neighbours, Mum. It's none of their business and besides he doesn't hurt you."

"*Doesn't 'urt me?*" Gladys sat up to her full height and waggled her shoulders. "*Doesn't 'urt me?* I only pay half my pension towards the housekeeping, don' I? So that means I'm helping to feed him two meals a week. Two good meals I might add."

"All right, Mum. I'll put in an extra couple of bob for Charlie, if that's what's bothering you." But the situation continued to gall Gladys.

"'Ere Dolly," Gladys said one evening after he'd left. "Why don't 'e never take you out for a meal or to the pictures?"

"Oh, Mum." Dolly's exasperation was evident in a deep sigh as she settled into an easy chair. "He travels all week up and down the line on that train. On Sundays he just likes to stay indoors." She snatched up the newspaper and buried herself behind the open pages.

"Yeah, and ea'," Gladys said. "'E don't half like your sherry trifle."

Dolly jumped up and threw down the newspaper. "Listen, you old nag, I'm not young and I'm not pretty and petite like Clary was. I've never had men flocking to my door." She threw herself back on the couch and covered her face with her huge hands, and began to cry.

Gladys bit her quivering lower lip. "I'm sorry g'ew. I didn't mean to 'urt yer feelings. It's just that I think you deserve better." She reached over and touched Dolly's arm but Dolly pulled away.

"I deserve better? Well, you're right, I do. I'm a nice person, but men never get beyond this ugly face. You don't understand what it's like, Mum. Charlie doesn't love me. I know that. But he likes me, and he's my only chance for marriage and a family." She pulled a hanky from her cardigan sleeve and mopped her eyes and blew her nose. "Oh, Mum, I want children more than anything else in this world, and I'm still young enough to have them. Don't begrudge me this one chance."

Gladys leaned over and wrapped her arms around Dolly's shoulders, gently rocking her in a rare cuddle. She loved this big ugly, kind-hearted daughter of hers.

Dolly was right about one thing. She wasn't a bit like her younger sister. Clary had been a pretty girl and men had flocked to her door. She'd had the pick of the bunch, but she'd married a handsome ne'r-do-well who left her before Lyn was born. Gladys closed her eyes and rocked Dolly, as her thoughts centered on Clary, so bright and full of life as a young girl. But she had turned into a sullen, bitter woman and had died soon after her only child had married.

Gladys never complained about Charlie Thomas again and a year later she died.

"I'll miss the old girl," Dolly said. She and Charlie walked slowly arm in arm out of the churchyard. "Cantankerous as ever right up to the end, wasn't she?" Dolly chuckled and shook her head at the memory of her mother sitting by the window day after day, keeping watch and reporting on the neighborhood. Mum would certainly have had plenty to say about today. It appalled even Dolly when Charlie picked all the flowers out of Mum's little window garden, and took them to her funeral.

"Here we are then." Dolly reached in her bag for her key to the front door. "Time for a nice cuppa tea."

"I'll not come in," Charlie said. "It wouldn't be right for me to call on you *yere* anymore, Dolly."

Dolly stopped, the key hesitating at the lock. She turned and stared at him. "What do you mean, you can't come to the flat anymore? Why ever not?"

"Look you now, Dolly," Charlie said. "Now that your mother is no longer *yere*, I don't think it's proper. What would the neighbours say?"

"Sod the neighbours." A shiver ran down her spine. "Does this mean we won't be seeing each other anymore?" She couldn't believe after she'd invested two years of her life into their relationship, he'd want to end it. Hot tears welled in her eyes and she looked away, up at the dirty windows above the little shops across the street. Hastily pulled curtains covered the inquisitive eyes of the people spying down at them.

"Well..." he hesitated. "I was thinking that perhaps you might want to get married."

Her heart almost leaped out of her throat. She turned back to face him. "Married? Do you mean it?"

He took a step back, gaping at her. "Well, yes...Is that what you want then?"

"Oh, yes." She threw her arms around his neck and kissed his flaming cheek, then turned a triumphant smile toward the fluttering curtains in the dirty little windows.

Charlie, she discovered, had anticipated a lengthy engagement. But Dolly reasoned that Gladys would understand if she didn't mourn her mother for long, and that Gladys of all people would encourage her to strike while the iron was hot.

She began immediate preparations for her wedding and set to scouring and polishing the little flat. On her lunch hour from work, she shopped for material for her wedding dress, and sewed it in the evenings.

Three weeks later, a radiant Dolly, in her new frock and floppy hat decorated with pink silk roses, walked out of the local registry office on the arm of her husband. Charlie hadn't thought enough of the occasion to buy a new suit. A friend from the bookstore where Dolly worked, and her niece, Lyn, had acted as witnesses.

Dolly invited a dozen friends and her family to the flat for a small celebration afterwards. Charlie didn't see the need to invite anyone.

It wasn't much of a marriage. Dolly was shy and uninformed about sex and Charlie, she discovered, could take it or leave it. And he preferred to leave it. Dolly continued working at the bookstore and became more and more Charlie's live-in housekeeper, except that she ached for a baby.

When she finally confronted Charlie, he'd faced her with his mouth agape and his black hooded eyes blazing. "No, woman. There'll be no children."

"But, why? Surely you've imagined having your own children around you."   .

"No," he bellowed. "I don't want children. I don't like children. They make noise and they cost money, don't you know. And just in case you think you can fool me—there'll be no opportunity." He never attempted sex with her again.

As her chances to have a family slipped away, she realized she'd been duped. She'd married him expressly to have children, but he had married her simply for a housekeeper, at no wages.

Dolly accepted her lot and she and Charlie drifted along in a more or less comfortable rut until one fateful day.

Dolly almost ran the last few yards to the station to catch her train home. A late customer kept her from closing the bookshop on time, and she thought she might miss Charlie's last run of the day.

She rounded the corner and stopped short. St. John's ambulances lined the curb in front of the station. Policemen turned back people who tried to get down to the platforms.

Dolly worked her way through the pushing crowd, panic and apprehension engulfing her. "What is it? What's happened?" The policeman straining to keep control, ignored her.

"Please!" She pulled at the policeman's sleeve. "My husband is the conductor on the 5:18 from Kings Cross. Has something happened?" The policeman grabbed her by the arm and pulled her free of the crowd. From under his helmet he looked straight into Dolly's eyes. "Yes, it's the 5:18. There's been an accident."

Her knees threatened to collapse and bile rose in her throat. She swallowed, staring at the policeman's troubled eyes.

"Are you all right, madam?" He struggled against the pushing crowd.

Dolly's mouth moved but no sound came.

Nursing sisters in starched aprons and veils supported the hobbling, bleeding wounded to the ambulances, and Dolly studied each agonized face.

Suddenly, she ducked under the policeman's arm and ran toward the platform. Halfway down the steps she stood aside to make room for a crew carrying a stretcher. As they struggled past her, she gaped at the injured man. His arm, protruding from the blanket, wore the sleeve of a conductor's uniform. Her heart lurched. Charlie's fringe of white hair was coated with blood.

Dolly gave up her job and spent days and weeks sitting beside Charlie's hospital bed, while he slowly healed. Then, supported by crutches, Dolly took him home to their little London flat. Just as her mother had been confined by her arthritis, Charlie became a prisoner of his injuries. Depressed and totally dependent on Dolly he turned surly and aggressive.

"Charlie," Dolly said one day when she'd had time to review their resources, "I'm going to have to find another job."

"No!" he shouted. "I need you *yere*. I can't do for myself."

"Well, without my pay packet we can't live on your pension from the railroad."

"I'll think on it," he grumped.

She hated scenes, but eventually she had to broach the subject again. "Charlie, I've been going over your pension papers. Did you know this is all you'd ever get? No matter how prices go up, your pension will always stay the same."

"Don't keep on, woman. Didn't I say I'd think on it?" Charlie set his jaw and scowled into the fire.

Their financial situation deteriorated with rising food prices, and matters finally came to a head when the county council notified them that the rent would be raised.

"Charlie, we have to do something. We can't manage on your pension. I have to find a job. You're well enough to do for yourself now."

"Stop nagging at me, you stupid cow," Charlie yelled. "I've thought on it."

Charlie's solution was the furthest thing from Dolly's mind.

"We're moving."

"What! Move where?" Dolly collapsed into a chair and gaped at him.

"Before I was on the London train run, I was on a small line. We used to go to this town called Stanton, and I've been thinking, there are probably some villages around that town that would be cheaper to live in than London. I'm thinking we should look into it."

Dolly stared at her husband. "Leave London? I've lived here all my life. I've never even been to a small village. I can't go." She clenched her fists and slammed them down on the arms of the chair. "I won't go and leave Lyn. She's all that's left of my family."

Charlie heaved himself up out of the chair with the aid of his heavy oak cane and limped two steps to stand glowering over her. "Don't you tell me what you will do and what you won't." Menace dripped from his soft, deliberate words.

Dolly's heart raced. Charlie's jealousy over Lyn had caused them words before. But this time, watching the anger in his black hooded eyes, she actually felt frightened. She knew there would be no further argument with him.

It took just about a month to find the right village and Charlie thought to pacify her. "You can 'ave a nice garden *yere*, Dolly. You could grow some vegetables for us."

The possibility of a flower garden had sounded inviting to her, but somehow, Charlie had figured out a way to make gardening more work for her. "Yes, Charlie," she sighed. "And perhaps you'd like me to grow enough to preserve for us, or even enough to sell."

Charlie almost smiled. "That's the spirit!"

Dolly packed up their belongings, and hired a moving lorrie to take them to a tiny cottage in the small village of Littlingham.

CHAPTER ELEVEN

LITTLINGHAM 1985

Barbara arrived at the Black Swan Inn to find Lilianne already there. The young Canadian sat at a small table in the corner of the public lounge sipping a glass of wine. Barbara caught her eye and returned her wave.

"Hi, glad you could make it." A wide smile animated Lilianne's face when Barbara reached the table.

Barbara pulled out a chair and sat. "Hope you haven't been waiting long. Peggy Hilton has invited me to stay with her for a few days. I had to check out of here and move my stuff to Peggy's."

"No problem. Want some wine?"

"Not right now, thanks. What've they got eat? I'm starving." Barbara studied the blackboard tacked over the bar with the day's special menu written on it in white chalk.

"The usual pub fare, but they cook it well here."

"Yes, I remember even when I was a little girl, The Black Swan had a reputation for a good meal. Of course, it had different managers then."

"And a different cook, I should think," Lilianne laughed. "So, you've lived here all your life?" She seemed eager to begin her interview.

"Oh, no. Only from the time I was about four years old. I left when I was almost eighteen."

"You said you went to school with my dad. So you knew my aunt."

"Yes, although we weren't friends. She was older than me."

"Dad said she was called Lilypad, but he couldn't remember why."

"Just silly nonsense. You know how kids give each other nicknames."

"Shall we order?"

"Let's see what's on the regular bill of fare." Without waiting for an answer, Barbara walked to the bar and selected two menus from a stack held upright between an empty glass and a donation can to Doctor Bernardo's Home for Orphaned Children. She handed a menu to Lilianne and sat again while she decided on her dinner.

"What shall I call you? Mrs. McNab or Barbara?" Lilianne regarded her over the top of the menu.

"Oh, Barb, or Barbara, please."

A waitress appeared beside them. "What can I get you, ladies?"

Lilianne decided on lentil soup, a crusty roll and salad.

Barbara tapped her index finger on the menu. "I haven't had real fish and chips for years. I know all that grease isn't good for me, but I'll repent when I get home again." Barbara closed the menu and exchanged a grin with the waitress. "And I'll have a shandy to wash it down."

Lilianne leaned her elbows on the table, cradling her wine glass in her hands. "Do you mind if I ask you questions while we wait, Barbara?"

"No problem. But remember, I was very young when your aunt was killed."

"Yes, but you obviously remember when it happened."

"Of course. There hadn't been a murder in this village in over a hundred years. Lily Ann's caused a sensation."

"Tell me what you remember."

"I believe your grandparents had been out for the evening. They didn't realize Lily wasn't in the house until the next morning when they went to wake her for school. At first it was believed she had run away. Apparently she threatened that periodically when she fought or argued with her parents. Although the village constable was called right away, they began checking the bus schedules to Stanton, and the train times to London. Then Stanton police were called in."

"Any idea how long that took?" Lilianne had opened a notebook and seemed to be checking Barbara's story against notes written there.

"Well, she went missing on a Sunday night...I don't know." Barbara bit her lip while she concentrated on the distant memory. "It was probably Thursday or Friday before the authorities got serious about searching for her."

"Then what happened?"

"A day or two later—Saturday afternoon, I believe—some kids found her body in the cave down by the river."

"You have a very good memory. According to the police reports that is exactly what happened."

The waitress brought their food to the small table and elbowed her way back to the bar through the increasing crowd.

"Tell me the reaction in the village."

Barbara placed her napkin across her lap and picked up her knife and fork. "Well, there were whispers that she'd been raped, but we little kids had no idea what that meant. We were very naïve in those days." She sprinkled her fish and chips with a liberal dose of malt vinegar and reached for the salt.

"Do you remember any details about the investigation?" Lilianne sipped steaming soup from the edge of the spoon.

"Every man who was in the village that night had to account for his whereabouts. The children wondered why only the men were being questioned, but it seemed obvious to everyone else. In the end, after every alibi had been checked, it was supposed the murderer was a passing opportunist. As you know, no one was ever charged."

Lilianne consulted her notebook. She stabbed at her salad and raised a forkful into her mouth.

Barbara had the distinct impression that Lilianne wasn't satisfied that she had all the pieces of the puzzle. "I'm sure I haven't told you anything you didn't know. How about you telling me why you're doing this after all these years."

Lilianne closed her notebook and chewed a bite of crusty roll before she answered. "I'm a recent graduate with a degree in journalism and work for a small newspaper. I've always wondered about my aunt, especially since I'm supposed to look so much like her. My grandparents are both dead now and I thought it sad that everyone, except my dad, has forgotten her. So, I decided to write a book about her murder. I'm not trying to solve the case or anything like that. I just don't want her memory, or what happened to her, to be entirely forgotten." She selected some salad then seemed to change her mind about eating it. She placed her fork on the plate, pursed her lips and studied her fingernails.

Barbara was afraid the girl was going to cry. "Have you had any luck with the official reports?"

Lilianne brightened and resumed her meal. "Not yet. But I have permission to dig in the basement where the files are archived. That's about all the police could do for me. I haven't seen the inquest report or the postmortem findings either." She raised her head and smiled. "But I've been promised access to them. Unfortunately, it was such a long time ago that most of those who lived here and might remember more about the incident are gone."

Barbara had been eating while Lilianne spoke. Now she pushed her plate aside and sipped her shandy. "There are still a few people living in the area who might remember more details than I can. Peggy Hilton for one. She lived here then. And I can tell you from personal experience, she is still as sharp as a tack. I'll try and get you two together."

"Thanks. I'd love to talk to her and I appreciate any help you can give me."

Barbara began to warm to the idea of helping the young woman seated across from her. "I've just thought of something. I'll bet old Reverend Morris was in on the whole thing right from the start. He was the vicar here then, and knew everything that went on in the village. He's still around."

The young woman looked up surprised. "Oh, really?"

"Yes, I saw him this afternoon, as a matter of fact. He's in his nineties now and unfortunately suffers from Alzheimer's. Still, he's lucid part of time, so it might be worth a visit."

"Great! How can I contact him?"

"You'll have to clear it with his daughter first. Her name is Elizabeth Smythe-Bickerton. I'll get the phone number for you."

"Would you? I'd really appreciate that."

Barbara nodded. "Sure, no problem. In the meantime, I'll ask Peggy if anyone else who was around when your aunt died still lives in the area."

"Thanks, Barbara. You've been very helpful. Would you like another drink?"

CHAPTER TWELVE

LITTLINGHAM 1985

The next morning as Barbara prepared to catch the bus to London the phone rang.

Peggy answered it and her eyebrows rose in a gesture of surprise. She held the receiver out to Barbara. "It's for you." Her little black eyes twinkled with curiosity.

Barbara automatically checked her watch. It couldn't be John at this hour. Puzzled she took the phone. "Hello?"

"Elizabeth Smythe-Bickerton here." The vicar's haughty daughter wasted no time with pleasantries and came straight to the point. "Barbara, as you know, my father isn't well, but he has periods when he's the old self."

"Yes," Barbara said.

"Well, last night Father and I had a conversation in which he remembered you coming to see him yesterday, and he also recalled something else." She sounded very self-important.

"Really?" Barbara's mental antenna engaged suddenly fully alert.

Elizabeth hesitated. "I think it would be better if you came around. Would that be convenient?"

"I'll be on the next bus. Thank you." Barbara cradled the phone, her heart pounding.

"Whatever's the matter?" Peggy's eyes widened.

Barbara ran up the stairs telling Peggy over her shoulder what Elizabeth had said. "Another minute and I'd have been off to London and missed the call." She grabbed her purse and flew out the door in time to catch the next bus to Piggen.

Elizabeth opened the cottage door to Barbara's knock. "Do come in. I'm very excited to have news for you." She led Barbara into the parlor.

The old man's chair in front of the window sat vacant. "Your father isn't here today?" She was genuinely disappointed not to see him.

"He's sleeping at the moment." Elizabeth eased her considerable bulk onto the sofa and using her ring-laden hand, indicated a chair. "Do have a seat."

Barbara 's stomach fluttered, and her fingers drummed on the arm of the chair. Impatiently she clasped her hands together in her lap.

Elizabeth sat facing her obviously enjoying the theatrical anticipation she'd created. She held her head slightly tilted with an air of drama about her and leaned forward, her eyes searching Barbara's face, expectant. "My father told me you had a brother." Barbara's heart sank. This was old news. "Yes, I know about the baby. He died with my mother."

"*Au, contraire*," Elizabeth flicked her hand, jangling her bracelets. "You had an older brother." A wide grin split her equine face.

Barbara sat rooted to the chair, her mouth dry. Pins and needles prickled her fingertips and her toes. She forced her tongue over her dry lips. "An older brother? Where is he? What happened to him?"

"Yes, well that's the other thing. Apparently he was evacuated to one of the dominions during the war."

Barbara's heart lurched and began to pound. "The dominions? You mean overseas?"

"Exactly."

"Did your father say which country?"

"No. That's all I could get out of him, I'm afraid." She studied Barbara's face as if judging the effect she was creating.

"He didn't by any chance remember my father's full name, did he?" Barbara held her breath.

"I'm sorry. That's all he told me." She spread her hand at the base of her throat in a condescending gesture. "Does it help you with your quest?"

Barbara sucked air deep into her lungs, surprised that she could even breathe again. "Oh yes. Thank you, Elizabeth. Thank you so much."

"*Noblesse oblige*," Elizabeth said with a royal wave of her hand. The superior air had returned.

STANTON 1985

The pinched-faced woman behind the counter focused her small pig eyes on Barbara's face. Breath rushed from the woman's lips in a noisy, exasperated sigh. "We are not a research center. We are a county council office and on Monday mornings we are very busy."

"Well, I really am sorry to disturb you." Barbara imitated the clerk's tone. "But all I need is a little information. Just tell me where I can find the records of adoptions that occurred in this county during the Second World War, and I'll leave you to your *busy* schedule."

The woman sniffed. "American, aren't you? We get a lot of Americans in here looking for their *roots* but the records aren't kept in this office." Her mouth turned up in a mean smirk.

"Where are they kept?" persisted Barbara in the same tone.

The clerk's thin mouth barely moved. "In London." She turned her back.

Barbara's cheeks burned. She clenched her fists, digging her fingernails into her palms. She had not slept well again, and the latest information about having another brother had jumbled her thoughts until her head throbbed. "Listen you arrogant, so-called public servant." The clerk swung around to face her. "For your information I was born in this country and if this is the way you usually treat Americans, I wonder you haven't caused another revolution. I'm asking you for assistance with public records. You may have worked here since your childhood, but you don't own the records. You are paid only to be their keeper and I have every right to examine them."

The clerk drew herself up and yanked on the bottom of her sweater with both hands. Her eyes blazed through the magnifying spectacles on the end of her thin nose. "The record you want is the Adopted Children's Register. It's kept at Titchfield in Hampshire. The office of the general registrar." Her lips turned up at the edges in the semblance of a smile. She began to turn away again.

"Just a minute. Are there copies at any other office or do I have to go to Titchfield?"

"Saint Catherine's House in London has an index and they can issue a certificate." She walked away.

"And what year did the index begin?"

Without turning around, she mumbled, "1927."

"Thank you." Barbara used carefully measured syllables. "Now that wasn't so hard was it?"

The woman turned and gave Barbara a withering look.

Barbara caught the next bus for London and hurried along Kingsway to the Public Record Office.

The once white Portland Stone of St. Catherine's House was grime coated and as dark as the cloudy morning. Barbara hurried up the wide, shallow steps and through the revolving door. The record office was crowded. Everyone in England must be researching their past, she thought as she made her way to the counter and collected the certificates she'd ordered on her first visit. There were no vacant seats, but a wide windowsill served the purpose. Had it only been four days since she ordered the certificates? So much had happened, not the least of which was finding out she was not whom she had thought.

She put her briefcase and bag beside her and made herself comfortable on the windowsill while she studied the two certificates in her hand. John's parents' marriage certificate coincided with the information on his birth certificate, except that the letter C as a middle initial for his mother was now revealed as Clarice.

Barbara stared at the paper, wondering what the odds were that this not too common name should be John's mother's as well as her own middle name. Another coincidence struck her. John had named their daughter Janet and gave her Barbara's middle name, Clarice. *Did he know that was his mother's name too?* She thought again how secretive he was about his family, especially his mother.

Dolly and Charlie's marriage certificate held no excitement for her now that she knew they weren't her parents, but it did tell her Dolly's maiden name. A thrill ran down Barbara's spine as she realized that since Dolly and her own grandmother were sisters they shared the same maiden name.

She put the two marriage certificates in her briefcase and inquired at the information desk about the adoptions index.

"I'm sorry, madam, special arrangements must be made with the Registrar General's Office to view it." The clerk had been pleasant enough.

"Before I do that, could you please tell me what information I can expect to find there?"

The clerk smiled. "Yes, it gives the child's new name, birth date, court, entry date and reference number and district, as well as the adoptive parents' names, address and occupations."

Barbara thanked her. She sighed and turned away from the counter. That information wasn't going to help her find out who she was, only who she became, and she already knew that—Barbara Clarice Thomas.

Disappointed, she left the record office and went to find a cup of coffee while she planned the next step in her search strategy.

The restaurant served a good cappuccino. Barbara sipped the hot, creamy drink while she mulled over her meagre information. Everything depended on her finding her birth name, and there seemed to be only one way, a very long and tedious way, but it would probably work.

She knew her birth date and place, and Peggy had assured her that her name was Barbara even before she was adopted. So she would search for a birth registered in the first quarter of 1936 in or around London. And pray she'd been named before her birth was registered.

She hurried back across the street, and ran up the wide steps to St. Catherine's House, and took down the first alphabetical index.

It was arduous work, made more frustrating because Barbara seemed to have been a popular name that year. To make it even more difficult, she wasn't certain which of the registration districts were in London. The queue leading to a clerk for assistance was too long to wait for each questionable find. Instead she wrote down all the possible entries and by the late afternoon, had a long list of likely candidates. Her shoulders ached and her head throbbed after hours of poring over the heavy books. She took her list to a very sweet, accommodating clerk, who crossed off the registration districts that weren't in or around London.

The clang of a bell shattered the quiet rustling of papers. Startled, Barbara looked around at everyone gathering up papers.

"Why is the bell ringing?" she asked a woman standing next to her.

"Oh, that means they're going to chuck us out and close up."

Barbara checked her watch and was amazed to find it was half-past four. No wonder she felt exhausted.

She put her papers in her briefcase, and left the building to take the tube train to Victoria. She caught the express bus to Littlingham and settled into the bus seat, grateful to Peggy for the invitation to stay with her for as long as she was in England.

Throughout the journey Barbara couldn't shake the feeling that she needed to take a different approach to her problem. But what could she do? Frustrated and discouraged she closed her eyes and dozed until she reached the village stop.

Peggy opened the door to her knock. "Oh, Barbara, you do look tired. Come and have a nice cup of tea. Dinner will be ready soon."

"Oh, thanks. A cup of tea would be wonderful." She collapsed onto the chintz sofa, inhaling the rich savoury aroma of lamb wafting from the kitchen. Her mouth watered. She hadn't eaten lunch.

"Something smells wonderful," she called out to Peggy.

"It's shepherds pie. Do you like it?"

"I love it, but haven't eaten it in years."

Over dinner she told Peggy about her day. "I'm sure there has to be an easier way to find my birth name. The way I'm doing it is slow going and will cost a fortune if I have to order all those certificates. I had no idea there would be so many entries." She yawned behind her hand and gave a tired shrug.

"You need a good night's rest. Tomorrow is soon enough to sort it all out."

Barbara smiled at the older woman, grateful for her company and her compassion. "Yes, I think I'll turn in." She rose from the chair, a goodnight ready on her lips, when suddenly all fatigue vanished.

"Of course! Why didn't I think of this before?" She could hardly contain her excitement.

"What is it?" Peggy's eyes widened with anticipation. "What's the matter?"

"Peggy, how well did you know my mum? Dolly I mean."

"We were friends. As friendly as neighbours ever are. You live so close together, you try to stay friendly but private, if you know what I mean."

Barbara nodded. She could understand that arrangement, especially when they shared common walls. It must have been hard not to know each other's business.

"Dolly was quite a bit older than me and she had your da to care for. I was a young widow with three lively children to look after when I came here." Peggy glanced at the portrait on the mantelpiece of herself and her husband George.

"Didn't you live in this house when my mum and da came here to Littlingham? I thought you were born in this village."

"I was born here. My parents had a little place across the river, over near Billy's farm. But I left and went to work in Stanton. That's where I met and married George." She smiled a gentle sort of secret smile, then continued. "I moved back to Littlingham with the children at the beginning of the war, when George went into the army. He thought I should be closer to my mum and dad. It was a good idea, as it turned out, and I've been here ever since. Your mum and da were already living next door. So I only knew them about a year before you came. We became good friends over the years, though."

"But you knew my mother, Lyn. You told me you met her when she visited a couple of times." An excited tremble ran through her. "What did she look like?"

"Well, she was a tiny woman. Full of nervous energy, she was. Reminded me of a little bird. Her hair was a bright coppery red and her eyes were…" Peggy gazed off into space, a look of concentration and a frown wrinkling her forehead.

Barbara didn't interrupt her.

Finally Peggy seemed to have the vision she was looking for. Her face cleared and her eyes twinkled with triumphant pleasure. "Her eyes were aquamarine."

Barbara swallowed, unable to speak. Her body trembled. "Peggy, you've just described my granddaughter Laurie."

Except for the tick of the clock on the mantle piece and Reggie's purring, the room was very quiet. Then Barbara had another question. "You told me Lyn's mother was Dolly's sister. Did Dolly ever mention her sister's first name?"

"No, dear. I'm sorry." Peggy stared down at Reggie curled up on her lap.

Barbara wondered if she answered without really thinking about it. "She never said her first name? Did she ever say anything such as, 'my sister so-and-so, or Lyn's mother…'?" Her voice trailed off.

Peggy stopped stroking the cat's head and looked up at Barbara. "Her name was Clary! Yes, that's what they called her." She sat up straight, her blackberry eyes bright with excitement. "But her name was Clarice. I remember Dolly saying your middle name was the same as your grandmother's."

A tingle beginning in Barbara's scalp radiated through her body. "Oh, thank you." She could barely see Peggy for the tears welling in her eyes.

"Does that help then?" Peggy looked astonished.

"Oh yes. Don't you see? Dolly's maiden name was Chandler. So my grandmother's name was Clarice Chandler. Knowing that, I can find her birth certificate, then her marriage certificate. When I know Lyn's father's name, I can get her marriage certificate. Then I'll know my father's name and I can get my own birth certificate."

"Oh, my dear." Peggy reached for Barbara's hand across the table and gave it a sympathetic pat. "It all sounds so complicated."

"Not really. It will take time, but you've made it so much easier."

CHAPTER THIRTEEN

USA 1985

John stared at his image in the bathroom mirror and contemplated the dark stubble on his chin. He ran his hand through his blue-black hair now flecked with white, and smiled, recalling Barbara's comments about the white streaks at his temples.

She had come up behind him and tickled his ribs. "You look distinguished and learned. You might even be mistaken for a professor of English at some Ivy-League university." He sure missed her. She'd phoned earlier to tell him she'd left the Black Swan Inn and was now staying with her former neighbor. The longer she stayed in England the more entrenched she seemed to become. He wanted her home. Suddenly every nerve in his body tingled. Glaring at his image in the mirror he gave voice to his thought. *Admit it—you want to make love to her.*

He assembled his shaving gear, listening to the rain beating on the skylight above him. He wished he'd been more attentive and sympathetic to Barb. What she'd said on the phone hadn't really registered with him until much later, after he'd had his coffee and cleared his head of sleep. She'd sounded devastated and at the same time excited, and his first thought had been to use it as an excuse to get her to come home.

He stared at himself in the mirror. "McNab," he said to his reflection, "sometimes, you're a real bastard." Black eyes stared back at him and he began to lather up his face with shaving soap. The rain beat harder on the skylight, and his mind drifted back to the rainy day he and Barbara had first made love.

LONDON 1955

They walked with arms around each other, under a dark sky, heavy with the threat of rain. Intent on each other, they'd ignored the first light raindrops. Suddenly, the roiling black clouds opened and the rain came down in torrents.

He gripped her hand and, dragging her, they ran for shelter. Restricted by her pencil slim skirt and high-heeled shoes, she struggled to keep up with his long strides.

His cap and greatcoat protected him from the rain, but by the time they found a dry place under the eave of a shop, she was soaked through. He wrapped his arms around her and as he bent to kiss her upturned face, the rain ran in rivulets off the peak of his cap onto her face.

She squealed with laughter and snuggled closer into his arms. "I'm freezing." She wore no coat over her dove-gray suit.

"Come on." He took her hand, and pulled her after him, as he ran.

She stumbled behind him. "Where are we going?"

"To my hotel. It's just around this next corner." He had to yell to be heard over the rain battering the sidewalk.

Her black patent-leather pumps squelched with each hurried step along the hotel corridor. By the time they reached the door to his room, they were breathless from running and laughing. He fumbled the key into the door lock while she shivered hopping from one foot to the other.

Inside the room, he shook the rain off this cap and draped his coat over the back of a chair. His uniform had stayed dry but his shoes and socks were wet.

She kicked off her sodden shoes, and pulled off her drenched jacket. Her black sweater was plastered to her skin outlining the contours of her breasts. Rain streamed off her hair and her teeth chattered. She looked absolutely pathetic.

"You'd better peel off and get warm." He yanked a blanket off the bed and handed it to her. "Wrap up in this while I run you a hot tub."

Twenty minutes later she came out of the bathroom hugging the blanket around her with her wet hair wound in a towel. Without make-up, her freckled pink face glowed.

He'd changed his socks and put his shoes near the heater to dry. Room service had just delivered hot tea and sandwiches.

"Oh, food. Good, I'm starving." She crawled across the bed dragging her blanket, and settled on the edge, beside him. Between bites of ham sandwiches they giggled together about how wet they'd gotten, and the sound her wet shoes had made when she walked.

"You looked like a half-drowned kitten." He grinned and kissed her gently on the nose.

"What am I to do about my clothes? They're draped all over your bathroom."

"Don't worry about it, they'll dry eventually." He unwound the towel from her head and used it to rub her hair, stopping to kiss her neck behind her left ear. She smelled of perfumed soap. "I love you," he said.

"I know you do, and I love you," she whispered turning her head to brush her lips along his cheek.

He nuzzled her throat. "I think I've been in love with you since I saw you dancing with Budd. I couldn't get you out of my mind. And I didn't want to." He spoke into her damp hair, savoring the fresh smell of her. "That first time I phoned you and asked you to meet me—it shocked me that I was able to do that. Love conquers cowardice, I guess." He laughed softly.

Barbara looked up at him. "Well, it certainly took you long enough to summon up the courage. You know, you never did tell me what took you so long."

"Cowardice." Even now, he was embarrassed to tell her how shy and nervous he'd been. He would never have made the call at all without Budd's coaching. "I honestly couldn't believe you'd be interested in me. Then I was scared that I'd waited too long and you'd found someone else."

"I felt the same way about you. I had just about given up hope when you phoned." She breathed against his ear and he tingled all over. "I didn't know that what I was feeling was called love. I just knew I wanted to be near you. And when you first held my hand, it made me feel all funny inside." Her eyes shone mischievously. "And that first kiss. I was such an innocent." She gave a self-conscious giggle. "You made my knees weak."

He remembered that first kiss too, and the memory brought an immediate physical response. He placed his hands on either side of her face and his mouth came to hers smothering whatever she would have said next.

She raised her arms to encircle his neck and the blanket fell away.

He leaned back in elated wonder to admire her firm young body. He didn't speak—he couldn't—he didn't know what to say to express his pleasure. He was very aware of his heart beating at twice its normal rate. He moved towards her and stroked the pale skin of her breast with his trembling fingers. He kissed her throat and trailed his lips to replace his hand. Her little gasp of pleasure was all the encouragement he needed. He kissed her parted lips and lowered her to the bed.

She hugged him to her, and responsive and trusting accepted him, her first love.

All that happened was in great silence of the afternoon, broken only by the rain pattering against the window, and their faint murmurings of love to each other.

Later, snuggled in his arms, under the warm blankets, she said, "I wish it could always be like this."

"Always?" he teased. "We can't make love all the time. We do have to eat occasionally."

"Oh, you! You know what I mean. I wish we could be together always."

"Why can't we?"

"Because tomorrow we have to go back to work. But I wish we could spend all our tomorrows together."

"I want that, too." He suddenly raised himself onto his elbow and looked into her lovely grey eyes. "Will you marry me, Barb?"

"Yes...oh yes!" She reached her lips to meet his.

Releasing him, she sighed. "But it will have to wait until we both finish our military obligations. After that when we're both civilians again. Then we'll be married."

"That's too long a time to wait." He pulled her to him and kissed her long and hard feeling the pressure of her body against his.

In the weeks that followed they shared many more wonderful hours of love. They'd plan and plot to make them happen. Sometimes he could only get a one-day pass. Other weekends she'd travel all night just to spend a few hours with him then make the journey back to Manby having gone without sleep.

The lack of sleep was taking its toll. Barbara walked around in a daze of exhaustion. She did her work by rote and collapsed at the end of the day when she got back to the billet. Her friend's mirth turned to concern when she almost passed out.

"I just need some rest," she protested. "I won't go to London this weekend. I'll stay here and sleep."

The next morning she threw up, and again the next morning.

That night, after lights out, Lorna and Jean came to Barbara's bed and sat, one on either side. Lorna took Barbara's hand and patted it reassuringly while Jean whispered to her. "You're pregnant."

"What! I can't be."

"Sshh!" Lorna slapped a hand over Barbara's mouth stifling her shriek. "Well, you certainly show all the signs."

A baby! Barbara couldn't stop thinking about it.

The lights had been turned out more than a half hour before, but the lamplights outside illuminated the billet and the rows of beds along each wall. The deep breathing of her twenty roommates told her she alone was still awake with her thoughts.

Becoming a mother frightened her, but at the same time, it thrilled her. She stroked her flat belly thinking that a new little being nestled there. The baby she and John had created.

John! What would he say?

She couldn't tell him over the phone. She needed to see his reaction. She loved him, and all his words and actions told her he loved her. Still, what if he wasn't pleased? The thought frightened her. What would she do?

In her narrow bed she tried to imagine John delighted at the thought of being a father—laughing, hugging her and making plans. Then she imagined him angry, sullen and telling her he didn't want to see her again. No! He'd never be like that. Of course he'd be shocked, she thought, but never angry or blame her.

What was it Lorna had said? "It takes two to tango, mate!"

She smiled to herself remembering the first time John had made love to her. How naive she had been—sitting wrapped in a blanket with nothing on underneath and then being shocked when it had fallen away—and the look of surprise and...what? Yes, admiration, on John's face!

A delicious sensation crept over her remembering John's tentative first touch on her bare breast. She hadn't objected, in fact she wanted it. His passionate kiss led to further exploration. She tingled at the memory. Her body had been alive with anticipation as he lowered her to the bed. She'd hugged him so close she could feel the drumbeat of his heart against her own.

She lay looking up at his face. His expression had been at once tender and fierce.

Her movements came naturally and instinctively, which surprised her. John must have known it was a totally new experience for her. Just as is it was obvious to her that it was not new to him. She'd been jealous and disappointed, but secretly she was glad that he'd been experienced.

John longed to see Barbara. It had been three weeks since they were last together. She'd had duty one weekend, and he'd had to work the next. He'd phoned her but she seemed distant and he was afraid she had lost interest in him. He couldn't bear it if he lost her now.

He'd never thought much about love, and he certainly hadn't thought he would want to get married—at least, not yet. But he hadn't counted on meeting someone like Barb and falling in love. She filled his thoughts all day while he worked and all night in his dreams.

They'd talked on the phone two nights ago and she assured him she still loved him. He'd begged her to come to London.

He lay on the bed in the hotel, smoking, idly examining the diamond ring he held in his hand. They'd never discussed a ring, but he needed to make it official—she was his and he wanted everyone to know it.

A tap on the door brought him out of his reverie. He shot off the bed and yanked open the door. He reached for her, and his excited greeting died in his throat.

She stood perfectly still, and looked up at him, appealingly. The freckles on her thin face stood out against her pale skin, and dark circles under her eyes emphasized their size.

And there was something else—fear?

"Barb, what is it? What's wrong? Are you ill?"

She burst into tears and flung herself into his arms. He pushed the door closed with his foot and led her over to the bed. They sat down and he held her close to him and smoothed her hair, all the time saying, "Please don't cry. Tell me what's wrong."

At last she stifled her sobs long enough to choke out an explanation. "I'm going to have a baby."

"Oh, sweetheart." His mind suddenly went blank.

"You're not angry, are you?" Tears continued to well up in her eyes.

"No. No, of course not. Are you sure about this?" He sucked air deep into his lungs and blew it out. "Wow! It's just that you took me by surprise." Surprise was putting it mildly. He was in shock. He held her close while she sobbed against his chest. He kissed the top of her head while his thoughts raced. *This is my fault. I knew what an innocent she was. I should have been more careful.*

She raised her head and looked into his eyes. "You are angry. I can tell."

"Honey, I am not angry." He wrapped her in a hug.

She sobbed again choking on her words. "Tell me what I should do."

"What *you* should do?" He tilted her chin and looked into her tear filled-eyes. "Barb, honey, we're in this together. I've loved you since we first met, and I've told you many times I want to spend the rest of my life with you. You said you felt the same way. You said you'd marry me."

"Yes, but that was before. Do you still want me?"

"What a dumb question. Wipe your tears and look what I have for you." He handed her the velvet box.

She blinked back her tears and opened the box. "Oh, John!" She gasped. "It's beautiful." She threw her arms around his neck and kissed him.

He unhooked her arms from his neck and took the box from her grip. "I love you, Barb." He slipped the ring on her finger. "Why don't we get married now, right away?"

She began to cry again. "I can't. I'm only nineteen."

He sat back and gaped at her. "What's your age got to do with it?"

"The legal age to marry without parents' permission is twenty-one. I can't get permission from my parents, because they're dead." She wiped her tears, and sniffled. "I won't be able to stay in the air force either. What am I going to do?" She looked very young and vulnerable.

John smiled at her. "Honey, just because you don't have parents doesn't mean you can't get married. There has to be someone who can give us permission. Can't we go to a judge or something?"

CHAPTER FOURTEEN

LINCOLNSHIRE 1955

Barbara, Lorna and Jean, dressed in their best uniforms and spit-polished, sensible shoes, waited at the main gate of RAF Manby. A warm sun shone in a brilliant blue sky. New pale-green leaves and blossom petals fluttered in the morning breeze. An occasional insect buzzed by, and a chorus of birds sang for their mates.

Barbara thought she couldn't have ordered a more beautiful day for her wedding. She had been so nervous and excited she'd hardly slept the previous night. "I wish they'd hurry up," she said exhaling a pent-up breath.

Lorna fidgeted from one foot to the other. "I'm so nervous you'd think I was the one getting married." She looked down at her legs. "Gosh, it was so nice of John to give us the nylons. I can't think of a present I would have appreciated more."

Barbara smiled. John had given each girl a gift of two pairs of grey nylons for being Barbara's wedding attendants. She knew the pleasure of wearing nylon stockings. He'd kept her supplied since their second date.

During their first weekend together in London, while she and John had strolled the streets and taken in the sights, Barbara constantly pulled her skirt away from her legs.

"Is there something wrong with your skirt?" John stopped walking and frowned at her legs.

"Not my skirt, exactly. It's these bloody cotton stockings." Irritated, she yanked at her skirt bunched up around her crotch. "They make the wool skirt climb."

"Do you have to wear those awful-looking things? Aren't you allowed to wear nylons?"

"Yes. As long as they're gun-metal grey, but they're as scarce as hen's teeth and twice as pricey."

The next weekend when they met, John gave her two pairs of gun-metal grey nylon stockings.

For the umpteenth time, Jean walked to the road and looked in the direction of Louth. "Not yet," she said and walked slowly back to her friends.

Startled by the sudden sound of a car horn, they turned in unison. A shiny black limousine glided to a stop beside them. The driver and passengers each wore a United States Air Force uniform and had a white carnation pinned to his lapel.

John bounded out of the back seat of the car and threw his arms around Barbara, crushing his flower, as he kissed her. "Sorry we're late, honey. I stopped to get this." He held a nosegay of pink rosebuds and baby's breath.

Barbara took it and inhaled the scent. "It's lovely. Thank you." She kissed his cheek.

John introduced his friends. Mitchell was a tall, swarthy, gentle man. Barbara immediately liked him.

She already knew Budd. She had danced with him the night she and John had first met. He had curly blonde hair, even white teeth and a flashing smile. Chiseled features, and bright blue eyes completed the handsome face. He was very good looking, and knew it.

Lorna couldn't hide her admiration of him. Her eyes sparkled as he pinned a pink rosebud boutonniere to the front of her jacket.

"He's smashing, Barb," she stage whispered.

Budd lapped it up.

"Okay. Let's get a move on." John steered Barbara to the back seat of the car.

Budd drove. "Geez, I wish these people would learn to drive on the right side of the road. I can't tell how much room I have to spare." He steered first too far to one side of the road, then overcompensated.

Mitchell sat on the edge of the front seat. "Well, for God's sake don't scratch the damn car. It's my butt in a sling if you wreck it." He gripped the dashboard peering anxiously ahead.

"Why don't you let me drive? I'm sure I can do better than you."

"Aw, shut up, Mitch. You're making me nervous. I'll get the hang of it before we get onto the main drag." Budd swerved the car around a bend, throwing them all to one side. They fell into each other in a heap of hats and flowers.

"Damn it, Budd. Take it easy. You'll kill us all," John said.

Barbara clung to John's arm and closed her eyes. She didn't open them again until the car jerked to a stop outside the Louth Town Hall. A delicious little shiver ran through her and she drew in a deep breath to calm her excitement.

John helped her out of the car and gave her a hug. "Nervous?"

"I'll say." Barbara blew out a long breath and turned to her friends. "Do I look all right?" she whispered.

"You look smashing. Come on, or you'll lose your slot," Jean nudged her towards John.

He took her hand and ushered her through the town hall door and down the hall. Outside the Registry Office he stopped, took her other hand and drew a deep breath.

"There's still time to change your mind." His eyes twinkled and his lips formed into a lopsided grin.

"Not likely!" She smiled and squeezed his hands.

A white haired, grandmotherly Registrar introduced herself. Barbara gripped her nosegay of flowers and willed her legs not to quiver, but the formality binding them in marriage took only a few minutes.

John removed the engagement ring from Barbara's finger and replaced it with a gold band. He slipped the diamond ring back on her finger and kissed her.

She could hardly hold the pen to sign the register. It was all over so quickly. They were married.

Back outside the town hall, Budd rubbed his hands together. "This calls for a celebration. Pub's just opened." He pointed across the street. "Come on. The first round's on me." He led the wedding party to The Red Rose and ordered drinks to toast the bride and groom.

Mitchell insisted they limit it to just one round. He was the best man and had other plans. John had asked him to make arrangements for a luncheon celebration and Mitchell had kept the location secret.

Budd managed to down a couple of extra drinks, then insisted on driving. He seemed to have only one speed—fast.

"Slow down, you idiot." Mitch became increasingly agitated. "We'd like to get there in once piece."

"Where the hell is *there*, Mitch?" Budd's irritation was showing.

Barbara held on to John in a tight grip. Budd's driving terrified her. She couldn't even enjoy the beautiful countryside flashing past. Even Lorna, who usually had something to say about everything, was strangely quiet sitting in the front seat wedged between Mitchell and the reckless driver.

A turn off the main road led along a country lane so narrow the high hedges on either side brushed the car doors. The lane suddenly gave way to a tiny stone bridge over a stream, ending in a pond where ducks paddled.

A gravel path separated the bridge from an ancient inn. Vine-covered red brick at ground level and white-washed above, it was topped with a thatched roof. Running alongside the building stood a row of thatched cottages, their postage-stamp size gardens ablaze with flowers. Over a belt of trees, the bell tower of a little church was visible.

"This is it. I hope you like it." Mitchell turned an anxious look on the wedding party to gauge their reaction.

"Oh, Mitchell, it's lovely." Barbara gazed in wonder at the tiny village.

Budd skidded the car across the gravel. "Jesus Christ! Where the hell are we?"

"The village is called Swigglesthorpe, and the pub is the Pig and Whistle." Mitchell laughed. "I just couldn't resist it when I found it."

"How the hell *did* you find it?" Budd stared about him.

Barbara was ecstatic. "It looks exactly like a Clyde Cole sketch. Oh, John, isn't it marvelous?"

A man ducked through the tiny door of the Pig and Whistle and came out to greet them with a rosy-cheeked smile. "Welcome. Welcome. I'm Jonathan Hannington, the landlord."

He could have stepped right out of a Dickens story, and Barbara immediately dubbed him Mr. Fezziwig.

He wrapped Barbara's hand in both of his. "Many years of happiness, my dear." He raised his ample eyebrows another notch and turned to John, "May I?"

John nodded, an amused smile on his face. The landlord kissed Barbara's cheek then he shook John's hand.

"Please, please come in. Your table is ready." He ducked through the door and led them inside to a table covered with a starched white cloth and set with pretty china and a vase of flowers in the middle.

"How about a drink on the house in celebration, whilst I see to your lunch?" The landlord hovered while they settled themselves and Barbara studied the surroundings.

Polished benches, like church pews, lined the wall beneath small leaded windows. Shiny horse and pony brasses hung neatly down the old exposed wood supports and around the unlit fireplace.

Mr. Fezziwig returned with their drinks and stage whispered to Barbara. "We have a couple of ghosts here at the Pig and Whistle." He nodded at a chair beside the fireplace. "The old chap who used that rocking chair for many years still visits us occasionally." On the back was a brass plaque bearing the name and dates of the dead customer.

Barbara played along. "How do you know when he's here?"

"You'll know when you see the chair rocking."

The landlord moved on and Barbara exchanged a smirk with Lorna across the table.

A dark wood shelf, beneath the sloped ceiling, held old china platters and plates. Behind the bar a dozen or so beer glasses and mugs, each labeled with its owner's name, sat in a row.

"How *did* you find this place, Mitchell?" Barbara stared in admiration at her surroundings.

"I like to explore the countryside, and came across it by accident several weeks ago. I fell in love with its quaintness. I can't tell you how pleased I am that you like it."

"Oh, I do. Thank you so much for bringing us here."

After a wonderful, enormous lunch, Mitchell sat down at the piano and played. They sang and laughed.

John came up behind Barbara and wrapped his arms around her. "Happy, darling?" He kissed the top of her head.

"Oh yes. But I was just thinking, I wonder if we should have invited my CO? She did go out of her way to get me permission to get married."

"Too late now. The deed is done and I'm never going to let you get away from me."

She turned to him grinning. "John, do you realize how funny the name of this place is? Years from now when someone asks where we celebrated our wedding, I can say 'the Pig and Whistle at Swigglesthorpe,' and nobody will believe there is such a place." She laughed.

At that moment the barman brought another round of drinks to the table. "Tell you what, missus—a drink on the house, to anyone who can say that three times, in a hurry." He winked at her.

"The Pig and Swiggle at Picklesport!" She laughed. "You try it, John."

"The Pig and Whistle at Swigglesthorpe," he said it slowly.

"No fair," Budd bellowed. "You gotta say it fast. Like this. The Swig and Pickle at Wigglespork." He'd drunk too much anyway and everyone laughed.

Several other customers had joined them around the piano, and they attempted the tongue-twister amid shouts and laughter.

As the evening wore on a barmaid worked behind the counter and Fezziwig continued to deliver drinks. He stopped between Barbara and John. "I didn't tell you about our other ghost, did I? Do you know the poem about the highwayman?"

"Yes, I remember learning it in school. It's about a girl who gave her life to save her lover. He was a highwayman."

"This was the inn and Bess, the landlord's black-eyed daughter of the poem, lived here."

"Go on with you. You're pulling my leg. *The Highwayman* is fiction," Barbara said, delighted by the myth.

"That's what most people think. But 'twas here she died saving her lover's life." He tapped his finger to the side of his nose. "Folks around here know the truth. She's been seen many times."

John chuckled at the man. "Have you seen her?"

"Aye. Beautiful she is. Raven haired, just like the poem says. You might see her. She likes lovers, having lost her own, like. Newlyweds such as yourselves might bring her to visit."

"Okay, we'll watch for her." John grinned. They joined the noisy crowd around the piano singing and laughing. The hours flew by.

John touched Barbara's arm and held out a key to her. "You seem to like this place so much, I got us a room here for the night."

"Oh, John. You really are a romantic." She stood on her tip-toes and kissed his cheek.

"Let's make use of it." He gave her his lop-sided smile.

"What about the ghost?" Barbara grinned at him.

"She's not invited." He took her hand and led her out from the noisy room and up the narrow stairway.

John and Barbara wandered along their favorite stretch of the Thames embankment, arms around each other's waist, content. The comforting smell of deep-fried Atlantic cod still clung to them. He kissed her lightly, his lips tasting faintly tart and vinegary.

"I wonder why fish and chips always tastes so good eaten out of old newspaper?" she said.

"I don't know. Perhaps yesterday's news has something to do with giving it flavour."

She chuckled. "But have you noticed how much better it tastes eaten outside instead of in a restaurant?"

"Hmm." He bent to her again, and kissed the tip of her nose. "I sure love you, Mrs. McNab."

"I love you, too." She smiled up at her husband and hugged his waist. "Oh, I'm so happy. But I wish it didn't have to end so soon." She drew in her breath and released it in a deep sigh. "But I promised myself I wouldn't complain. It just means we're that much closer to being together again, forever."

This was the last day of their honeymoon. They'd had seven glorious days together but tomorrow they had to return to their respective bases.

His squadron was soon to return to the United States. She would be discharged from the Royal Air Force in about a month, and would join him at his base in California. All week they'd been planning their future.

"I know you don't want to make the Air Force your career, John. What do you want to do?"

"I planned, long before I met you, to earn a degree in aeronautical engineering. What do you think of that?"

"It sounds marvelous, but how will we live? I won't be able to work after the baby is born."

"You won't have to, my love. After I complete my four years of service I'll be eligible to receive a college education. Compliments of the United States government."

"You mean they'll actually finance your education?"

"Not only that, but they'll pay us a stipend. That was one of the enticements that made me enlist in the first place. We won't get much money to live on, but we'll manage. Lots of other couples are making it."

"That's incredible. I've been wondering how we would support ourselves." She grinned up at him. "You had this all figured out, didn't you?"

"Don't you worry, sweetheart. Just take care of our baby." He reached over and placed his hand on her still firm belly.

The May afternoon hinted at a warm summer to come. Blossoms scented the air, even over the smell of the traffic. They sauntered along awhile, in silence. But her thoughts raced and she tried out the words in her mind first, before she tentatively asked, "Did you mind that we had no family to invite to our wedding, John?"

He looked down at her, a momentary frown creasing his forehead. "No, of course not. Besides, I don't know about you, but the wedding was just a formality, as far as I'm concerned. It's how we feel about our marriage and each other that really counts."

"That's a smashing thing to say. For the rest of my life, I'm going to remember that you said that." She tightened her arm around his waist again. Caution guided her next question as she concentrated on keeping her voice casual. "Do you remember once telling me that I was nosey when I asked about your family?"

"Yes." He looked into her upturned face and scowled. "What about it?"

"Now that we're a family," she patted her stomach. "I'd like to know about your parents and brother and sister. Tell me what sort of a child you were. I'll bet you were always a good, kind little boy, weren't you?" She laughed at him, teasing, sensing she was treading on thin ice, remembering how evasive he'd been the last time she'd tried to bring up the subject.

"Why are you always on about my family? Let's not spend our last day together talking about the past." He gave her his impish grin. "Want to go back to the hotel?"

"John! I thought we weren't going to keep secrets from each other, ever."

"I love the way the freckles kinda dance when you wrinkle your nose." He bent to kiss the tip.

She pulled back from him, and set her face in what she hoped he'd see as her most stern expression.

"Okay, you win." He took her hand and led her to a vacant bench nearby, overlooking the river. He draped his arm around her shoulder. "I don't have any secrets. It's just that I don't really remember anything about my parents, or my brother or my sister. I was only seven the last time I saw them. So there's nothing really to tell." He fingered a curl behind her ear.

"But I want to know all about you. Tell me about John, the little boy. Tell me what it was like for you here in London when the war first broke out. Were you frightened?"

"No. I can't remember ever being scared in those early days. I suppose there were a lot of peed trousers during the first air raids." He tipped his head back and laughed. "But like most of the kids, I thought the war was great. There was a kind of holiday atmosphere and an excitement."

"If you weren't scared, what made it different?"

"For one thing, all the dads started disappearing, then came home in brand new uniforms. The mums went off to work in munitions factories, or became bus conductors or electricians. The old guys from World War One felt needed again. They strutted about in steel helmets and Home Guard armbands. Those with better eyesight or who were more nimble climbed up on the rooftops as plane spotters. At night the air-raid wardens roamed the streets, looking for chinks of light showing through the blackout curtains."

"In Littlingham we had blackouts, but I never could understand why." Barbara shrugged.

"Well, everyone in London understood why. Without the lights of the city to guide them, the German bomber pilots couldn't see their targets. But once they'd dropped their incendiaries, the blackout didn't matter. The whole city was lit by the fires."

John gave a derisive laugh and turned to kiss the top of Barbara's head. "I don't suppose Littlingham felt the food shortages either, like they did in the cities."

"I remember clothing being in short supply. But that may have had more to do with economics. My parents were very poor. And, of course, there were never enough sweetie coupons. Otherwise I think we ate pretty much the way we always had. Nothing fancy."

"I expect you had lots of space to grow vegetables in the country, too. In London, they dug up the parks and golf courses and turned them into victory gardens."

"When your dad was gone to sea, did your mum have a victory garden, then?"

John played with her hair, winding the curl at her neck around his little finger. "No, not with three little kids to take care of. But we had a neighbour, Old Mr. Kennington, who had a garden allotment on the golf course. He kept us in vegetables. I remember one day I went with him, and on the way a German spotter plane swooped over us."

Barbara sucked in a breath of anxiety. "Oh! What happened?"

"It was the most exciting thing that had ever happened to me. I can still see it." He grinned at the memory, and using his free hand demonstrated the angle of the aircraft. "The plane came from behind a stand of trees. It banked then swooped down over us. I shielded my eyes so I could see it. Old Man Kennington yelled. 'Cor, blimey! Get down Johnny-boy.'"

"Johnny-boy! He called you Johnny-boy? Hey, I like that."

He gave her a sidelong glance and his crooked grin. "Don't you even think about calling me that."

"Ah-ha," she chortled. "At last. I know a secret about you."

"Forget it." He poked her gently in the ribs and grinned.

"Oh, all right. I'll forget it. For now." She turned and kissed his cheek. "Tell me the rest of the story."

"Well, Old Man Kennington had bad legs so I didn't think he could move that fast, but he grabbed me by the scruff of the neck and pushed me into the gutter. The next thing I knew, he landed on top of me.

"The plane engine seemed to stall, cough and start again as it roared over our heads. I can still remember the sounds. I couldn't resist a peek, and squirmed out from under the old guy. I managed to get my head up just as the plane passed over us. It was so low I could see the German pilot's eyes behind his goggles. The plane roared off and I waved as it disappeared over the horizon.

"I helped the old guy to his feet and he stood there shaking his fist at the sky hollering, 'You bloody Hun. We'll get you yet. Bastards!' I liked that old man and learned some great swear words from hanging around him."

"What was the plane doing there if it didn't intend you any harm?" Barbara said.

"I guess it was just on reconnaissance. The pilot was probably looking for signs of troops among the trees. Or perhaps the ack-ack gun emplacements and barrage balloons on the edge of the golf course." He gazed off across the river as if picturing it all in his mind. "Did you have Hilter jokes when you were a kid?"

She frowned. "Hitler jokes?"

"Yeah, like, why doesn't Hitler ride a motorcycle?"

"I don't know." Barbara turned to grin at him.

"Because when it starts up it says 'Britain, Britain.'"

"You just made that up!"

"No, I didn't. Do you know why Hitler didn't keep a monkey for a pet?" She shook her head, grinning at him.

"Because he'd sent all his apes to fight for him."

"That's terrible. Just the sort of joke little boys would make up, I suppose. Did you spend much time in an air-raid shelter?"

"Yeah, almost every night during the Battle of Britain, and until I left for South Africa."

"It must have been really cold and uncomfortable," she said.

"Yeah." He seemed to be far away as if remembering something. Then suddenly said, "That's enough of that."

"Do you know or remember anything at all about your real father?"

He took his arm from around her neck, pulled out a cigarette and lit it. He drew the smoke deep into his lungs and blew it out in a long blue stream before he answered. "I never knew my real father. He was a sailor and died in an accident at sea before I was a year old. I don't know when my mom remarried."

Eager to hear more but afraid to hurry him, Barbara waited while he dragged on the cigarette again. The smoke drifted from his lips as he continued.

"My step-father was in the Royal Navy too, and I always thought of him as my dad. I suppose Babs was born when I was about three or four, but I remember the day my brother was born—it was the day war was declared." He drew on the cigarette again and smoke drifted from his lips as he spoke. "The following year I was evacuated to South Africa." He put his arm around her shoulders and hugged her. "There you have it. Now you don't need to ask any more questions."

Barbara watched the variety of emotions flicker across her husband's face and etch deep lines around his eyes. He blinked and gave a small shake of his head as if trying to clear it of a painful memory. He slowly turned to her with his lopsided grin. "We're wasting some valuable time. Wanna go make use of that overpriced hotel room?"

"Later. You're being evasive again. Tell me about your mother. What was she like?"

"What difference does it make now? It's all in the past."

"Well, I don't understand. I've told you all about my parents. Why is telling me about yours so difficult?"

He just shrugged and drew on the last of his cigarette before he dropped it and ground it under his heel. "It's not that it's so difficult. I've told you all that I can remember."

Barbara stroked his hand. "Couldn't you at least tell me what they looked like? Tell me about your baby brother."

John tensed under her touch. "The baby? Well, he was just a baby." He was beginning to show signs of irritation. "I dunno what he looked like. Bald. And he crawled around and always got into my stuff."

But Barbara was determined to learn all she could about his family. After all, she reasoned, this was her baby's family too. What if one of them had a serious illness? A cold hand of fear clutched at her midriff. Maybe that is why John was so secretive about them. She pressed her questions. "What about your little sister? What did Barbara look like?"

"She was just a kid with red hair and freckles." He suddenly stood and grinned. Taking her hand he pulled her to her feet. "Come on. Let's not dwell on the past."

"No. Wait! What about your mother? You've never mentioned her or told me even what she looked like."

He released her hand in an angry gesture. "Dammit! Can't you leave well enough alone? For God's sake, Barb, forget about them. They're all dead! Gone!" He clenched his jaw and turned from her, glaring off across the river.

Barbara was stunned by his angry outburst. This was a side of him she hadn't seen before. She remembered again how reluctant he was to talk about his family when they were on their first date. He seemed to be especially sensitive about his mother. She knew she was pressing him by asking so many questions, and now she'd gone too far and he was angry.

Seeing his scowl and watching his jaw clench and unclench, a lump rose in her throat. She brushed away the hot tears coursing down her cheeks.

She loved him so much and now she'd upset him. *He's right*, she thought. Did it really matter if she knew everything from A to Z about his family? She'd never know them personally and if John wanted the subject closed, she guessed she could go along with that. Even as she made a solemn vow not to ever speak of it again, she couldn't help wondering what he was hiding. She wiped the tears away with her fingertips.

Suddenly he turned and wrapped her in his arms. "I'm sorry." He blew out a long pent-up breath. "What an ass I am! How can I love you so much and act this way? Our last day together, too." He looked down into her face and ran the back of his hand along her cheeks, stroking away the remnants of her tears. His lopsided grin spread across his face and an impish sparkle crept into his dark eyes. "Wanna make up?"

She nodded, feeling a smile tugging at the corners of her mouth. "Sure." His anger had passed. Relief washed over her.

He took her hand and with their step quickened by the now familiar urgency, they retraced their steps to their hotel room.

CHAPTER FIFTEEN

LITTLINGHAM 1985

Barbara lifted the brass doorknocker and gave it three hard bangs. The door opened and a hefty built, sandy-haired man filled the doorway, glaring down at her.

"Yes. What do you want?" He spoke quietly, but anger blazed in his periwinkle-blue eyes.

"Hello, Gordon. I'm Barbara…"

"I know who you are. What do you want?"

Barbara drew back, surprised and confused by his hostile attitude. "I uh…I came to see your father or Elizabeth."

"I sent Lizzie packing back to London. And my father is resting after the berating and badgering you women have put him through." He pushed on the door.

"Wait!" she said.

He hesitated with the door still half open. "What?"

"Gordon, what's the matter? What have I done?"

"Strewth!" He flung the door open with such force it crashed into the wall and bounced against his back. "What you've done is upset my father and I won't have it. You and Lizzie—working over a poor old man. Putting him through an inquisition." He leaned toward her. His nostrils flared and his blue eyes blazed with anger. "Don't you understand, he's lost his memory and he can't remember the past on demand, no matter how much you prod and question him!"

Barbara took a deep breath and ran her hand through her hair, letting her breath escape slowly. "I'm sorry, but I don't know what you're talking about. The last time I saw your father he was fine. And I certainly didn't berate or badger him. I came a second time, at your sister's invitation, but I didn't even see your father."

"Well," he leaned forward, and his angry voice boomed in her face. "*You* may not have bullied him, but Lizzie did it for you."

Barbara staggered backwards and almost lost her footing off the doorstep. Gordon followed her. The veins in his forehead pulsating and beads of sweat glistened on his beet-red face as he loomed over her and continued his tirade.

"Bloody Lizzie. Mrs. High-and-Mighty. Likes to play Lady Bountiful, trying to impress the Littlingham peasants. She's supposed to come down here to give me a hand with Dad and she upsets him every time. I came home this evening and found her yelling at him to remember something for you. I know you were here, and Peggy Hilton an' all." He sucked breath deep into his lungs and stepped backwards into the doorway, shouting, "Now bugger off out o' here." With one swoop of his ham-like hand, he dismissed her and slammed the door in her face.

Barbara leaned across the small table tucked into the corner of the Black Swan Inn. She shouted so that Peggy could hear her over the noise around them. "Well, I certainly didn't mean poor Reverend Morris any harm. And I think Gordon Morris was very rude and unreasonable." She'd barely poked at the plate of sausage and mash in front of her. Her cheeks burned with resentment at the memory of being humiliated by the old vicar's son.

Laughter bubbled above the conversation in the crowded pub, and a lively darts game over near the bar raised periodic loud cheers. At the opposite end of the room someone played ragtime on a tinny upright piano.

Peggy pushed her plate to one side and sat stiff-backed with her arms resting on the table. She pursed her lips, narrowing her shiny black eyes as she strained to hear Barbara.

"I'm sorry you had to go through that." She reached over and patted Barbara's arm. "Gordon is a good bloke, really. He hires a local woman to stay with his father during the day when he works, otherwise he seldom leaves the old man. He's just started having Lizzie come one weekend a month." A wicked smile lit her wrinkled face and she gave a big wink. "I think he's found a lady friend in Stanton. Anyway, the poor bugger deserves a break. And he's right about Lizzie. She does put on airs and graces."

She raised her head and looked beyond Barbara's shoulder. Immediately her demeanor changed. Her eyes widened. Her mouth gaped open. "Oh Lord," she breathed.

A hand rested lightly on Barbara's shoulder and she turned to face Gordon Morris. She stiffened, dreading another outburst from him, especially here in public.

"Mrs. McNab. Uh...Barbara. I've been looking for you." A contrite smile turned up the corners of his mouth and he nodded at Peggy. "G' evening, Mrs. Hilton."

Peggy nodded once in response without taking her eyes from him, but Barbara sat perfectly still, frozen, holding her glass halfway to her lips.

Gordon reached behind him and grabbed a chair. He swung it in front of him, and self-assured, threw one leg over the seat. "Do you mind?" Without waiting for a response he sat and took a deep gulp from the drink in his hand. Flicking his tongue across his lips he set the glass on the table. He ran the back of his hand across his upper lip wiping away the last specks of brown foam. Leaning both arms on the back of the chair he rested his chin on them and looked directly at Barbara. "I have something to tell you."

He straightened up and looked away seeming to be embarrassed. "But, first, please accept my apology for the dressing down I gave you. I really am sorry for being so rude and taking my anger at my sister out on you."

He leaned down across the back of the chair again and grinned at her. At that moment, Barbara thought he seemed more like a teddy bear than the grizzly bear she'd first encountered at his front door. She glanced at Peggy glued in place, her hand still wrapped around her glass.

Gordon stood up and gulped the rest of his drink. "How about a refill?" He was gone before they could answer.

"What was that all about?" Peggy sounded astonished.

"I don't know, but he's certainly different from the last time I saw him. I wonder what he has to tell me."

At the door Lilianne Paddington craned over the crowd.

"Oh, there's Ben Paddington's daughter. Do you mind if I invite her to join us?"

"Of course not. Please do. I'd like to meet her," Peggy said.

Barbara caught the young woman's eye and motioned her over. She introduced the women to each other and Peggy shuffled her chair to make room for Lilianne between them.

The crowd parted, allowing Gordon through. He carried two drinks in one huge hand, and a large foam-topped pint of brown liquid in the other. He put the drinks on the table in front of Barbara and Peggy and swung his leg back over the chair. Reaching for his beer, his gaze suddenly glanced off Lilianne then quickly returned to stare at her. He sat perfectly still, gaping, his hand poised just short of wrapping itself around his beer mug. His usual ruddy complexion paled and his lower jaw sagged.

"Oh, Gordon," Peggy was the first to recover. "This is Lilianne Paddington. You remember Ben Paddington? This is his daughter. You probably remember Ben's sister Lily."

Gordon mumbled something unintelligible and stared almost panic-stricken at the young woman.

"Lilianne is visiting from Canada." Barbara glanced back and forth between the girl and Gordon, fascinated by his reaction to the Canadian.

"She's writing a book about her aunt's murder. They never caught the man who killed her, you know..." Peggy's voice trailed off. She glanced at Barbara, clearly puzzled.

Gordon's Adam's apple rose and fell as he swallowed hard. "Is that right," he mumbled. He seemed unable to take his eyes from Lilianne's face.

Under his scrutiny, the Canadian girl's cheeks turned bright red.

Barbara cleared her throat. "So, Gordon, what were you going to tell me?"

His gaze broke and he turned to Barbara as though finally remembering why he was there. "Um...yes." He reached for his beer. "My father remembered you coming to see him, and it started him talking."

An excited flutter began in Barbara's stomach. Her spine slowly straightened until she sat upright, waiting. "Yes?" The word came in a husky whisper, inaudible above the noise of the crowd around them.

Gordon took a long draught from the glass clutched in his large hand. Barbara held her breath waiting for him to continue.

"Dad remembered your father's name. It was Brown."

Gordon Morris gulped the last of his beer, draining the glass before he set it down on the table. Then without a word of explanation, he stood and backed away from the table. Suddenly, he turned and elbowed his way through the milling crowd. Ignoring the protests of the man taking aim at the dartboard, he forged a path to the door of the Black Swan Inn and fled.

Outside, separated from the noisy throng, he leaned against the wall. His heart raced. He drew the cool night air into his lungs and concentrated on breathing slowly until he had time to think about what had just happened.

Jesus! Coming face to face with a vision from his past, his heart had threatened to jump out of his chest. Seeing Lilianne Paddington was like looking at Lilypad, and the events of that night came rushing back at him like a blow to the belly.

He'd been home on a fourteen-day leave from the army after his initial training. He was eighteen and full of himself in his stiff new khaki uniform. He'd spent every evening down at the Black Swan, drinking beer and playing darts. Since it was his last night, his friends and neighbours had treated him to several rounds of drinks, and his head buzzed. The pub wouldn't close for another hour, but he still had to pack his kit and he hadn't spent much time with Mam and Dad.

"I'd best be off." He rolled down his shirtsleeves and reached for his battle dress jacket.

Old Man Woolsey clapped him on the shoulder and handed him a pint. "Here you are, lad. One for the road. Off early tomorrow then?"

"Cheers," Gordon said and took a long swig of the beer before wiping the foam off his upper lip with the back of his hand. "Yeah. I'm catching the four o'clock milk train." His head hummed. He blinked and squinted his eyes but nothing he looked at stayed in focus. Bracing his leg against the side of the table, he managed to button his jacket and set his forage cap at a jaunty angle. "Night all." He waved and stepped clumsily out the door into the night. The cold smacked him in the face but did nothing to clear his head.

"Boo!"

"Christ a' mighty. Who the hell is it?"

"Ooh. Naughty boy. What would the vicar say if he heard his little boy taking the Lord's name in vain?"

"Lily Paddington. Is that you? What the hell are you doing? Hiding out here?"

"I'm supposed to be home with Ben, but he's asleep and I got bored."

"Your mam and dad are inside." He jerked a thumb towards the pub.

"I know. I've been watching through the window." She suddenly burst into a high giggle. "I looked through a crack in the curtain and there was my mam on the other side, not six inches from me, she was. She couldn't see me, of course." She placed her hand on his arm. "I saw you playing darts."

"Well, you better get on home now." He stepped around the girl and staggered.

She grabbed his arm and steadied him. "Here, let me help you."

He didn't object. In fact he sort of liked feeling her so close. She had a bit of a reputation as a flirt, but she was too young for him. He thought she might be fifteen.

"Where are you going?" Lily slipped her hand between his arm and body.

"Home. I've got things to do." He concentrated on placing one army-booted foot carefully in front of the other.

"It's early. You don't need to go yet, do you? Why don't we take a stroll? You need to walk that load off anyway." She hung on his arm with both hands and steered him in the direction of the vicarage, chattering about God only knew what, until he realized they were on the road beside the river. The path veered steeply away from the river's edge. He was having trouble navigating and allowed her to push him along. At the top of the path he stopped and kissed her. She kissed him back enthusiastically.

"Give me a minute. I drank too much beer." She let go of his arm and he staggered off behind a bush. He managed to undo the buttons on his fly, but fastening the buttons was another matter. They kept slipping out of his grasp.

"Oh, bugger it," he mumbled, fumbling for the buttonhole.

"What's taking you so long?"

He didn't hear Lily approach.

"You've been gone a long time." She was suddenly there. "You need all sorts of help, don't you?" She giggled and began to help him fasten his fly buttons.

Gordon couldn't remember what happened next except that he had her on the ground and she was screeching. "Stop! I didn't mean it. Let me go."

As he thrust into her, he realized she hadn't meant to have sex with him. She was just a tease but there was no way he could stop now. He wished she would just shut up.

Her pain was real. He swore the scream she let out could be heard all the way to Stanton. He covered her with his body and pinched her nostrils shut. He used the heel of his hand to cover her mouth and held her fast with his other arm across her throat until she stopped struggling.

He stood unsteadily and fumbled with the buttons on his fly. His head buzzed but he planted his feet firmly and concentrated. Finally satisfied he was properly buttoned, he turned his attention to Lily. She hadn't moved. "Come on. Get up. We both need to go home now." She still didn't move.

"Bugger all, Lily. Don't blame me. You started this. Get up." He retrieved his cap from among the fallen leaves, and slapped off the dirt against his thigh. He tucked his cap in his epaulet and brushed the debris from his trouser legs.

"Stop messing about. Come on. I've got to go." He grabbed her upper arms. She was a hefty girl and without her help he couldn't sit her up. He let go of her arms, and as she fell backwards, her head hit the hard packed earth with a dull thud.

His head cleared instantly. Strewth! She'd been knocked out. He patted her face and got no reaction. He grabbed her wrist and groped for a pulse. He must have been touching the wrong spot because he couldn't feel anything.

He took a deep breath to calm his jitters, and clear the beer-induced fog from his brain. He placed his hand on her chest, just below her breast.

Nothing.

Jesus, she is dead!

Tangled thoughts raced through his brain. Her parents thought she was at home. Nobody had seen them together. He couldn't just leave her here. The pub would close soon and Nell and Jack Simmons used this path to shortcut to their place.

Gordon's heart raced. What should he do? He hoisted her on his shoulder in a fireman's carry and staggered back towards the river road.

Running with his heavy burden he clambered down the steep bank and along the edge of the river. One of her shoes fell off and he couldn't pick it up with Lily slung across his shoulder so he kicked it. The shoe rolled down the bank and splashed into the river. By the time he located the cave tucked in the highest part of the riverbank, he was staggering and gasping for breath.

Generations of children had played in the cave during the warm days of summer, but it was early autumn. He'd have time to get away before anyone found Lily.

He pushed her through the crevice then clambered over her. Sweat born of exertion and fear saturated his back. His breath came in rattling gasps. He grabbed Lily under her arms and hauled her deep inside the cave. In the darkness he kept bumping into boulders. He left her behind a large rock and staggered to the mouth of the cave. He stopped, straining his ears, but heard only his own ragged breathing and the wind stirring the near naked tree branches. Just as he was ready to jump down on the riverbank he saw Lilypad's other shoe. It had fallen off just inside the cave entrance. He grabbed it and tossed it in the direction of her body.

Jumping into the soft dirt along the river he wondered about his boot prints, but couldn't see how anyone would know the tracks were his, and not some farmer's out looking for his wandering sheep.

Gasping to fill his starved lungs, he raced along the river's edge until he reached the road. He stopped and brushed at his uniform, but it was filthy. He'd have to wear his other uniform and he'd spend the rest of the night polishing his boots.

The moon had been playing in and out of the clouds, and it chose the moment he heard the voices to peek out. He recognized Old Man Thomas leaning heavily on his skinny red-haired daughter, Barbara.

Cursing his shiny brass insignia, Gordon ducked into a shadow but his hobnail boot scraped on a stone.

Barbara looked in his direction but she and her father continued up Primrose Lane.

He sucked in a breath and let it escape slowly, softly. He was safe.

The vicar and his wife were still up when Gordon reached the vicarage. He could hear the radio and his parents' softer laughter.

Gordon crept in the back door and made straight for his bedroom, changed into his other uniform and went back downstairs to see his parents before they went to bed.

He couldn't sleep but even if he'd wanted to, he didn't have time. His uniform trousers had earth imbedded in the knees. The elbows of his jacket were coated in mud and black streaks of dirt covered the rest of the uniform. He doubted he had enough spit to ever get his boots clean and shiny enough to stand up to the sergeant's eagle eye.

He sponged his pants and jacket with soapy water, but couldn't get it dry. He ended up having to stuff it still wet in his kit bag. He managed to get a passable shine on his boots before he crept out of the house long before dawn.

Pacing up and down the station platform he relived the nightmare with Lily Ann and worried that he may have left some clue that would tie him to her death. With relief he climbed aboard the train, and with each turn of the wheels on the track, he felt more certain his secret was safe.

His mother's next letter was full of details about Lily Ann Paddington's disappearance. Her parents had come home from the Black Swan and gone to bed believing Lily was asleep in her room. The next morning the village constable had begun a search, but it was thought Lily had carried out a frequent threat to run away. The Stanton police had concurred.

Weeks later the vicar's wife had written with the news that Lily's body had been found. Since it was obvious she'd been "molested" the police had questioned every man and boy who had been in the village the night she disappeared. Everyone could be accounted for so the police had no clue as to who had killed the girl. Mrs. Morris described in detail every mourner who had attended the funeral and, of course, Reverend Morris had conducted the service. The little church had been packed.

Gordon stared at the letter in utter disbelief. He'd got away with it. Nobody had remembered he was there that night.

It had taken him years to get over what he'd done, and now Lily's niece was here in Littlingham, looking the spitting image of her aunt.

CHAPTER SIXTEEN

LITTLINGHAM 1985

As angry as she had been with Gordon Morris for yelling at her, Barbara had to admit he had redeemed himself. He didn't have to search her out at the Black Swan to tell her her father's name.

She had lain awake for hours in the night, listening to the rain, her mind going over and over the information she'd gathered from Peggy and the Morris family. She eventually fell asleep imagining herself actually looking at the entry of her birth.

She awoke to a typical April day, showery, with dreary grey clouds broken by periods of marvelous sunshine. Even the lack of sleep and the thought of hauling the huge ledgers up and down from the shelves in the General Registry Office all day couldn't dampen her enthusiasm for her task.

Riding on the bus to London gave her time to review all the information she'd gathered. There wasn't enough to answer all her questions, but she'd learned a lot in just a few days. Her father's name was Robert Brown and her mother was Lyn. Her grandmother had been Clarice Chandler, and somewhere, she had an older brother. A shiver of excitement tickled her spine.

What a lot she had to tell John the next time she talked to him!

By the time the bus reached London, the clouds were thickening again. She mentally kicked herself for being in such a hurry to get to the record office, she'd forgotten to bring her umbrella. She ran from the bus stop to St. Catherine's House eager to begin the most important genealogical search she would ever undertake—the record of her own birth.

Her hands trembled as she pulled the first index book off the shelf. She took a deep breath to calm her jitters and ran her finger down the first page of Bs. She turned the page and began searching the next column, then the next and the next, until she came to Browne. She stopped when her eye caught a Barbara Browne and her heart almost stopped too. But there was no middle name given.

Not knowing her mother's maiden name was a definite disadvantage, but she refused to be discouraged. One thing she'd learned in genealogy class— there was more than one way to skin a cat. She'd just order a birth certificate using the information she knew.

In a shaky handwriting she hardly recognized, she filled out the form to order a certificate of birth for a child named Barbara Clarice Brown or Browne, born 25 February 1936, father's name Robert Brown or Browne, a mariner, His Majesty's Royal Navy. Possible district Lambeth, possible mother's name, Lyn.

The wait until she could return and pick up the certificate would be the longest three days of her life.

With nothing more to do at St. Catherine's House, Barbara walked out into the light drizzle to catch the bus back to Littlingham. The afternoon threatened to remain dark and dreary and Barbara looked forward to spending it with Peggy. Many times since she'd come to the village, she'd reminded herself of her good fortune in finding her old neighbour.

Peggy lit a fire and turned on the lights.

It was the perfect atmosphere for drinking cups of tea, and sharing memories of Littlingham. Peggy told Barbara what changes had taken place in the village since she'd left, and who had died and who had moved away.

The conversation led to the comical things that had happened in Littlingham. Each funny memory led to another story until they were laughing like a pair of teenagers.

The cat, curled up beside the hearth, unwrapped his tail to peer at the women with a wary eye. His ears twitched signaling his disapproval of the noise.

Peggy stopped to take a breath. "Do you remember when the doodle-bug hit Littlingham?"

"A rocket? Here?" Barbara frowned. "No, I don't remember that."

"Late in the war, it was," said Peggy wiping away the tears of laughter from the last story. "Let me see." A frown wrinkled her forehead and she rubbed her chin. "It was probably in late summer of 1944. Everyone reckoned it must have been off course. Do you remember how they screamed going overhead? But they were no threat then. Not until the noise stopped. Then they dropped nose first, straight down. That one landed at the far end of the village near the road to London."

"Was anyone hurt?" said Barbara.

"Well, we had a couple of casualties." Peggy grinned. "Nothing life threatening, mind." She covered her mouth stifling the laughter already bubbling behind her hand. "Elsie Mercham was having a bath when the flying bomb came screaming in. She climbed out of the tub, wrapped herself in a towel and stood on her toilet. Just at the moment she opened the window to see where it was going, the scream stopped and the bomb fell. The blast knocked her off the toilet, ripped off her towel and sent her flying out the door. She landed at the other end of the passageway with a broken hip. She couldn't move and lay there for a couple of hours before one of the farm lads delivering milk heard her yelling. He found her, propped against the wall in her birthday suit." Peggy sputtered through her laughter. "Elsie said the poor lad turned so red from embarrassment he looked as if he would burst into flames. He could never look any of the village women in the eye after that." Peggy chuckled.

"What about the other injury?" Barbara could hardly speak for laughing.

"Well, it wasn't an injury exactly. More like an insult, really." Peggy leaned back against the chair. Merriment twinkled in her little black eyes. "Do you remember the Leatherbets? Jem and Tilly? They had a little cottage just this side of the London road."

Barbara shook her head trying to picture the couple. "I think I remember them. We used to call them Mr. and Mrs. Spratt. You know like the nursery rhyme? He was skinny Jack Spratt who could eat no fat and she was fat and could eat no lean."

"That's the ones."

"So, what happened?"

"They had no indoor plumbing and Old Jemmy was using the outdoor loo at the end of the garden, when the flying bomb hit. The loo shack fell over onto the door trapping Jem inside. The only opening was through the bottom, across the pit. Tilly had to fetch a couple of neighbours to free him. He was a right mess. He crawled out followed by a swarm of blue-bottle flies and Tilly made him strip off out in the garden. More neighbours had gathered by then, and the descriptions of poor old Jem dancing around in his combinations while Tilly squirted him off with the hosepipe provided entertainment for months down at the Black Swan." Peggy threw herself back in the armchair, and using the hem of her pinafore, wiped her cheeks, rosy and shining with tears of laughter. "You're good for me, Barbara. I haven't had such a good laugh for a long time."

Barbara wrapped her arms across her ribs and swayed back and forth, rocking with gales of laughter. She groaned, rubbing her aching sides.

"Ooh, oh," Peggy suddenly shrieked. "I have to go to the loo, or I'll wet my knickers." She jumped up with the agility of a young girl and ran for the door.

Her loud yelp was the final insult to the sleeping cat. Reginald sprang out of his chair, his eyes bulging and his tail as stiff as a bottlebrush. Barbara pointed at him through tears streaming down her cheeks.

Reggie threw one last startled glare over his shoulder before he skulked out of the room.

Barbara was still chuckling at the vision of skinny old Jemmy Leatherbet jumping around in his underwear followed by a swarm of flies, while his very fat wife hosed him down.

Peggy padded down the stairs and straight to the kitchen. The sound of water running into the kettle and the rattle of china meant they were to have more tea.

Barbara wiped her eyes and composed herself before Peggy returned with the tea tray.

"I've got some old photographs you might like to see." She set the tray on the table and rummaging in the sideboard, brought out two albums. "I think you are in some of them when you were a little girl."

Peggy identified the people in the photos and reminded Barbara when the various shots of her had been taken. "Would you like to take these? Your children might enjoy seeing what you looked like as a child."

Tears welled in Barbara's eyes. She was too choked up to answer and accepted the pictures with a grateful hug to Peggy.

The old woman took off her spectacles and talked sadly of her daughter. Since Mary's death she hadn't seen very much of Mary's children. She told Barbara about her sons and their families. "Jim, and his wife Lucy come often and bring their young boys. Such bright little lads they are too." She ended with a smile. Her black eyes disappeared into the folds of wrinkles. "But Ben works up in the north now, so I only see them a couple of times a year.

"Barbara, you haven't yet told me very much about your family. Do you have any photos of them with you?"

"Do I—you're kidding, right? I'll be right back."

She ran upstairs to the bedroom and returned with her wallet bulging. "I'll have to start carrying them around in a suitcase if I get any more." She laughed at her joke and began shuffling through the stack of photos. "The trouble is, I have pictures of my grandchildren taken every month of their lives, and I just keep adding them to my wallet." She shook her head.

Peggy replaced her spectacles and took the photo Barbara held out to her.

"This is my husband John when he was a young man and here is a more recent photo. This is Jack, my eldest, and his wife Chris. Jack is the image of his father at the same age." A tall, slender young man with shining eyes and dark tousled hair smiled shyly for the camera. His right arm was draped around the shoulder of a willowy blonde woman with a big smile. "Here's a recent picture of Michael, their little boy."

"Do you see them often?"

"Oh yes. They live near enough that we get together almost every week, when they're not too busy with their own lives. The Sunday before I left the States to come here we all got together for a barbeque. It was sort of a *bon voyage.*"

Peggy smiled and returned the photos. Barbara pulled another one from the stack in her wallet.

"Here's Janet and Ken her husband, and Laurie their little girl. They have a little boy now too." She rattled on describing the children. "And this is Donald. He's a rascal—full of fun and such a tease. He gives Janet a hard time every chance he gets. John and I always said the hospital made a mistake and gave us the wrong baby."

Peggy smiled at Barbara's joke.

"We don't know where the blond hair came from, although friends say they can see a resemblance between Donald and me."

Barbara studied the features of her youngest child. She stroked his smooth face with her fingers—but it wasn't her son's face.

Baby fingers caressed the cheek. "D...Daddy, d...don't go," a child's voice begged. The smell of smoke, dust and sulfur filled her nostrils and burned her throat. Then she was standing on the ground looking up at him. A sailor's hat rested on his blond curls and bore the letters HMS.

"Oh!" She gasped. The sound escaped her lips before she could stop it.

Peggy looked up. "Whatever's the matter? You look as if you've seen a ghost. Are you all right?"

"I just had the funniest sensation." Barbara pressed her hands against her midriff. Her breath came in shallow little spurts. "I...I...I looked at Donald, but it wasn't Donald."

CHAPTER SEVENTEEN

LITTLINGHAM 1985

The cold rain beat a tattoo on the umbrella shielding Barbara's upper body. Blasts of March-like wind drove the downpour against the front of her slacks and into her shoes.

A car pulled close to the uneven sidewalk and slowed to Barbara's brisk pace. Out of the corner of her eye she saw the passenger side window lower and a vaguely familiar male voice called out to her. "Can I give you a lift?"

Barbara ignored the offer and focused her attention on the umbrella tugging in her hand like an eager child.

"Hey, Barbara. Barbara Thomas, uh…McNab," the voice called again.

She stopped and peered into the window of the car pulled in beside her— and met the startling blue eyes of Gordon Morris.

"Come on, get in. I'll give you a lift," he said.

"That's okay, thanks." The wind lifted the umbrella up over her head. "I'm just going up the road to the bus stop."

"I'll drive you. You're getting drenched." He reached over and opened the passenger side door.

"Well…all right. Thanks." She stepped into the swollen gutter and threw her briefcase in the back seat of the car. With blue-cold hands, she fought her stubborn umbrella into a fold, slid into the passenger seat and slammed the door. Blessed warmth wrapped itself around her shoulders and across her frozen ankles.

"Thanks," she said. "I had no idea the weather would be so awful today." She pushed a handful of dripping wet hair off her forehead. "I'm not sure I would have started out."

Gordon nodded toward the umbrella. "That brolley didn't do you much good. You're soaked." He adjusted a pair of rimless glasses. "Well, where to?" Shoving the car in gear he accelerated away from the curb.

"Oh, just to the bus stop, thanks. I'm catching the bus to London." She reached for the seatbelt and fastened it.

"I'm going to London. I could drop you."

His sudden show of friendliness after his performance in the Black Swan took her off guard. She shook her head and scowled. "No, really. I don't want you to go out of your way."

He took his eyes from the road long enough to give her an amused glance. "Don't be silly. Where are you going on this dreadfully cold and wet morning?"

"To Kingsway. The General Registry Office at Saint Catherine's House."

"Ah, yes. You're going to find your roots." A touch of mockery echoed in his voice. "No problem. I have an appointment not far from there."

She shrugged. "Well, okay. I'd appreciate it." She agreed, but not without apprehension. Riding on the bus she could look about her and not watch the road. Here in his Mini, zipping along on the left-hand side of the road, she experienced an uneasy sensation in the pit of her stomach every time they passed another vehicle. She forced herself to relax and concentrate on his easy chatter instead of the oncoming traffic.

"I was meant to be painting the trim on the house today." Gordon glanced at her. "But with this weather I had the perfect excuse to take care of some business in London instead."

"Peggy Hilton said you worked just outside Stanton. Are you off today?"

"All week, actually. The firm closes for a week in the spring every year."

"I thought the British were very big on their holidays in the summer. I remember businesses closed for two weeks every August, and everyone trooped off to the seaside."

"Yes, well, my govn'r has a young family and carries on the practice just as his father did. He closes the business for a week in the spring when the kiddies are out of school, and two weeks in August."

"That seems so strange to me now." She chuckled glancing out at the green fields dotted with shallow puddles. Beneath newly leafed tree branches, sheep and young lambs huddled together.

"Is this your first trip back to England?"

"Yes. It's been thirty years."

Gordon expertly maneuvered the little car along the country lanes. "You must see a lot of changes."

"Especially London. Hearing all the foreign accents it's hard to remember you're still in Britain. Here in the country I don't think it could ever change. This is the real England." She indicated the blurred landscape shimmering through the rain as the car flashed past.

"What's changed the most?"

"London, of course. And the money!" She laughed. "The decimal system doesn't bother me. I'm used to that from American money, but I can't tell just from their size what the British coins are worth. No more farthings, and ha'pennies. And no more one-pound notes." She shook her head. "One change I've noticed and that I'm pleased to see is the class system disappearing."

"Class system?" He gave her an exaggerated sidelong glance. "Whatever do you mean?"

"You know. You went to public school so you were considered upper middle-class and university material. The rest of us were subjected to that damn eleven-plus exam." She turned to look at him and thought a smirk played at the corners of his mouth. Perhaps not. She didn't really know him, and so she continued. "Imagine, your whole future being decided by an examination you took at eleven years of age! If the poor kid suffered nerves or wasn't feeling well the day they took that exam, he or she never even had a chance at high school, but was kicked out at fifteen and sent off to find a job."

He didn't comment and stared straight ahead.

"Isn't the school-leaving age sixteen now?" She thought she'd read that somewhere, but did he really care? She was just prattling for the sake of something to say.

He nodded. "Yes, I believe that's right."

"That's still a bit young, isn't it? But until 1947, it was fourteen. Can you imagine how many truly talented people were deprived of any further education? And what a waste of their potential." She stopped talking and turned to him. "I do sound preachy, don't I?"

He smiled over at her. "Today, in this country, the fight is against discrimination. Whatever that means. Is America big on *discrimination*?"

"I can't believe you'd ask that. You've obviously never experienced discrimination." She shook her head in disbelief and turned to watch the mist-shrouded landscape again.

"Why, have you?" He sounded utterly amazed.

"Yes, right here in England, several times. First of all there's that eleven-plus exam. Then women are traditionally paid less than men for doing the same job, of course. But the military was the worst offender. When I joined the WRAF the minimum service was four years. Men, on the other hand, could do their two years national service in the RAF and still get paid better than the women. But if they signed up for three years, they were considered regular military and paid even better. It's time the whole world recognized women as equals and rewarded us accordingly." She turned to look at him, and found him grinning broadly. "Gordon Morris, you've been laughing at me!"

"I was ready to take you to Hyde Park and get you a soapbox." He chuckled out loud.

Her cheeks burned and she turned from him. Mercifully he left her to her embarrassment and they rode in silence.

Gordon merged the car into the increased flow of traffic at the motorway and joined the vehicles speeding to London.

When her face had cooled she attempted conversation again. "Who's taking care of your father?"

He glanced at her. "Mrs. Cruickshank."

"Should I know her? I don't recognize the name."

"She came to live in Littlingham a few years ago, just about the time my father got very bad. She's a widow, and used to be a nurse. I heard she was looking for a position and it's worked out beautifully for us both. She cares for Dad during the day and I have him at night and weekends." He gave a derisive laugh. "Except when Lizzie comes to do her token duty."

"And you've never married?" The words were out before she could call them back. "I'm sorry. Don't answer that. It's none of my business." Her cheeks burned again. She ran her hands through her hair, releasing the tight curls that had formed as her hair dried.

"That's all right. No. I never found anyone who wanted me." He paused. "Especially you."

She turned sharply to gaze at him. "What?" He stared straight ahead peering through the rain-covered windshield. She studied his somber profile, the lines around his mouth, the crows feet at the corner of his eyes, and the white patches at his temple blending with his thinning, sandy-blond hair. The wipers beat a rhythm in time to her pounding heart.

"Just my little joke." He laughed, but it wasn't a joking laugh. "I had a bit of a crush on you, you know."

"No!" She watched his face but it was very still.

"Do you remember those dance classes my mother taught at the church hall?"

"Oh, yes. I loved those classes." The dance lessons had been the highlight of Barbara's week from the time she was twelve until she left Littlingham. His mother, young and blond, had been Barbara's idol because she knew all the dances and did them so well. Peggy told her that his mother, Agatha Morris, had died of a brain hemorrhage in about 1954. Barbara did a quick calculation. The vicar's wife would still have been in her forties and her husband near seventy then.

"My mother insisted that Lizzie and I attend, 'to set a good example for the village children,' she told us. But I hated them." His glasses had slid down and he pushed them back in place before he continued. "Then I discovered you loved to dance and wouldn't have missed a lesson for anything in the world. And that if I'd go, and dance with you, I got to hold you in my arms." He was laughing and Barbara was relieved. He was just relating a young boy's pleasant memories of many years ago.

Barbara remembered the tall, sandy-haired teenager, self-conscious of his acne. She'd felt sorry for him because the other kids thought him aloof and called him "toffee-nosed" because he went to public school and, so they thought, he considered himself better than they. All the village kids knew Lilypad had a crush on the vicar's son but he tended to avoid her.

Barbara experienced a fleeting image of being about fourteen and going to her first *big* dance at the town hall in Stanton. She and Mary Hilton had felt so grown-up, wearing their best dresses and applying a little lipstick to their smiling mouths. And when the town boys from Stanton asked them to dance, they found that what Mrs. Morris had taught them really worked.

The traffic increased even more entering the city, but Gordon seemed comfortable and confident driving in it. "You never guessed I had a thing for you?"

She turned to stare at him, astonished. "I had no idea. Why didn't I know?"

He was grinning. "No one knew. You were so young. Then when I was eighteen, I went away to the army to do my national service, and when I came home, you had gone."

"Gordon, that's impossible. When you were eighteen I was still just a child. No more than about eleven."

"Yes, but remember I was in the army for six years. I never forgot you."

He's lying! Why is he trying to flatter me?
He glanced sideways at her. "Do you still dance, by the way?"
"No, I haven't danced in years. My husband doesn't dance, you see."
The wind had dropped and the rain slowed to a drizzle. The car eased smoothly up to the curb at the Aldwych entrance to the General Registry Office and Gordon switched off the ignition. He took off his spectacles, and turned to gaze directly into her eyes, an ever-so-sad, gentle smile across his face. "What a pity. You were such a great dancer."
Somehow she knew he wasn't talking about John being a non-dancer and in the quiet of the parked car, she was sure he could hear the pounding of her heart. His mood changed suddenly. "Well, will this do?"
"Yes. Thank you so much for the ride, Gordon." She undid her seatbelt and picked up her handbag and umbrella from the floor.
"I could pick you up and drive you back so that you won't get wet again." He leaned toward her, his face almost eager.
She felt out of breath. "Oh, no thanks. I'll be here all day. Besides, look, the rain has stopped and the sun seems to be trying to shine. It will be gorgeous later on." She slid out of the car and tugged her briefcase from the back seat. Suddenly, she was all thumbs. The strap of her bag slid off her shoulder and the loop on the umbrella handle caught on the car door. She pulled it free it and shut the door, glad to be away from him. His confession and the way he looked at her had confused her. She had the distinct feeling that he was hiding something and suddenly she was very afraid of him.
Someone unlocked the doors to the Public Record Office, just as she reached them. She dismissed Gordon Morris from her thoughts and hurried to be the first in line at the counter.
Waiting for the clerk to bring the certificate seemed to take forever. Barbara's stomach flip-flopped. Her breath came in short gasps as though she couldn't fill her lungs.
Finally her wait was over. Her hand trembled when she accepted the piece of paper from the clerk behind the counter. At last she'd know her real mother's name.
Normally crowded, the General Registry Office still had a few vacant seats this early in the morning. Barbara found a seat and laid her birth certificate on the table, never taking her eyes from it.
She took a deep breath and, letting it out a little bit at a time, unfolded the paper. Her hands shook, banging her rings against the wooden tabletop.
She scanned the information. Carefully she studied each entry again, the

date, the place, the names. Something jarred. She squeezed her eyes shut, then opened them and looked once more at her mother's name. Her stomach knotted and her pulse thumped in her temples. She'd seen that name before— *on her husband's birth certificate.*

Her immediate impulse was to phone John, her best friend, her confidante, to ask his advice and seek his comfort. Then realization set in. *Oh, my God!* If the same woman's name was on John's birth certificate and her own, it could mean only one thing—*she was married to her own brother!*

The ramifications were too horrifying to contemplate.

Gripped by a wave of nausea, she levered herself from the table. She staggered across the record room, her legs heavy by imagined lead weights. Her head spun and she knew she'd pass out before she made it to the ladies' room. She groped her way out of the record room, away from the crowds of researchers. In the hall she sank into a chair just as the room spun in a dark yellow haze. She closed her eyes and dropped her head onto her knees, only vaguely aware of her bag and briefcase slipping from her grasp and clattering to the floor.

A sudden vivid recollection filled her reeling mind…

"Insy, winsy spider, climbed up the spout, again." She giggled. This time she'd remembered all the words and Mummy laughed and hugged her. Mummy's coppery hair smelled like summer as it fell across Babs' face and tickled her cheek.

"Are you alright, m'dear?" A middle-aged woman had crouched beside her and was peering at her face.

Barbara raised her head. People wearing concerned frowns had gathered around her.

"I'm okay. Just tired." She tried to make sense of the vision. But she knew a small window to the past had just opened and she needed to look deeper into it.

Suddenly she could see herself quite clearly as a little girl. She remembered where she had lived, and she knew that's where she could recapture some more of her past.

Someone placed her bag and briefcase in her hands. "Thanks." She pushed past the knot of people and stumbled to the door.

CHAPTER EIGHTEEN

LONDON 1985

The entrance to Royal Gardens looked familiar, yet strangely different. Barbara remembered it as a straight little street blocked at the end by the railway embankment. Now it curved to the right and she couldn't see the end from where she stood. Two streets to the left had been the train station. From around the bend in the road the incessant thumping bass of reggae music vibrated in her head.

Eager to see the street as she remembered it, and hoping she had only imagined it different, she crossed to the other side. The dilapidated remnant of the once little green park clung brown and overgrown to the corner plot. The wrought-iron gate was gone and the railing, rusted and bent, hung out of the broken brick wall. Weeds grew between the cracked concrete paths.

A wall, obscene with graffiti, ran the full length of that side of the street. She leaned against it and put her head in her hands, trying to make sense of the rags and snatches of visions that played around the corners of her memory.

"You awrigh', missus?" The flat intonation of a Londoner startled her. She looked up into the frowning face of a young black man.

"Uh. Yes. Thank you." She still couldn't get used to Jamaicans with Cockney accents. "I'm fine."

"Wachyer doin' arahnd 'ere?"

"I used to live on this street. Number seventeen." She indicated the direction with a nod of her head.

He stared at her and shook his head. "Nah, missus. There ain't no seven'een Roy'aw Gardins. The old 'ouses only go to number nine. Then its flats."

Scowling at him in disbelief, she walked a few steps along the sidewalk and craned to look around the curve. He was right. A Chinese take-away occupied the corner where, before the war bombed it out of existence, the George and Dragon public house had stood. Three old, once elegant Victorian terrace houses, now dirty and neglected, looked quite out of place next to the huge blocks of ugly, square, utilitarian flats filling the right side of the little cul-de-sac.

"Thank you..." Her voice trailed off.

"Crikey." The young man hurried away, out of the street, darting a last quick glance over his shoulder at her.

Barbara stood looking at the unattractive street, trying to remember what it had looked like when she was a little girl. She thought it had been grimy, but homey. But that's not all she recalled about that time...

LONDON 1940

She squatted on the sidewalk in front of her house with a piece of coal held firmly in her hand trying to make a hopscotch, as she had seen the big girls do. Her blue print frock, stretched over her bent knees, had coal dust on the skirt. Barbara thought Mummy would be cross when she saw it so she tried to brush it off and added another streak. Hunkered over the crooked lines she'd drawn, she contemplated another black smudge on the sleeve of her white cardigan.

A loud, dull thud startled her. A strange grey-white piece of metal rocked to a stop just within her reach. A wisp of smoke curled from one end. Just big enough for her small hand to grasp, she reached to pick it up but it was hot. She pulled back without touching it.

She gazed about her wondering where it had come from, but no one else was in sight and there were no sounds. A silver flash high above her, and then another, caught her eye. Two planes darted and weaved between black puffs that smudged the clear blue sky. They banked, and caught in the sunlight, flashed again like flying fish darting in and out of the ocean.

Fascinated, Barbara stretched her neck, resting the back of her head on her shoulders, and rocked back and forth on her heels.

Eager to share the spectacle, she jumped up and raced to her house.

"Mummy, Mummy," she yelled as loud as she could. "Come and see, in the sky."

Mummy ran to her. "What it is? What's all the excitement?"

"It's planes, Mummy. Come and look." She pulled Mummy by the hand out onto the street. "See, they're writing in the sky." She pointed up to the dog fight still raging overhead.

"Oh my God," Mummy screamed. She scooped Barbara up and ran for the house. Then the air-raid siren began to wail.

Mummy seemed to be running everywhere at once. She tucked the baby under one arm, grabbed the gasmasks and pulled Barbara by the hand to the air-raid shelter out in the back garden.

LITTLINGHAM 1985

Barbara hardly remembered the journey back to Littlingham. She made her way slowly to Peggy's front door just as dusk settled over the little village. It had been a ghastly day. Emotionally exhausted and confused by all that had happened to her, her greatest wish was to climb into bed, pull the blankets over her head and wake to find she was at home in California. Her limbs felt leaden and she could hardly lift her hand to grasp the doorknocker.

Peggy opened the door and gasped. "Oh, Barbara. Whatever is the matter?" She flung the door wide and helped Barbara into the cottage. Taking the briefcase from Barbara's hand she set it in the entry. "Come on through. You need a nice cup of tea and something to eat."

A delicious savoury aroma filled the cottage but it did nothing to increase Barbara's appetite. Her stomach had been in a knot all day and the way she felt at this moment, she wasn't sure she could ever eat again. She sighed as she sank into a kitchen chair and ran her hands through her hair.

Peggy picked up the steaming kettle and poured water into the teapot. "Tell me what happened," she said over her shoulder. She covered the teapot with a cozy and set it on the tray with two cups and saucers, a jug of milk and a sugar basin.

"I wish you'd pinch me and tell me I've had a horrible dream. Oh, Peggy. It's been just the most awful day of my life." She covered her face with her hands

Peggy touched Barbara's arm. "Oh, it can't be all that bad."

Reginald interrupted with a loud *purr-ump*. He sat at Peggy's feet looking up at her expectantly.

"Oh, Reggie. I forgot. You want your dinner, don't you?" Peggy fed the cat before she carried the tea tray to the table. She sat and took Barbara's limp hand. "Tell me all about it."

Barbara sucked in a deep breath and let it escape in a series of little sobs. "I was really excited at the prospect of finding my birth mother's name. My hands trembled so much. I could hardly focus my eyes on the words. Then I had to look at them over and over just to be sure I wasn't mistaken." Barbara took her hand from Peggy's and covered her eyes again.

"Take your time." Peggy patted her arm.

Barbara swallowed a sob. "My mother...and John's mother...had the same name." She let out a long wail. "Peggy, I'm married to my b...brother."

"Oh, my dear. What are you saying?" The variety of the emotions Barbara had experienced all day reflected in Peggy's face, but the warmth and compassion in the older woman's voice encouraged Barbara to continue.

Ignoring the tears streaming down her cheeks, Barbara held her chin in her hands. "How am I going to tell John?" Her voice sounded hoarse and whispery to her. "And what about my children? They'll have to know, but what can I say to them? They'll probably hate us, John and me. They'll be so ashamed."

"Nonsense! Of course they won't be ashamed. But aren't you putting the cart before the horse? You don't know for certain that you and John are brother and sister. Couldn't both mothers have had the same name and not even be related?"

"What?" Barbara gave a short laugh. "Don't you think Emmalyn Clarice Hayes is an unusual combination of names for two different women to have? Especially since they were both born in London. They would have been the same age too. No, the coincidence is too much." She shook her head dismissing the idea. "They had to have been the same woman."

"Stranger things have happened." Peggy's face broke into a smile. "Now, I think we should have something to eat, and you need to get a good night's sleep. Tomorrow you can decide how you're going to resolve your quandary." She patted Barbara's hand again and started to lever herself up from the table.

"No, wait. That's not all. I felt sick and dizzy and thought I was going to faint. Then the strangest thing happened. I remembered the feel and smell of my mother's hair." She trembled. "I don't how I recognized it. But instinctively I knew it was my mother, and it was almost tangible."

Peggy's frown suggested she was having doubts about the mental state of her houseguest. "Where have you been all day, then?"

"I wandered around. I'm not sure where. Just thinking. Trying to recapture anything about the past. I found myself on the street in Lambeth where I used to live and I had a sort of vision about the war." She shuddered and hugged herself, rubbing her arms. "Oh, Peggy, I've always thought myself stable and sensible, but I think I went a little insane today. How can I forget the past so completely for forty-five years and recollect it now, just as I find...I...I'm married to my b...brother?" She blinked back the tears pooling in her eyes.

"Oh, my dear." Peggy patted Barbara's hand. "Do you think that the shock you had today jogged your memory?"

Barbara stood and began pacing. "I don't know. I don't understand what is happening to me. I feel as though I've completely lost control of my faculties."

"I've heard that children often block out painful memories. You were such a little girl when you came here and you'd been through so much trauma." Her white hair moved as she shook her head from side to side. "Your injuries were so severe. I wonder if you even remembered when you came out of the coma that you even had a Mummy."

Barbara stopped pacing and faced Peggy. "So what made me remember today?"

"I would think the shock of finding your mother and your husband's mother had the same name may have done it." She pushed herself from the table. "Now, you must eat something. I'll give you a tablet to help you sleep and tomorrow things will be clearer to you."

The beef stew tasted delicious, but Barbara couldn't seem to swallow. Peggy finally gave up urging her to eat and instead encouraged her to go to bed.

Barbara climbed the stairs to her bedroom, and turned on the lamp. She peered at her reflection in the mirror above the dressing table, noting that the light accentuated the dark circles under her red-rimmed eyes. She studied every inch of her face, turning it this way and that, trying to see any similarity between her face and John's.

She saw several features that she and her children shared. The arch of Janet's eyebrows and her full lips. The shape of Donald's face and the set of his eyes. Jack least resembled her, but he looked exactly like John as a young man. Remembering John started the terror all over again. She gripped her midriff and fought back tears.

A tap at the bedroom door made her straighten up and flick the tears from her eyes. She opened the door.

The light from the hall beyond turned Peggy's silvery white hair into a halo. Her shoe-button eyes twinkled in the shadow of her face. "May I come in, dear?"

Barbara stepped back and opened the door wide. "Sure."

"Ever since you came back to Littlingham, something has been in the back of my mind to tell you. Something from the past. I'm not sure this is the right time to give you this, but perhaps it will help you." Peggy held out a faded black and white photograph.

Barbara took the picture of a young couple. One corner had been torn off. A crease ran diagonally across the woman from her hips to her knees, but it didn't mar her face, or that of the young man. The woman's light-colored hair hung in waves around her shoulders and some sort of clip held it off her face. She was smiling, but her facial contours shadowed the features. The man had his arm around her waist. He wore the uniform of a naval petty officer but no cap. His hair was smooth and dark. He looked nothing like the blond-haired sailor who Donald resembled.

Puzzled, Barbara shrugged and held the photograph out to return it.

"Turn it over," Peggy said.

In large, old-fashioned, square handwriting that Barbara recognized as her mum's, Dolly Thomas had written *Lyn and Dan Loder*.

"That's your mother," Peggy said.

Barbara gasped. She held the photo closer to the lamp and studied the image of the woman again.

"Of course, she's very young in that picture," continued Peggy.

"Who's Dan Loder?"

"I don't know, but perhaps Reverend Morris does. Remember he said he didn't know the other one? We didn't know what he meant. Perhaps he was saying he didn't know your mother's other husband."

"Oh, God." Barbara moaned. "Do you think she was married to this man before she married my father?"

"I don't know, dear. I'm not sure." She held her lower lip between her teeth and her brow furrowed in concentration. "I can't remember Dolly ever saying Lyn was married more than once."

"The inscription isn't clear. It could mean this is Lyn and a man called Dan Loder. Or it could mean this is Lyn Loder and Dan Loder."

"Oh, dear. I'm sorry. I thought it would help." Peggy wrung her hands and looked as if she would cry. She was obviously distressed and Barbara tried to comfort and reassure her.

"Thank you, Peggy. I'm sure this is a valuable clue. Where did you get this photo?"

"From Mr. Hotchkiss."

"Who?"

"Remember the old rag-and-bone man? You sold him your furniture before you left to join the air force. He brought it to me. It was stuck in the back of a drawer of the sideboard you'd sold him."

Barbara's hand flew to her mouth, stifling a gasp. "All those photographs I burned before I left! They must have been of my parents and my brothers." Her shoulders sagged and she sat heavily on the edge of the bed. "How could I have been so stupid?" She buried her face in her hands. "I just can't take any more, Peggy. I can't even cry. I'm depressed beyond tears."

Peggy sat beside her and put her arm around Barbara's shoulder. "What's done is done. You can't bring back those photos. Try to put it out of your mind now. And do get some rest. I worry about you." She turned at the door. "Goodnight, my dear."

CHAPTER NINETEEN

LITTLINGHAM 1985

Barbara stacked the coins according to their value on the narrow shelf next to the pay phone. The old red booth, the only one in the village, had seen far better days. Names and numbers had been gouged into the metal wall behind the phone. One windowpane near the floor was missing. Into the gaping hole, generations of dogs had lifted their leg, evidenced by the rivulet of fresh urine dribbling onto the thick black grime coating the floor.

Waiting for the operator to put her call through, apprehension tensed Barbara's spine. She was about to break the promise she had made to herself never to ask John about his mother. Knowing he might respond to her questions by becoming confrontational, she'd offered to shop for Peggy so that she could make the call in private.

The connection sounds stopped, and the clipped voice of the operator instructed her to deposit the money.

"Thank you, operator." Barbara reached for the coins but in her nervousness she swept them onto the floor. "Oh…just a minute," she pleaded. "I've dropped the money." She bent to scoop the coins off the filthy floor and collected the grime from countless shoes under her fingernails. Her hands shook as she pushed the coins, one by one, into the slot and heard them drop into place. She wrapped one arm across her middle and drew a deep breath

"Thank you," said the operator. "Go ahead."

"McNab," John answered absently.

Barbara sucked in air to calm her nerves and keep the anxiety out of her voice. "Hi, honey. Are you busy?" Her cheerfulness sounded forced.

"Barb! This is a surprise. No, I'm not too busy to talk to you. How's it going, sweetheart?"

"Pretty good." She winced hating herself for sounding like some damn Pollyanna. "But I need to ask you some questions."

"Is something wrong? You sound, uh…different."

She swallowed hard. She should have known she couldn't hide anything from him. He'd caught the strain in her voice. When she'd first decided to call him, she'd thought she could tell him that their mothers had the same name. Perhaps she'd make some joke about it. But after thirty years of being best friends as well as lovers, she should have known that wouldn't work. She needed to be looking right at him when she told him they might be brother and sister.

Oh, God!

Swallowing the bile rising in her throat, she sucked in a breath in an effort to control her nausea. It was imperative that she sound casual, but it took more effort than she'd thought it would.

"No, nothing's wrong," she lied. "My research just raised some questions and I thought you might know the answers."

"What kind of things?" Just the mere hint of suspicion colored his voice.

Through all the years, she had kept her vow. They hadn't discussed it. She just didn't ask, and he'd never volunteered any significant information about his family. She hesitated, wondering what his reaction to her question would be.

"What was your mother called?"

"My mother? Good God! I thought you took a copy of my birth certificate with you. Her name is on there. Emmalyn."

Barbara's heart skipped as she replayed the way he said his mother's name. He had said "Emma-LYN," emphasizing the last syllable. She could hardly breathe.

"Barb? You still there?"

She cleared her throat. "Yes…yeah. Honey, is that what she was called? Did she have a nickname?"

He was silent for several seconds while she held her breath. Finally he answered. "God! It's been so long, but I don't think so."

"Well, okay." She breathed again. "One other thing. Does the name Loder mean anything to you?"

"Loger? No. Who's Loger?"

"Not Loger, darling, Loder." She spelled it for him.

"I've never heard it. What's it got to do with me?"

"I don't know that it has anything to do with you. I just came across it in my research."

"Barb, what the hell is this all about?"

"Nothing. Don't get so upset. I just asked."

"Well, I can't help you. This genealogy thing is your game. Leave me out of it."

Barbara kept her voice steady. "John, calm down. You knew before I came here that I intended to look for information on your parents' backgrounds. And you didn't object when I said I wanted to do this for the kids and our grandchildren. I don't understand why you are so mad about it now."

"Dammit! Barb, I can't stop you from searching records in England. But there's a difference between that and you submitting me to your damn third degree."

"Third degree!" Her voice sounded shrill even to her. "You're being ridiculous and I'm sorry I even called." She slammed the receiver into the cradle and swept the rest of the coins into her purse.

USA 1985

John stared at the phone. Had she really hung up on him, again? Well, he couldn't blame her. What was he so mad about? Geez, he must be nuts or something flying off the handle like that.

He pulled Peggy Hilton's telephone number out of his wallet and dialed it.

"Hello," said the voice on the other end of the line.

"Mrs. Hilton, this is John McNab. I'd like to talk to Barbara."

"Oh, I'm sorry, Mr. McNab, she isn't here. She went to do a bit of shopping for me in the village. Shall I have her give you a jingle when she comes back?"

"No, thanks. Just tell her I called and that I'll get back to her." He replaced the receiver and rubbed his chin, thinking. *So, that's what all that clicking had been when she phoned. She placed the call from a pay phone. Why not from the old lady's? I wonder why she did that?*

The day dragged by and he was glad it was Friday. He needed the weekend to think. As a young engineering student he'd learned that the first step in solving a problem is to define it. Throughout his career he'd continued to remind himself of that. He needed to examine why Barb's questions made him so mad.

On the way home he grabbed a pizza and ate it with a beer while he watched the six o'clock news, but he couldn't concentrate. He wanted to talk to Barb, but it was two in the morning in England. She'd be asleep.

John grabbed Tigger's leash, alerting the dog to their nightly ritual. A couple of miles run around the neighborhood.

The mutt barked and jumped until the leash was in place and they headed out the door. Usually John enjoyed this time with his thoughts, but he'd spent too much time alone lately. He missed Barb and looked forward to her coming home. But the way she was stretching out this research thing, it didn't seem as if he'd be seeing her any time soon.

It was this obsession with family, *again*. She'd always had this fascination about his family. The first time he met her she wanted to know about his parents and siblings. Hell, even on their honeymoon she couldn't leave it alone. It was the cause of their first argument.

The phone was ringing as he let himself into the house.

His daughter's cheery voice greeted him. "Hi, Dad. How are you coping?"

"Hi, Jan. I'm doing okay."

"Is this a bad time to talk?"

"Give me a minute to feed the dog." He put Tigger's dish of food on the floor and returned to the phone. "I'm back, Jan."

"Dad, have you heard from Mom?"

"Yes. As a matter of fact I talked to her today." He flopped on the couch and put his feet up. This could be a long conversation. Jan was a talker.

"Great. How is she? Has she learned who her real parents were yet? Did she say when she was coming home?"

"Hold it! So many questions." He could hardly tell her about their conversation. *Your mother hung up on me.* "No, honey. I didn't ask, but I did get the feeling she didn't plan to be home any time soon."

"How come?" Her voiced sagged with disappointment.

"Well, she's busy. You know what she's doing over there, Jan."

There was a long pause. "Dad, are you and Mom having problems?"

"What makes you think that?" He never could hide much from Jan. Daddy's little girl could read him pretty well.

"She never goes anywhere without you, and you guys seemed to be cool to each other before she left. Knowing the two of you, I'm surprised she's stayed away as long as she has, unless there's a problem."

"Yeah, we have a problem but it's not what you think. In fact it's more of a misunderstanding, that's all. It will work out."

"What exactly is the misunderstanding about?"

"Jan, I don't think…"

"Hey, Dad. I'm a big girl now. You can tell me. Maybe I can help."

He couldn't resist her anymore than he could resist her mother. "It's no big deal. She just keeps asking about my parents and my brother and sister."

"So? Why don't you answer her questions?"

"I can't, Jan. I don't know why. I've always kept that part of my life tucked away where even I couldn't see it."

"That's weird, Dad. Why is it a secret?"

"Now you sound like your mother. It isn't a secret. I just don't talk about it."

"That's an old trick, Dad. Deflect and conquer. Well, not talking about them doesn't change the fact that you did have parents and siblings. They did exist and they all died in the war, didn't they?"

"Jan, I…"

"Answer the question. Did they all die in the war? Come on, Dad, say it."

"Yes. Except for my real father. He died in an accident at sea when I was a baby. My mom remarried and had my sister and my brother."

"There. That wasn't so hard, was it?"

"Geez, Jan. You make me sound like a little kid."

"I hate to say this, Dad, but you've been acting like one. So, what's the rest? Your stepfather died when his ship was torpedoed and your mom and sister and brother died in an air raid. Isn't that right?"

"How the hell do you know so much?" He was really shocked. He didn't ever remember laying out his whole family story like that.

"Not hard to figure out, Dad. Over the years I've listened to bits and pieces and put things together. So where's the problem?"

"I dunno. I don't really want to talk about this right now, sweetheart. Okay?"

"No, Dad. It isn't okay. Why don't you want to talk about it? Do you have something to hide?"

"There you go again, sounding just like your mother. No, I guess I feel uncomfortable talking about it. That's all. I always felt sort of guilty for some reason."

"Well, here it comes." She gave sort of chuckle-cum-snort. "Didn't you take psychology in college, Dad?"

"What are you talking about?"

"Psychology 101. It's classic. The guilt. It's called survivor syndrome. Soldiers suffer it when a buddy standing beside them is killed and they live. You feel guilty because you survived, and your parents and siblings didn't. I bet you knew that all along, didn't you?"

"You're pretty smart for an old school teacher." That's exactly how he felt, but he certainly wasn't going to admit it to Jan. "But I'm not sure that's it."

"No, I don't think that's all of it, but it's at the root of the problem."

"Yeah...you could be right at that." He tried to lick his lips, but his mouth was as dry as Death Valley in August.

"Dad." Jan let out a long sigh. "I'm sorry. I don't mean to make light of it. I've often thought you had a deeper problem than just the guilt. Think about it, Dad. There's more, isn't there?"

He chewed on his lip. It seemed strange that his own daughter could make him so uncomfortable.

"Dad, I love you."

"I love you too, hon."

"I'd have spoken to you about this before, but I thought it wasn't my place to tell my father he maybe needed therapy."

"What the hell for?" *Geez! Had she been talking to Barb?*

"Don't fly off the handle. When I was in college, I took a course on child abandonment and rejection. Wait, Dad. Let me read something to you. Don't go away while I find it."

She was gone for several minutes while he fumed. He was tempted to hang up but he still smarted from Barbara doing that to him earlier in the day. Besides, he knew it wouldn't be the end of it. He might as well listen to what Janet had to say. She wasn't being insolent. She apparently thought she could honestly help him. So he hung onto the phone and calmed his anxieties until she returned.

"Dad, are you still there?'

"Yes, Jan. I'm here and all ears."

"Don't be sarcastic. Just listen. Okay? It's kind of long but worth wading through. Listen. 'In the condition known as post-traumatic stress syndrome the commonest symptoms are flashbacks, loss of concentration, sleeplessness, high anxiety and aggression.' It goes on to quote the *Diagnostic and Statistical Manual of Mental Health Disorders,* used by American psychiatrists. You still there, Dad?"

"Yeah, I'm listening."

"Well, it goes on to say, 'The symptoms are'—and this is a quote—'precipitated by the sort of stress that would evoke distress in most people and is generally outside the range of such common experiences as bereavement, chronic illness, business losses or marital conflict.'

"This is the part I found most interesting. It says, 'The disorder may be especially severe or long lasting when the cause of the stress is of human design, such as child abandonment or rejection.'

"What do you think, Dad? Does that sound like someone you know?"

"Your mother?"

"Don't be facetious, Dad. Anyway, Mom faced her demons and she's doing something about them."

"Okay. But I don't lack concentration." Now he was really getting mad. "I wouldn't be able to do my job as well as I have all these years if I couldn't concentrate."

"Now you're being defensive. You don't necessarily have to have all the symptoms. It's possible you aren't even aware that you felt you were abandoned when you were sent away to South Africa. Your resentment seems targeted at your mother. Probably because you loved her so much, and she's the one who actually sent you away. Anyway, Dad, the reason I thought you need to see a therapist is that the treatment is based on bringing your resentment to the surface. Sometimes, just by talking to someone who listens and is sympathetic will do it. That's what Mom did. She talked to the therapist and acted on the advice she was given."

"Sure…" What could he say? "Well, thanks for thinking of me, Jan." The sooner they got off this topic the better.

"Let's change the subject."

"Not too soon for me."

"Okay, Dad. Now I have a bit of a problem. I didn't want to have to tell you, but the boys and I have planned a big party for next Saturday night for you and Mom to celebrate your anniversary."

"Next Saturday? That's sort of short notice, Jan."

"Not really. We planned it long before Mom even left. We weren't worried though because we figured she'd be home in plenty of time. It's too late now to call it off. We sent out RSVPs and got a lot of takers. We've ordered food, drinks and a band. Oh, God, Dad." Her voice cracked as if she were about to cry. "Could you try to get Mom to come home in time? But don't tell her about the party. We'd like it to be a surprise for *somebody*. I'm sure sorry we had to spoil it for you."

"Sure, Jan. I'll try."

"Thanks, Dad."

"No, Jan, thank you. I love you, honey."

He hung up the phone, and adjusting the pillow behind his head, closed his eyes. He thought back on the fight he'd had with Barb about going to England. Secretly he'd gloated about the new plane's unveiling. It had given him the legitimate excuse not to go with her, but he felt really bad about being deceitful.

That Jan! He smiled to himself. Was it really as elementary as she said? He'd feel like a fool if all these years he'd never come to grips with something so simple.

He watched the late news and went to bed—*alone*. Damn. He really missed Barb, and if Jan was right about his mental block being guilt, as soon as Barb came home he'd sit down with her and tell her everything he could remember about his mum and his brother and sister.

Long before the dawn light crept into his bedroom, John awoke gasping for breath. His throat felt as if he'd swallowed a sponge. He swung his legs over the side of the bed and stood. Sweat clung to his back and under his arms. Through the darkened house, he made his way to the refrigerator and took a long drink out of the water container. Barb hated when he did that instead of pouring it into a glass. He shrugged, replaced the container and padded back to bed.

Anxiety still gripped his stomach. He clasped his hands under his head and scowled up at the darkened ceiling wondering what had scared him so badly. A dream. That was it! He'd had *the* dream. He recognized it now. But why had it happened again after all these years?

He's standing on a beach wrapped in a warm, contented glow. He isn't aware of any landmarks around him, but he knows instinctively that it's Durban beach. The sun blazes off the white sand and hurts his eyes. He squints out across the ocean. In the distance he sees a sailor holding a baby, and a woman holding the hand of a little red-haired girl. They are waving to John. The baby's bald head shines in the sunlight. As he watches, they slowly sink beyond the horizon, their fluttering hands at last disappearing into the ocean.

He'd always known the dream people were his step-father, mother, baby brother and Babs. And when he was a little boy, the dream had confused and terrified him.

It had been years since he'd woken in the night, sweating and fighting the dream back into the deepest recesses of his mind. The last time he could remember having the nightmare so vividly was soon after he and Barb were married. So why now after thirty years?

This time he didn't want to forget it. If Jan was right he needed to confront it.

Ignoring the sweat trickling from his forehead and running down his face, he concentrated on what had happened to trigger the dreaded dream.

He sucked in a sharp breath as his mind made the connection. Barb's phone call! She'd asked him about his mother's name.

LITTLINGHAM 1985

On the other end of the line, Peggy Hilton called Barbara to the phone. "It's John."

Barb took her sweet time picking up then sounded as dejected as a wounded puppy. "Hi, John."

"Hi, sweetheart. Did I wake you?" He didn't wait for her to think up a reason. He knew the reason. He'd screwed up, royally. "Honey, I'm really sorry for the way I acted yesterday. I just don't know what gets into me sometimes. I love you so much and yet I yell like that."

"John. Forget it. All right? I know how it upsets you to talk about it. I shouldn't have asked you about your mother."

"No, I can't forget it. But let's call a truce. Okay? We'll talk about this just as soon as you come home. But over the phone, long distance, is not the time."

She didn't respond. She must still be mad at him but he couldn't blame her.

"Barb?"

"What?"

"Don't stay mad at me." He wished he could reach out and touch her, to make her forgive him. "When are you coming home?"

"Soon. It's taking longer than I thought it would."

"How come? What's the big deal?"

"Well, it takes three days between ordering certificates and actually picking them up."

"Won't they mail them?"

"Sure. But that will take even longer. Anyway I don't have a deadline."

"Barb, I miss you. Let's not ever do this again."

"What? Do what?"

"Be apart. Don't let's ever spend time away from each other."

She responded with a big sigh. "Oh, honey, I miss you so much."

Good! Does that mean she isn't mad anymore? "Barb, about that deadline. The kids are really anxious that you get home by next weekend."

"Why?"

"You're not supposed to know, but they've planned something for our anniversary. Will you get home in time?"

"I don't know, John. What day?"

"Saturday night."

"I'll try. "

"Okay. But I was thinking. How about if I join you for a couple of days and we could travel back here together in time for the party?"

Barbara's insides suddenly turned into a frozen lump while her brain screamed *No! No!* The last thing she needed right now was John coming to England before she got to the truth about their relationship. Her mouth went dry as if a big cotton ball stuck in the back of her throat was soaking up her saliva.

"There's no need, John. I should be able to get back before next Saturday. I still have a few loose ends to tie up and they aren't the kind of things you'd enjoy. So I wouldn't be able to spend any time with you. Just tell the kids I'll do my best."

"They'll be really disappointed if you don't get back here in time. Don't let on I told you about the celebration, okay?"

She agreed, and they talked a little longer. He told her he'd run out of the food she'd left for him in the freezer. Barb told him about the village and the weather.

She cradled the phone receiver and wiped her clammy palms. She hated being deceitful to John, but she just couldn't tell him that she was afraid to come home. And she sure didn't want him to come to England right now. If only he would talk about his family, he might give her enough clues to help answer the questions. Instead she was forced to harbor the most unmentionable suspicion.

But what if she were wrong? She'd be blowing this thing way out of proportion unnecessarily.

But what if I'm right and John really IS my brother? A dreadful ache throbbed under her heart, but there were no tears left to relieve the pain.

CHAPTER TWENTY

LITTLINGHAM 1985

"Mom?"

Janet's familiar voice on the other end of the phone momentarily startled Barbara. She'd been wondering how she would react when she had to speak to her children. Would her guilt betray her? Now that she was being forced to speak to her daughter, she was surprised at how outwardly calm she was. Inside was a different matter. She had to force herself to breathe. Her heartbeat pounded in her ears. Bile rose. "Hi, sweetheart. This is a nice surprise. How are you? Are the children okay?" She spoke a little too quickly and made a mental note to take control of her next sentence.

"Hi, Mom. Yes, everything is fine here. The kids are great. But what's going on with you? Why are you still in England?"

"Jan, you know very well why I'm still here. I'm doing research." Her stomach recoiled at the memory of why she was still doing research and why she couldn't go home until she had some answers.

"But you were only supposed to stay two weeks." Jan's voice rang with accusation.

"Why are you so upset? Does it matter if I stay a few days longer?"

"Well yes, as a matter of fact it does. Did you remember that it's your thirtieth wedding anniversary next week?"

"Of course I remember." She laughed out loud, a mirthless laugh. "I'm not likely to forget something as important as that."

Not likely to forget I've been married for thirty years to my brother!

"That's what we thought too. That's why we figured you'd be home by now and we—that is Jack, Chris, Brad, Donald and I—planned a surprise party for next Saturday for you and Dad. Now you've spoiled it." Her voice caught and she stopped talking for a moment. "We had to ask Dad to try and talk you into coming home in time. But he said you weren't ready to come back yet." The sound of her breath escaping in a long sigh felt like a knife piercing Barbara's heart.

"Oh, Jan." She was afraid to say any more. Tears were already welling in her eyes.

"Mom, everyone has worked so hard. You know how talented Chris is. You should see the great decorations she's made. They're wonderful."

"Yes, sweetheart. I know if Chris created them, they're perfect." She couldn't imagine her daughter-in-law turning out anything less than perfection.

"Yeah, and we've invited a hundred and fifty people."

"You're joking!" The very idea seemed ludicrous. "Where did you find that many people to invite? Do we even know a hundred and fifty?"

"Oh, Mo...m!"

"Darling, I'm so sorry. I had no idea you'd go to so much trouble." Her heart ached for her daughter. A lump of emotion was forming again in her throat. She'd ruined her children's surprise and she couldn't even tell them why. Their hearts would be broken if she didn't attend the party. But how could she face them if their father really were her brother? Tears clouded her vision.

"I don't understand why you can't come home. I talked to Dad and I think he's going to get therapy so you don't have to be mad at him anymore."

"What are you talking about?" This was something new. "I'm not mad at your father."

"Well, you were. Jack told me you and Dad were having problems. We were afraid you'd gone away and would get a divorce."

"Good grief! Where ever did you get that notion?"

"It's okay, Mom. Jack told me your therapist suggested you try to find out what it was in your childhood had caused your fears and nightmares. And Dad told us that you found out you were born in London during the war, and went through air raids, and God only knows what other terrors. How awful for you, Mom."

"Dad told you, huh?"

"I hope you don't mind. He also told us about you being in a coma and all that."

"I'm glad you know, but I wish I'd been able to tell you myself."

"Me too. We would have been there for you when you needed some support."

"Thanks, sweetheart."

"Mom, I'm really proud of you for facing up to all that alone. Dad's sorting out his problems too, so everything should work out."

"Dad? What do you mean?"

"Oh, I should let him tell you." She didn't wait for a response from Barbara but hurried onto the next subject. "And now that you know about the party, you'll come home right away, won't you?"

Barbara took a deep breath. Jan mustn't know how close she was to breaking. How could she tell her child that her father was her uncle? "I'll see what I can do."

"Call and let us know when you'll arrive, okay?"

"Jan...I..."

"It's okay, Mom. See you in a couple of days. Gotta go, the baby needs to be changed and fed. Love you. Bye for now."

The phone went dead. Jan hadn't given her the opportunity to say she might not be able to make it.

Barbara hung up the phone. *John is 'sorting out his problems.'* He'd need her to be with him. But how could she go home? She put her head in her hands and sobbed.

Half an hour later, Peggy found her still red-eyed and miserable.

"Why don't you take a break from all this? Phone Lilianne and see how she's getting on with her research."

"You're right, Peggy. I'm spending far too much time worrying over something I can do nothing about tonight. I'll phone the Swan and see if Lilianne wants to have a drink."

"That's the spirit. Wash your face and put on some fresh make-up."

"Come with me, Peggy."

"No, dear. Thank you, but I think I'll turn on the telly and catch up on *Coronation Street*. You go and have a good evening. You can tell me all about it when you get back."

Barbara phoned the inn and found Lilianne was not only there, but eager to tell Barbara what she'd been able to learn. "Is Peggy coming with you?"

Her excitement was almost palpable.

"No. I asked, but I think she's tired."

"Okay, I understand. But ask her to do me a favor. She said she was at the Black Swan the night my aunt went missing. I need to check her memory of everyone who was there against the list the police gave me."

"Sure. I'll ask her." Barbara hung up the phone and relayed Lilianne's request to Peggy.

The old woman's brow furrowed. "I'm not sure I can remember that particular night." She rubbed her chin and pursed her lips. "It was so long ago and, at the time, seemed like any other night. You go and get ready and I'll work on it."

Peggy settled into her favorite chair with a pad of paper and a pencil. She'd completed her list of names by the time Barbara was ready to leave.

At the Black Swan Inn Barbara craned around the high-spirited crowd cheering a soccer game being played on television. Lilianne waved Barbara over to a small table in the far corner of the room. The young Canadian beamed.

"Boy, am I glad you phoned. I've been busting to share what I've found out with someone." Lilianne positively bounced with excitement. "I'm glad it's you."

Barbara laughed and shook her head at her young companion's enthusiasm. "Okay. Let's get a drink and you can tell me all about it."

She fought her way through the crowd and returned with their drinks. "Whew! What a mob. I hope we can hear each other in here." Laughing, she plonked herself in a chair opposite Lilianne. "Okay, let's see what's got you so excited."

The young woman reached into her briefcase and pulled out a stack of documents. "The Stanton police have been very helpful to me. I just wish they had been as diligent at the time of my aunt's murder. I think they really blew it."

"In what way? I remember everyone here thought the constable and the Stanton police were pretty thorough, but that there wasn't much evidence to go on." She tasted her drink.

"That's just it. There were a lot of clues. But whether by carelessness or incompetence, they overlooked things. For one thing, they never found one of her shoes. They were certain she wasn't killed in the cave and she wasn't wearing shoes when she was found. One was with her body. Presumably it fell off and the murderer threw it in after her." Lilianne sipped her Bailey's while she consulted her notebook. "They never checked it for fingerprints."

"Why do the police think the killer threw her shoe in the cave? Maybe it just fell off."

"No. It was laying partly on her hair."

"Oh, I see."

A cheer erupted from the television watchers.

Lilianne leaned across the table and shouted. "They speculated that the other shoe may have been thrown, or fell into the river. They never looked for it. If they had, they may have determined just where she was killed, and been able to glean other clues from the site. Instead they stomped all up and down the riverbank obliterating any footprints, etcetera."

"Boy, you are really into this, aren't you?" Barbara took another sip of her drink.

"I've done a lot of research on forensic evidence. Not that it was available back then, but I still think they did only half a job with the evidence they had." She sipped her drink.

Barbara patted Lilianne's arm. "I know it must be frustrating for you, but don't be too hard on the local constable. The Stanton police probably didn't have much experience conducting a murder investigation either. It was a big deal at the time, but very unusual."

"I know. It's just maddening." She drew in a deep breath and let it escape in a noisy sigh.

"Okay. So, where did all this lead?"

"I looked at the autopsy report and the inquest findings. Not much new to report there. Lily Ann was raped and suffocated. The evidence shows she had been a virgin. I wish I could tell Grannie that. She always thought Lily Ann was a bit of a tart—her word, not mine."

"Yes, I remember, that was the general opinion of her. It was rather cruel really. The gossips insinuating she had brought her death on herself."

"My Grannie even speculated that Lily might have been pregnant and was killed by her child's father. What a narrow-minded old woman she was."

"How sad. I'm really sorry, Lilianne."

"Don't feel sorry. Right now, this is just research to me. I have to write the story and I mustn't let my emotions get in the way." She riffled through her papers pulling out one particular document. "The inquest report is interesting. Did you know they interviewed most of the adult men in the village?"

"Yes, I do remember that. All of them as I recall. They even talked to my old Da."

"Well, as I said, the police blew it." She sat up straight with a triumphant smile. Her eyes sparkled with excitement. "Reading through the reports I discovered there was one person they didn't interview."

"Who?"

"I can't say right now. Did Peggy remember who was at the Black Swan?"

Barbara reached into her bag and retrieved the piece of paper Peggy had given her. Lilianne studied it in silence then sat back with a satisfied grin.

"Well? You look like the proverbial cat that swallowed the canary. What did Peggy's list of names tell you?"

"I think she confirmed the missing piece of the puzzle. Or should I say, the missing man."

"Oh, Lord! And you're not going to tell me who it is, are you?"

"No. Not until I've checked something at Stanton tomorrow. I can tell you this. During the interrogations a particular name was repeatedly mentioned. This person was in the village the night Lily was probably murdered. But he'd left by the time her body was found and the police never followed up on it. What I know about him now fits. If I'm right, the police can still charge him."

"You mean you actually know who it is and he's still around?"

"I can't say any more right now." She carefully replaced the papers in her briefcase, but her face revealed her excitement.

Barbara could sense the young Canadian's exhilaration. "Wow! I can't believe you may have found the murderer after all these years. I see why you are so excited. Will you tell me about it tomorrow after you know?"

"Sure. Let's have dinner tomorrow night. Bring Peggy. If I'm right, she'll be shocked."

CHAPTER TWENTY-ONE

LITTLINGHAM 1985

Barbara closed Peggy's front door and turned to run down the steps. Gordon's car was parked right outside the gate. She paused, wondering why he was there.

"Good morning," he called through the open car window. "Are we off to London again?"

"Well, I am, I don't know about you." She stooped, and peered into the car. "Aren't you supposed to be painting your house today?"

"I'd rather help you, if you'd let me."

"Help me? How?"

Suddenly he seemed very serious. "Barbara, please get in the car. I'd like to talk to you."

Apprehension gripped her. "Why? What about?" This was crazy—or maybe he was. He certainly had the wildest mood swings.

He opened the passenger side door. "Come on."

Her stomach knotted, but she couldn't think of any excuse not to get into the car. What could he possibly have to talk to her about? Diffidently, she slid into the passenger seat and sat very straight, looking ahead, avoiding eye contact with him. She felt, more than saw, his sidelong glance at her.

"Barbara, I'm sorry if I embarrassed you telling you about my adolescent crush. Forget I ever told you." He laughed. "And stop being so edgy. Let's go to London and find your family."

She looked at him, puzzled. His periwinkle-blue eyes sparkled and he wore the same rueful grin as when he'd found her at the Black Swan Inn.

Relieved, she chuckled. "Why would you want to help me do my genealogy?"

"Because I'm still feeling contrite about yelling at you the other night, and I'm fascinated by what you're doing. I can't imagine just finding out that you're adopted and having to start from scratch to find out who you really are." He gave a short laugh, shaking his head. "My family history is recorded in the family Bible for several generations back, so there are no skeletons hiding in the Morris family closet. But you, now!" He sounded as excited as if he really were going to solve a mystery. "Let me help."

"I appreciate the offer, Gordon, but what can you possibly do?"

"For a start I can drive you to London." He put the car in gear and turned it around to head down Primrose Lane.

He didn't speak again until the car had almost reached the London road.

"What made you decide to come and do genealogy in the first place? I understand you didn't know, until Peggy Hilton told you the other day, that you were adopted by old Charlie Thomas and his wife."

She forced herself to relax. "I guess it really started with my youngest son. Donald is twenty-two now, but when he was a little boy of four, he came to me one day, very excited because his friend's grandmother had come to visit. He didn't even know what a grandmother was." She chuckled at the memory. "After I'd explained, he wanted to know if he had one. My husband's family was killed during the war, and my parents—I thought they were my parents— were dead. I realized my children knew nothing of their ancestry. Donald's questions had a tremendous impact on me at the time. I suppose that stayed with me until the children were grown. Then one day, about six months ago, I saw a genealogy class advertised." She was starting to relax. "I've always enjoyed history and genealogy seemed like the next step. I took the class, and got hooked." She laughed. "The problem was I had no family to research. Until now."

"Tell me about your family and life in America." He glanced quickly away from the road. "What does your husband do?"

"John is an aeronautical engineer." She felt a lump in her throat at the mention of his name. "As for my family, well…" She told him about her life in California and enjoyed some mild bragging about her children and grandchildren.

The day was so different from the last time they had driven to London. It had bucketed rain then and she'd made such a fool of herself—preaching. Today the weather was typical for late April in England with the sun playing hide-and-seek around the clouds, and the lambs frisking in the fields. The conversation flowed much easier.

"Why didn't your husband come with you to England?"

"He had planned to, but at the last minute, the aircraft company he works for decided to unveil a new design right in the middle of our vacation. They'd messed him about for months telling him first he couldn't have this particular time off." She jerked her head first to one side and then to the other. "Then it was okay, and then it wasn't."

She turned to gaze out of the window, appalled that she had just calmly told this kind man a bare-faced lie! Why was she making excuses for her husband? Because no matter how mad she'd been at him, she loved him. She wouldn't betray him by telling a virtual stranger of their differences.

Gordon was speaking. "A pity you couldn't have waited until after the unveiling." His voice brought her back and her cheeks burned at her memories.

"What? Oh, yes, but that's only the half of it. This was to be our thirtieth wedding anniversary gift to ourselves." She shrugged her shoulders. "I still get mad thinking about it."

"Thirty years," he said. "And you're still in love with him." He slipped the car into a parking space not far from the Public Record Office.

"Of course I still love him." She was mildly shocked that he would even suggest otherwise.

"No." He turned to gaze at her. "I said you're still *in* love *with* him. I hope he knows how lucky he is and that he's still as deeply in love with you."

She tried, but couldn't control the tears beginning to blur her vision. She turned her head away to stare out of the car window. For the past hour, talking with Gordon, she had forgotten the terrible fear. Now it threatened to smother her.

He reached over, and taking her chin in his hand, turned her to face him. "Do you want to talk about it?"

She shook her head and flicked the tears away with her forefinger.

"I'm a good listener and you'll feel lots better if you tell someone."

Suddenly she covered her face with her hands and sobbed. He put his arm around her shoulder and pulled her close to him.

With her face against the front of his soft sweater she cried for several minutes. Reluctantly, she left the comfort of his embrace and the warm smell of him. "I'm sorry, Gordon."

"Right." He offered a large handkerchief. "Now, let's have it."

"It's nothing." She shook her head at his handkerchief. Reaching into her bag she pulled a wad tissues. She folded one, precisely lining up the edges.

"What? All those tears, over nothing!"

"Homesickness, I guess." She dabbed at corner of her eyes with the tissue, carefully avoiding her mascara

"Homesickness? Well, why in the world don't you just go home?"

"That's only partly true. It's just that I came here so blissfully naïve, and now I feel I've been deceived." She blotted her tears and sniffled. "I can't help but wonder how much different my attitude to life would have been, had I known the truth about being adopted." She told him about her efforts to learn more about her parents and how that had opened up memories of her childhood. It was good to put it all into words. She shared everything with him, except for the part about her fears that she was married to her brother. That was too devastating.

"No wonder you're so upset. What a burden you've been carrying around." He reached over and patted the tears on her cheeks with his handkerchief. "Have you thought what you are going to do about it?"

"That's why I'm here today. I'm ordering my parents' marriage certificate." She sucked in a breath to keep from crying again.

"Well, I'd say you're taking the right course in trying to prove one way or the other. And," he smiled broadly at her, "it's a good thing I came along. I knew these solid shoulders had to be good for something. Come on." He got out of the car and came around to help her out. He took her hand and tucked it in the crook of his elbow. "Chin up," he said.

She stopped in her tracks. "No, Gordon. I need to do this alone. I appreciate you driving me all the way here and letting me unload on you, but I don't need any more help."

"Are you sure?"

She nodded. "Yes, thanks anyway. I don't want to keep you. I can get the bus back to Littlingham."

"Nonsense. Tell you what. I'll find something to do for a couple of hours and come back to get you for lunch."

She started to protest, but he raised his hand to stop her. "I won't hear of it. Good hunting." He turned and strode away along the sidewalk beneath the London plane trees.

Barbara ran up the steps to the door of St. Catherine's House.

Now familiar with the layout of the record center, she hurried through the main aisle to where throngs of searchers poured over the marriage indexes.

She'd given her course of action a lot of thought. According to John's birth certificate, his mother was twenty-three when he was born in 1933. So she must have been born around 1910. Barbara's birth certificate said the mother was twenty-seven, making her born about 1909. She shuddered. Depending on the mother's birth month, those dates matched.

Then there was Dan Loder. Whoever he was. If he was Lyn's first husband, and John's real father was McNab, it only added to the confusion.

Barbara gave a big resigned sigh and reached for the index to marriages, January through March 1932, to find Emmalyn Clarice Hayes.

The first ledger didn't produce any likely candidates, but after about forty-five minutes, she caught her breath. Her hand flew to her mouth. *That's my mother!*

She grabbed the B index book for the same year, the same quarter, and quickly ran her finger down the name Browne. Suddenly she was staring at an entry for Robert Browne with the same reference. She'd found her parents. The pounding of her heart vibrated in her ears. A tingle ran through her entire body and her hand shook as she wrote the information on the certificate order form. *Now that she was so close to the truth—did she really want to know?*

She'd come this far. She couldn't stop now but the certificates would take the usual three days before she could collect them. The urge to be home when she finally learned the truth prompted her to write her California address.

The search had gone as far as she could take it.

It was too early to meet Gordon and for that she was glad. She needed to compose herself and just think. She found a seat in the hall and people-watched.

As he had promised, Gordon was waiting by the door for her. "Did you find what you were looking for?"

"I hope so. I've ordered the certificate anyway."

He rubbed his hands together in anticipation. "What do we do now?"

"I can't do any more here."

"Well, let's celebrate that." Gordon squeezed her shoulder as he opened the door to the outside.

Hot diesel fumes blew into her face as a red double-decker bus rushed by. "Phew." Barbara turned her face away from the offensive smell. "I guess I don't really like London."

"Let's have some lunch." Gordon sounded exuberant. "In all your many trips to this place in the last couple of weeks, have you tried any of the restaurants around here?"

"That place over there serves a great cappuccino," She pointed across the busy street.

"Great! Maybe they serve a good sandwich, too."

She was suddenly very hungry, not having eaten much in the past several days. She shook her head to clear it of any further thoughts that two women named Emmalyn Clarice Hayes could, in fact, be one and the same woman. She just couldn't deal with the ramifications.

Her mouth watered at the aroma of succulent lamb marinated in oil, garlic and herbs, wrapped in pita bread and topped with yogurt, fresh tomatoes and mint. Gordon ordered two gyros.

He ate one and started on the other before he even spoke again. "How's that young woman getting on with her research?"

The question was so unexpected Barbara had to stop and think what he was asking. "Young woman? Oh, you mean Lilianne Paddington?"

"Yeah." He sounded nonchalant yet there was something tense about his demeanor.

"Actually she's done better than the police."

"Oh?" He gripped his sandwich and leaned forward eagerly. "How's that?"

"She's discovered there was someone else in the village the night her aunt was killed. Someone the police overlooked in their investigation."

His eyes were suddenly very bright. "Who? Has she told the police? Do the detectives in Stanton know yet?"

"Whoa!" She laughed at his intense excitement. "No, she was going to reread the affidavits again today, just to be sure of her facts. I believe she was planning on taking her evidence to the police in Stanton tomorrow. She was very excited."

Gordon's mood suddenly changed. "Did she tell you who it was?"

"No, only that he still lived in the area."

He dropped his half-eaten sandwich on the plate. Wiping his hands, he pushed back his chair and stood. "Let's go."

"Oh, okay." She had been enjoying her food, but he fidgeted as she stood and gathered her belongings. "Before we head back to Littlingham, may we go to Selfridges? I'd like to pick up some gifts for my grandchildren." Having done what she came to do, she'd planned to relax and enjoy the rest of the day, but Gordon's sudden mood change had dampened her spirits.

He didn't speak but drove her straight to the big department store.

"I won't be long, Gordon." She suddenly had a thought. "If you're in a hurry, you can leave. I'll take the bus back." She wished he would. She found his moodiness very uncomfortable.

"Take your time." He didn't even look at her. "I'll wait in the car park."

Later, as they rode back to Littlingham, she turned to him. The gathering dusk cast shadows across his unreadable face. "I appreciate you driving me these last couple of days, Gordon. I hope I haven't done or said something to upset you."

"No, of course not. I'm sorry, Barbara. I didn't mean to spoil your day."

She was at a loss to understand his sullenness and he had obviously dismissed her. The sun slipped behind the horizon leaving scarlet streaks between the clouds. They rode the rest of the way to Littlingham in silence, but her thoughts and imagination were in high gear. *This man is very strange. I don't think I like him and I don't like being here with him.* Her heartbeat increased and her stomach knotted.

By the time Gordon stopped the car at Peggy's front gate, Barbara had her bag and briefcase already in her hands. "Thanks, Gordon." She jumped out and slammed the door.

The car sped away down Primrose Lane. When the taillights disappeared around the corner, Barbara walked slowly to the front door. She stood for several seconds composing her thoughts and willing her heartbeat to slow. She let herself into the house and found Peggy in the kitchen, preparing the habitual cup of tea.

"Hey, Peggy. You're not fixing dinner, are you? Remember we're meeting Lilianne at the Swan." She was surprised at how normal she sounded. She sure didn't feel too normal, but she had nothing to base her fears on and she didn't want to alarm Peggy. After all, Gordon had done nothing to her. She just didn't know how to react to his irrationality.

"Oh, yes. I remembered. I'm looking forward to it. I just thought a nice cuppa now would be in order."

"That's fine but let's go to the inn early. I'm eager to see how Lilianne's day went."

Lilianne was not in her room but the landlady assured Barbara and Peggy that she had returned from Stanton.

They enjoyed a drink while they waited for her, but she never did join them so they ordered dinner.

Barbara's anxieties about Gordon had subsided and she relaxed enough to ask Peggy about him.

"Peggy, do you know if Gordon Morris has a medical problem?"

"Not that I know about."

"I wondered if he took medication that would alter his temperament." She hoped she wasn't out of line telling Peggy about Gordon's mood swings. Maybe is could be construed as gossip.

"I've never heard anything about him being ill. But then he doesn't live in the village anymore. Why do you ask?"

"He drove me to the London this morning and later we had lunch together. In the middle of it, his mood suddenly switched from happy and congenial to angry and agitated."

"Why? What happened?"

"I don't know what brought it on. We were talking casually. Then he asked how Lilianne was getting on. He seemed to get very agitated and suddenly he was grilling me about her."

"Lilianne? What did she have to do with it?"

Barbara was still puzzled by Gordon's actions and told Peggy about him driving her home in silence. "It was very uncomfortable, but he assured me I hadn't done or said anything to upset him. I just don't understand it."

They finished their meal and had an after-dinner drink, but Lilianne had still not shown up.

They headed for home with their arms linked. Chatting comfortably they crossed the cobbled stone village square and turned towards Primrose Lane. A vehicle without headlights suddenly roared out of the entrance to the river road. Barbara grabbed Peggy and together they fell against the hedges to avoid being hit as the car sped by them.

"Who is that idiot?"

In the twilight the driver's profile appeared white and fierce.

"I've seen that car before." Peggy tried to lift herself out of the hedge.

Barbara helped Peggy to her feet and stared after the disappearing car. "I have too. In fact, I rode in that car today. That was Gordon Morris behind the wheel."

CHAPTER TWENTY-TWO

LITTLINGHAM 1985

Barbara slept well for the first time since she came to Littlingham. It was a relief to have decided to go home regardless of the consequences. She'd done all she could and her fate was now in God's hands.

She washed and dressed with a freedom from anxiety and dread that she hadn't experienced since Peggy told her Charlie and Dolly Thomas were not her parents.

Peggy was already hanging the wash and greeted Barbara from behind the sheets flapping on the clothesline. "Well, good morning, sleepy head. How are you feeling today?"

"Hi, Peggy," Barbara yawned, and blinked in the bright sunshine. "What a beautiful day. I can't believe I slept so hard and so long. I feel absolutely wonderful."

"You must have needed it. Can you help yourself to breakfast? I'm in rather a hurry this morning. I have that Celebration of Spring *do* today."

"Yes, of course. I'm sorry I'm so late. I hope I haven't slowed you down. I remember you told me about the luncheon." She chuckled. "For the Wrinklies, right?" She hadn't heard the descriptive expression before Peggy referred to herself as a Wrinkly. It made Barbara laugh again to say it.

After breakfast of tea and toast, Barbara made her bed and helped Peggy straighten up the house. She declined Peggy's offer to join her for the luncheon at the church hall.

"I think I'll say goodbye to Lilianne and Reverend Morris. You go and enjoy yourself. I'll see you later this afternoon."

They set off together down Primrose Lane and parted at the church. Peggy turned toward the community hall and Barbara turned to the churchyard.

Under her touch, the wrought-iron gate opened with a loud squawk. The protest disturbed the quiet of the morning and sent a flurry of birds out of the trees.

Unhurried steps brought Barbara to the graves of her adopted parents. Listening to a pair of thrushes in the oak tree branches above her, she smiled to herself thinking it fitting that their nesting would bring new life here, where death had brought generations of humans.

Thirty-two years before, she had hurried from this spot, the smell of fresh-turned earth piled on her da's new grave still heavy in her nostrils. Mum's grave had lain flat and unmarked. It had been difficult for her to leave them then and she never expected to be here again. A wave of emotion washed over her. Why had they deceived her into thinking she was their daughter? Still, had she known as a child, would she have recognized the sacrifices they made for her, or felt this gratitude? What if they hadn't adopted her and she had been raised in an orphanage? How differently her life might have turned out. She might never have met John.

John!

The thought of him jolted her back to reality. Her heart jumped at the prospect of facing him in a couple of days. Her reservation for a flight back to the States had been confirmed.

Was her life about to make a new turn?

She gazed one last time at the two flat graves with their granite markers and wondered if she would ever see them again. Somehow—perhaps because the beautiful morning promised a continuation of life—it was easier to leave them this time.

She retraced her steps out of the churchyard and wandered to the Black Swan Inn.

Lilianne was not there and Annie, the landlady, said they hadn't seen her since the previous evening.

"I don't know her very well, but that does seem a bit odd." Barbara shrugged. "I expect she's hot on the trail of another clue. When she comes back, please ask her to call me at Peggy Hilton's. I'm leaving Littlingham and would like to see her before I go."

Barbara left the Black Swan and crossed the village square. She bought an apple at the greengrocers and continued across the cobblestones to a footpath leading to the River Little.

She sat down on the grassy bank and leaned back on her elbows soaking up the warmth of the sun. The air was heavy with the scent of wild primroses and the carpet of bluebells stretched out as far as her eye could see.

She crunched on the apple and watched a dragonfly dart across the water. The scene around her was timeless. Sheep grazed on the green hills beyond the river. Young lambs frisked about leaping into the air as if delighted to be alive on such a beautiful day. A few cows jostled each other for the same space on the opposite bank.

If only it could stay this way and she didn't have to leave it. Barbara took off her sunglasses and hugged her knees to her chest. She wondered if she were doing the right thing in going home. She was no closer to the truth than when she'd first looked at her birth certificate.

She could stay in England until she was certain, but then she wouldn't be home for the anniversary party. The kids would be disappointed, especially Janet.

On the other hand, what if she went home and it turned out that she and John had an incestuous relationship? She lowered her head onto her knees, trying to imagine telling John they were brother and sister. What would he say? What would we do?

John loves me as much as I love him. Can we just pretend we don't know and go on loving each other?

She lifted her face and ran her hands through her hair fighting back tears. She thought she'd put all the doubts and anxieties to rest, but now they were returning. Peggy's solution was to ignore it and hope that it will all go away. That wouldn't do. Gordon was very supportive but he didn't have an answer.

Anyway, she couldn't expect her friends to solve her problems. Her dilemma was her own and she would have to come to grips with it. Tears spilled down her cheeks. Irritated she flicked them away and stood. Crying wouldn't help, either.

She tossed the remains of her apple aside for some small animal to find. Brushing off the seat of her jeans, Barbara threw her jacket over her shoulder. Wandering farther along the riverbank she startled a large blue heron. It lifted from the river and settled on the bank eyeing her as she passed. In the distance a flock of rooks rose out of the trees like bits of a black feather duster. Anxious moorhens gathered their chicks and hastily tucked them into the grasses near the riverbank.

Barbara gained the towpath and quickened her step to Piggen. She had one more question to ask the Reverend Bartholomew Morris before she left England.

Barbara ambled along the towpath, her footfalls muffled by the soft dirt, and silently approached the Morris cottage.

Gordon clung to the top rung of a ladder propped against the house. His paintbrush swished back and forth along the window trim. He hadn't seen her coming, and so as not to startle him, she called out from the garden gate.

He grabbed the top of the ladder with one hand and turned. "Where did you come from? I didn't hear you."

"I took the footpath. Isn't it a beautiful day?" She took off her sunglasses and shaded her eyes with her hand as she peered at the newly painted house. "It looks very nice. I like the color."

He braced himself on the top of the ladder, and looked down on her. "What are you doing here?" His face was flushed and not entirely from the sun. He was angry and Barbara didn't understand why. His mood pendulum seemed to be in the grumpy mode this morning. She sympathized with him. Caring day after day for an elderly father suffering from Alzheimer's disease had to be a tremendous strain.

"I didn't mean to disturb you, Gordon. I just came to say goodbye to your father. I'm leaving tomorrow."

The hint of relief darted across his forehead, and was gone. "Dad's sleeping. Anyway, he's off with the fairies today."

"He's what?"

"He's not having a very good day. He isn't lucid."

"Oh, I'm sorry. Well, maybe I can come back later. Right now I have to see if I can find Lilianne. Nobody's seen her since yesterday."

He abruptly turned from her and picked up his paintbrush. "Won't do you any good to come back." Dipping the brush in the bucket of paint, he resumed swishing it across the house.

She'd been dismissed with no hope or invitation to see the old reverend. She wasn't going to get the opportunity to find out if he knew how Dan Loder was related to her mother.

In his present mood Gordon probably couldn't be reasoned with. He hadn't said goodbye, so she didn't either.

She'd walked part way back to Littlingham still smarting at Gordon's rebuff before she remembered she hasn't asked Gordon why he was down on the river road the previous evening.

CHAPTER TWENTY-THREE

LITTLINGHAM 1985

Barbara woke with a start. It was still dark, but a hint of light glimmered a promise of dawn. She sat up in bed and hugged her knees. Her heart pounded under her ribs. She strained to hear any sounds, but the house was very quiet. Had she screamed, or only dreamed it?

A cold shiver ran down her spine and gooseflesh prickled her bare arms. She snuggled back into the blankets and stared at the ceiling. Snatches of a scene long forgotten inched around her memory and she felt herself begin to tremble. It was happening again. Another long-forgotten memory was emerging…

She stood beside her mother on the platform of the train station near their Lambeth home. They waited with their heads tilted up to watch the little boy behind the train window. He seemed to be kneeling on the seat. A large cardboard tag was safety-pinned to the maroon piping on the lapel of his navy blue blazer. He held the palms of his hands pressed hard against the glass and made no attempt to wipe the tears away from his dark brown eyes.

The vision seemed to be getting mixed up with other memories. The child in her mind looked like her son Jack as a little boy—and Jack was the image of his father as an adult! Barbara shivered and not because she was cold.

She couldn't hear the sobs, but the little boy's face shuddered each time he opened his mouth and gasped for air. The train lurched, stopped, and moved, slowly at first. The boy pushed his face against the window, knocking the maroon and navy blue school cap to the back of his head. A lock of dark hair fell across his forehead. The train picked up speed and he was gone.

Sleep eluded Barbara. A plan formulated. Daylight couldn't come quickly enough now. At breakfast she had told Peggy her plan for the day. "It was really a blessing that I couldn't get a reservation on the plane home until tomorrow night. Now I have time for one last trip to the record office and I'll still be home in time for the party on Saturday night. Wow! I feel lucky today."

Peggy's black eyes sparkled. "I'm so happy for you."

Barbara grabbed her papers. "I just have one thing to do. It should be a piece of cake, so I'll probably be back early." She rushed out the door to catch the early bus from Littlingham so as to arrive at the record office when the doors opened at 8:30. Amid a jumble of wet coats and umbrellas she joined the early morning commuter crowds and even found a seat on the bus.

Barbara's heart raced as she hurried up the steps and through the revolving door to St. Catherine's House. But her shoulders sagged with disappointment to discover the records she needed were kept at the Chancery Lane Public Record Office.

A light drizzle fell as she hurried along the wet sidewalk. Just inside the door of the record office she stopped short. A long bench on either side of the entrance was jammed with people, all staring at her. They each clutched a briefcase or folder of some kind.

A tall, elegantly dressed gentleman sitting near the door turned to her. "Are you lost?"

"I'm not sure." Barbara laughed at how silly she sounded. "I'm looking for the Public Record Office."

"Well, you've found it." He smiled and several others in the queue turned to her smiling and nodding.

"What are you all waiting for?"

"To use the microfilm readers," a merry, rosy-cheeked woman answered. "They're all in use at the moment. When one is free, the lady at the head of this queue gets it."

"Oh, I see. Then where do I go to ask about the availability of records?" Three people pointed toward a counter.

Relieved that she didn't have to wait through the line, she thanked them and made her way to the desk where a clerk ruffled through some papers. "Excuse me, can you tell me where to find information about children evacuated oversees during the Second World War?"

The clerk looked up. Her smile was one of apology. "I'm afraid you're in the wrong place."

"Oh, no! At Saint Catherine's House I was told the Public Record Office had them."

"Yes, but they meant the Public Record Office at Kew."

"Kew? Do you mean Kew as in Kew Gardens, Surrey?" Barbara ran her hand through her hair.

"Well, yes." The woman chuckled. "But not the gardens, of course."

The day seemed to be turning sour and Barbara clenched her jaw to keep from screaming.

The journey to Kew took much longer than she had anticipated and she wished now she had a car. But no, not really, she thought, watching the cars and buses going the wrong way on the roundabouts. She shuddered thinking how scary that would be after driving so many years in the States.

In answer to her inquiry, the clerk at the Public Record Office at Kew handed her an enormous stack of papers.

Barbara gasped. "All these children were evacuated overseas?"

"Oh, no. I misunderstood your request when you said you wanted to see the list of applicants for overseas evacuation. Less than 2,300 children actually went to the dominions."

Barbara found a seat and the clerk left, returning a few minutes later with a smaller sheaf of papers. She spread them on the table and sat down next to Barbara.

"Here are the ships and the dates and countries to which they sailed, with the dates of arrival and the total number of evacuees each one carried." The clerk bent over the paper and ran her finger down the columns as she spoke. She picked up a second paper. "And here are the children's names and ages, and their places of residence in Britain, listed by the country to which they were evacuated. You'll see that each sailing was coded. 'D' for the Dominion of Canada, 'U' for the Union of South Africa, 'Zed' for New Zealand and 'C' for the Commonwealth of Australia." She straightened up. "Can you manage?"

Barbara smiled at her. "Yes, thank you." She settled to the task, thinking the small lists would be a piece of cake she'd anticipated.

A tingle of excitement radiated through her body. She decided to search the South Africa list of evacuees first, for the fun of finding John's name. And there he was—John McNab, age 7 from London. He had sailed aboard the *Llanstephan Castle* from Liverpool August 24, 1940 and arrived in Cape

Town on September 20, 1940.

She continued to run her finger down the list of ships. Suddenly she stopped. The next ship showed no arrival date and the word torpedoed jumped out at her, followed by a second identical listing. Her mouth went dry. What did this mean? She pushed herself up from the table and stood on rubbery legs. She steadied herself and holding her finger on the entry, took the list to the clerk.

"What does…?" Her voice cracked. She swallowed and ran her tongue around her parched lips. "What does this mean?"

The woman bent her head and looked at the entry. She straightened and her face softened. "It means that the ships were torpedoed and sunk."

"With children aboard?" Barbara was incredulous.

"I'm afraid so." The clerk stared straight at Barbara.

"Were any of the children rescued?"

"All from the first ship, but just a few from the second one." The clerk shook her head and looked off across the room, blinking. "The program was halted after that. It actually lasted only three weeks."

Nausea crawled in Barbara's belly. *This will be a piece of cake,* she scoffed silently at her own naïveté. "Oh, God!" she breathed, and sat down at the table beside her. Propping her elbows in front of her, she covered her eyes with her hands and took several deep breaths. Composed at last, she looked up into the agonized face of the clerk. "I had no idea."

"No. Most people are not aware of the danger in which this country placed her children during the Second World War." She emphasized each word. "It's one of Great Britain's dirty little secrets that children were used as shields by placing them on troop ships and sending them in convoys into the middle of German submarine wolf-packs." She spat the words like venom.

Barbara stared at the woman. "Did you know one of those children?"

The clerk didn't answer immediately, but took the papers from beneath Barbara's hands and shuffled through them, then handed a page to Barbara. "This was my older sister." Her finger rested under the name of a five-year-old girl.

"She was only five?"

"Yes. The age bracket for evacuation was between of five and sixteen."

"Oh, the poor parents." Barbara immediately thought of her own grandchildren.

The clerk composed herself then turned back to Barbara. "Did you find the child you were looking for?"

Barbara shook her head, blinded by the tears burning in her eyes.

Later, having satisfied herself that no Daniel Browne or Daniel Loder had arrived safely in any of the commonwealth countries, she forced herself to search the list of children who were lost at sea.

CHAPTER TWENTY-FOUR

It was time to go home.

Barbara walked down Primrose Lane from Peggy's house to the Black Swan Inn. A mixture of apprehension and excitement gripped her. She'd done all she could to solve her genealogical puzzle. Her search of the evacuee records was supposed to give her the proof she needed. She'd found John among the records, but as far as she could determine, it didn't prove he wasn't her brother.

She'd done the only other thing she could think of—ordered her parents' marriage certificate. She already knew John's grandfather's name and his occupation. Now she had to wait to see her own maternal grandfather's name and what he did for a living.

Please God, let him be a different John Hayes than John's grandfather.

She could do nothing more, and if her worst fears were realized, continuing to hide wouldn't make it go away. She needed to go home and face John with her suspicions. Just the thought made her stomach do a flip-flop.

Nearing the Black Swan Inn, she forced her mind away from whatever dilemma awaited her back home in California. She had come to celebrate with Lilianne. If the young Canadian's theory had been right the police now knew who had killed her aunt, Lily Ann.

The usual gathering of old men sat on the bench outside the pub in the sunshine quaffing pints of dark ale.

The morning shone as bright and sunny as the day Barbara had arrived in Littlingham, but she was a completely different woman. Her life as it was then, she now knew was a complete lie. Not only was Littlingham not her birthplace but also Dolly and Charlie Thomas were not her parents. And worst of all she might have married her brother.

She massaged the lump of trepidation forming in her stomach again. *I can't keep thinking that. I must think it is all a big mistake. My life has to go on and I want to believe it will not be changed. John and I will go on loving each other as we always have without a shadow of doubt about our relationship. I must believe that…I will believe it.*

The old men touched their old gnarled hands to the bills of their checkered caps in greeting to Barbara. She was recognized now as a village daughter returned, and no longer regarded as an outsider.

"Good morning," she greeted them with a wave and a smile.

Stepping through the door to the public lounge, she blinked to adjust her eyes to the gloom. The characteristic smell of stale beer and old tobacco stung her nostrils.

Dave, the barman, stood at his usual station polishing up the beer pump handles. "Hello, Mrs. McNab. How are you this lovely morning?"

Barbara grinned at him. "How would you know what sort of the morning it is? Do you ever leave here?"

"'Course I do. Got a family, don't I?"

"Well, you always seem to be here. Day and night. I thought you never ventured any farther than the trash bin out back."

"Sometimes it feels like that. What can I do for you today, m'dear?"

"Dave, do you know if Lilianne Paddington is in her room?"

"Can't say, luv. Nobody's seen her for two days."

"What? Has she checked out?"

"No. We expected her back."

"I was in a couple of evenings ago looking for her. Peggy Hilton and I were supposed to have dinner with her. I thought she'd call if she decided to spend the night in Stanton. You say she's never been back? I wonder if she's still there."

"Well, I thought it was funny she didn't let us know how long she'd be away. She's our only guest, and Annie didn't know if she needed to prepare meals for her."

Barbara's instincts were suddenly alert "That is so strange. She didn't strike me as being irresponsible." She pulled a pound note from her purse. "Change this please, Dave. I'm going to call the Stanton police. We should find out where she is."

"Yeah. You're right. Here, use ours." The barman pushed the phone across the bar towards her. "Hope she hasn't had an accident. She was driving and she's not familiar with our roads." He stayed on the other side of the bar automatically wiping imaginary droplets while Barbara made her call.

Frowning, Barbara replaced the phone. "The police haven't seen her." Fingers of apprehension crept up her spine. "The detective I spoke with said she never kept the appointment she made with him. He thought she'd changed her mind so they've dismissed the whole thing." Barbara climbed on a barstool and propped her chin on her hand while she thought.

Dave busied himself straightening glasses behind the bar. "Want anything?"

She shook her head. "No, thanks. Dave, I'm really worried about Lilianne. Where could she be?"

Dave picked up his polishing cloth and rubbed a spot on the counter. His eyebrows suddenly knit together in a frown and he stopped polishing nonexistent stains. "The police are going to follow up on what she told them, aren't they?"

"No. Without the evidence she said she'd found, they don't think it worth reopening the case." She bit her lip, concentrating. "Is Annie around?"

"I'll get her for you." He hoisted a crate of beer bottles and started for the back door.

A minute later Annie came in drying her hands. "Hello there. What's all this about Lilianne?"

"Nobody seems to know where she is and I'm worried about her. She didn't keep her appointment with the Stanton police, either. When did you last see her?"

"She hasn't slept here for two nights. We thought she must have stayed in Stanton."

"Do you think it would be all right if I looked in her room? Perhaps she left something that will tell us where she is. If nothing else, I'd like to find her to say goodbye. I'm going home tomorrow."

Annie opened a drawer under the bar counter and pulled out a bunch of keys. She selected one and motioned Barbara to follow her.

Lilianne's bed was unused. Her cosmetics and brush and comb were lined up on the dresser. A bracelet and a pair of earrings looked as if they'd been casually dropped next to the lamp. A suitcase protruded from under the bed and a piece of hand luggage sat in the far corner of the room. A notebook and several loose pages with a pencil on top were on the bedside table.

Barbara picked up the papers and scanned them. "I think this is the list Lilianne compiled of the men who were living in the area when her aunt was killed. I recognize most of them." She picked up the notebook and checked some of the writing. "Annie, I'm going to take these to the police constable to look at."

"You go right ahead, Barbara. I think that's a good idea."

"When Lilianne comes back, I hope she'll understand I'm doing this out of concern for her and doesn't get mad at me."

"She'll appreciate it, I'm sure."

Barbara caught up with Constable Flood cycling into the village square, back from his daily rounds of the surrounding farms. His eyes narrowed while he listened to her. "Something is definitely amiss. Come on, let's go and talk to Dave and Annie."

At the Black Swan Inn the landlord and his wife recounted the last time they had seen the young Canadian while Barbara's apprehension grew.

Constable Flood completed his notes and phoned the Stanton police. Within hours a massive search was organized. The road between Stanton and Littlingham showed no evidence of a car having wrecked, so the search then focused on Littlingham. The entire village turned out to offer advice and speculation.

Peggy and Barbara sat on a grassy bank overlooking the river. They clasped their trembling hands together seeking mutual comfort. Surrounded by the morbidly curious onlookers, neither woman spoke, but there were plenty of rumors being passed around them from one villager to another.

Kids, caught up in the tense excitement, ran around yelling for no apparent reason other than exhilaration. Younger children sat wide-eyed clinging to their mothers, watching the searchers probing the bushes between the bank and the river's edge.

Volunteers fanned out through the woods surrounding Littlingham. They could be heard calling to one another as they probed the low-growing shrubs. One old farmer brought along his lurcher. The dog, unsure of the game, bayed when he picked up the scent of an animal that crossed his path, and caused a moment of frenzy among the people waiting on the riverbank.

Nervous speculation reached new heights when Lilianne's rented car was found abandoned in the nearby woods, with the keys in the ignition. Her purse was intact on the front seat, but the briefcase she carried everywhere was missing.

Every spectator had an opinion on what had happened to the young driver. The general consensus was, not without some degree of eagerness, that she had met with foul play.

The search reached the edge of the village. Shadows lengthened in the late afternoon, but nobody seemed ready to abandon the hunt for the young woman.

Someone thought it prudent to examine the cave where Lily Ann Paddington's body had been found almost forty years earlier.

Three shrill blasts on a police whistle froze everyone into statues. Several seconds of silence followed, broken by a shout.

Searchers poured from the woods and ran from the fields to converge along the riverbank.

"They've found something," someone stated the obvious.

Police officers exploded into action, dashing in every direction. Some went to the cars parked along the road. Others slid down the riverbank. A policewoman sprinted from her car clutching a folded black body bag. She threw it to a police sergeant waiting below the bank. He caught it on the fly and carried it away. Minutes later several uniformed officers reappeared carrying the black bag between them.

Barbara thought she might be sick. She squeezed Peggy's hand.

Peggy's gasp turned into a sob. She returned pressure on Barbara's hand. "Who would hurt that lovely young woman?"

"What's happened?" The woman peered at Peggy as if she expected an answer.

"Is it the girl?"

"How did she die?" It was obvious whoever was in the black bag was dead.

The village constable scrambled up the grassy slope. People ran towards him and gathered in a clamoring knot. The constable bent over gasping for air and held up his hand to calm and silence the barrage of questions. "I can't tell you anything at the moment."

A red-faced farmer elbowed his way through the crowd to confront Constable Flood. "Well, somebody needs to tell us what's going on."

"Do we have a murderer in our midst?" A young woman with a child perched on her hip pushed through the crowd. "I've got children to protect." People turned and stared at her as if she had just blurted out a revelation.

"Yes. Tell us what you know. We have to defend ourselves."

The constable surveyed the sea of faces. His expression said he intended to make the most of his few minutes of recognition. "Here are the facts. The body of Miss Lilianne Paddington of Ontario, Canada, has been recovered from the well-known cave in the riverbank."

The butcher, still wearing his bloodied apron, craned over the heads of the crowd. "How did she die?"

"She appears to have been murdered, but that will be decided by an inquest to be held first thing tomorrow morning." Constable Flood rocked back and forth on the balls of his feet.

The spinster librarian's timid voice was easily recognizable. "Was she raped like her aunt?"

Plod ignored the question.

"The Stanton police will be conducting an investigation and will, of course, be interviewing a number of people." The constable seemed disappointed that his brief fame had faded.

A very young police officer appeared beside Barbara. "Mrs. McNab, would you please come with me?" He spoke very quietly but several people heard him and gave Barbara suspicious glares.

"Me? Why?"

"The detective you spoke with earlier would like a word with you."

Barbara followed the policeman to the Black Swan Inn where a makeshift interview room had been set up away from the lounge and bar. A middle-aged man in a rumpled coat introduced himself and offered her a hard chair to sit on. "You are aware, I'm sure, that the body of Miss Lilianne Paddington has been recovered."

"Yes. Oh that poor girl." Hot tears burned in Barbara's eyes. "Please tell me what happened to her."

"I see no reason for keeping information from you. She was quite obviously murdered. Her body was found in the cave along the riverbank."

"The same cave where her aunt's body was found?"

"It appears so. There will be questions so I will tell you. The difference between the two murders is that in this case she does not appear to have been raped." He shuffled through a handful of papers in front of him. "Now, Mrs. McNab. You seem to have been most closely associated with her. How well did you know her?"

"I wouldn't say I knew her. I was acquainted with her. Her father and I had gone to school together when we both lived here in the village. I think Lilianne felt a certain ease with me for that reason."

"How often did you see her?"

"We had dinner together a couple of times. She wanted to ask me what I remembered about her aunt. You know Lilianne is...I mean, was writing a book about her aunt's murder? Oh God—this is awful." Barbara stopped and sucked in a breath.

The detective produced a box of tissues and offered it to Barbara.

She wiped the tears now coursing down her cheeks. "She was gathering background information from anyone who knew her aunt. Lilianne also shared some of her research findings with me, but I didn't really *know* her."

"She apparently talked more to you than to anyone else here. You say she told you about some of her findings."

"Yes. She was very excited to have found something the police had overlooked during the investigation of her aunt's murder."

"When did she tell you that?"

"The night before last. We had a drink together here at the inn." Barbara crumpled the tissue. "Oh my God. I can't believe this."

"Did she tell you what she planned to do with the information she had?"

"Yes, first she had to check something out in Stanton. Then if she was right, I believe she intended taking her proof to the police."

"You don't know what she was going to check, or if she did in fact find what she was looking for?"

"No. I didn't see her again. Why are you asking me all these questions? You surely don't suspect me?"

He chuckled. "Oh, no. A man, a very strong man, committed this murder. But tell me, why didn't you see her as you planned?"

"I don't know. I looked for her, but she wasn't here. I came to find her to tell her goodbye. I was supposed to leave today to fly home to the States."

"But you obviously didn't leave." The brindle-haired detective regarded Barbara.

"No, I had one more search of my own to do in London, so I postponed my departure and changed my plane reservation."

"So why didn't you look for her after you came back from London?"

"I'd had a very emotional day and was tired." She tore a little corner off the tissue.

"You said you had a search to do in London. What were you searching for?"

"Oh, family history. Nothing to do with Lilianne's research."

"I see." The detective consulted his notes before he spoke again. "You know that Miss Paddington was last seen just before you and Mrs. Hilton came here to the inn to have dinner?"

"I didn't know when she was last seen. I just assumed, since she'd said she was going to Stanton, that she'd decided to spend the night there. I was disappointed that I'd missed her. We…Mrs. Hilton and I hoped she might join us for dinner."

"You had dinner. What did you do when you left here?"

"We just went back to Peggy's…Mrs. Hilton's house. I've been staying with her." She tore another piece off the tissue.

"What time was it when you left the inn and walked back to Primrose Lane?"

Barbara was surprised he knew where Peggy lived. "I don't know. Probably eight, eight-thirty."

"It would have been just getting dark by then. Did you see anything out of the ordinary along the way?"

"No. I don't think so…" She ripped at the tissue.

"Think. Take your time. You had just missed Miss Paddington. She was last seen just before you arrived at the inn."

"Yes…wait a minute. We did see something. A car without headlights came tearing out of the river road and almost ran us down."

"And did you see who was driving?"

"Oh, God…yes." Barbara leaned her elbows on the table. She rubbed her temples while her brain did cartwheels.

"Take your time, Mrs. McNab."

"I remember now. It was Gordon Morris. Do you think…?"

"Gordon Morris? Does he live here in Littlingham?"

"No. He's from Piggen. I recognized him, but I also knew the car because he had driven me home from London in it, just that afternoon."

"Did you and Mrs. Hilton discuss the incident?"

"Only to the extent of wondering what he was doing driving down on the river road with no lights. Do you think he had anything to do with Lilianne's death?"

"We won't know until we have all the facts. Tell me, did you and Mr. Morris talk about Miss Paddington?"

"As a matter of fact, he was very interested in her progress in her search for her aunt's killer."

"Tell me about that conversation."

Barbara told the detective all she could remember. He plied her with questions about minute details, and was especially interested in Gordon's sudden mood change.

"What did Miss Paddington tell you she had discovered?"

"She said there was someone else in Littlingham the night her aunt was killed and that the police had overlooked him because he was gone before they found her body."

"You lived here then, didn't you?"

"Yes. I was just a child. But I remember how all the men were questioned and had to provide alibis for the night the police thought Lily Ann Paddington had been murdered. They only looked at the men because she'd been raped. They even talked to my elderly father, but I was his alibi. I used to go and meet him at the pub and walk him home."

"You walked him home that night?"

"Yes."

"You lived on Primrose Lane, so you had to pass the river road. Did the police talk to you about that night?"

"No. As I said, I was just a child and I think the police questioned only the men in the village. They may have interviewed some women, but I never heard of them talking to any children."

"I know it's a long time ago, but do you remember anything about walking your father home that night. Anything you saw or heard that was different from other nights?"

"No. We rarely saw anyone. Most people coming from the Swan would have gone in the opposite direction. We lived almost at the end of the village. Only the church and the vicarage were beyond Primrose Lane."

"Who was the vicar then?"

"Reverend Morris." The hair raised on the back of her neck. She shivered and shredded the last of the tissue.

"Mrs. McNab, you have become very pale. Would you like a glass of water?"

Barbara shook her head. "I do remember something." She hugged herself to keep from trembling When next she spoke her teeth chattered. "Because Lily Ann's body wasn't found for several days after she disappeared, I didn't realize until now that it had actually happened the night she was probably murdered."

"What? What happened?"

"Oh...I feel sick."

"Take your time." The detective poured a glass of water from the pitcher on the table. "Drink this."

She dropped the tissue and gripped the glass with both trembling hands, taking several gulps. The glass clattered as she set on the table in front of her. She drew air deep into her lungs and exhaled before continuing.

"My father and I were walking home, just as we did every Saturday night. I remember as we passed the corner of the river road I heard something scrape. I remember thinking it was a strange sound, and couldn't have been an animal. It sounded more like metal on stone. As I turned and looked across the road someone stepped back into the shadows. I caught a glimpse of a uniform and shiny metal buttons. I couldn't see who it was."

The detective blew out a breath signaling his disappointment.

Barbara ran her fingers through her hair then continued. "I wondered who was hiding in the shadows but I wasn't concerned because my da had his heavy oak cane with him. And although he was crippled, he was still very strong." The mental image of her da and his cane brought a smile to Barbara's thoughts.

"Please continue," the detective's voice interrupted Barbara's reverie.

"There isn't any more, really. We walked on. But…" The image was as clear as the night she had witnessed it. "As my da and I turned the corner into Primrose Lane, I looked back. A man wearing a military uniform stepped out of the shadows and ran towards the vicarage."

She sucked in a gasp before she spoke again. Her voice was a hoarse whisper. "Oh my God," she breathed. "*It was Gordon Morris.*"

CHAPTER TWENTY-FIVE

USA 1985

John stood naked before the mirror and grinned at the clean-shaven face in the mirror. "I'm a lucky son of a bitch!" He patted his flat stomach. "I'm healthy. I have three successful kids. Terrific grandkids. I'm paid well to design beautiful aircraft. And I don't know many men who can claim to still be in love with the same woman after thirty years." He slapped at his bare thigh in satisfaction.

Some people never seem to find the right mate and he and Barb had it all. Their love had grown deeper and more intense over the years, and he couldn't even entertain the idea of another woman. He knew without a doubt that she never had, nor ever would, be unfaithful to him. "And she's on her way home to me!" He turned to leave the bathroom but a backward glance in the mirror stopped him. He grinned at his reflection remembering a remark Barb once made. "Women always wrap themselves in a towel or a bathrobe and seldom study their nude form. But men can never seem to resist checking out their naked bodies—several times. Heck, they even have to come back and look again just in case something went missing while they weren't looking."

Towel or bathrobe, it didn't matter, he knew Barb's form very well and he was eager to see it again.

Barefoot, he passed back into the bedroom and picked up the long velvet box on top of his nightstand. Inside lay the beautiful necklace he'd had designed just for Barb to celebrate their anniversary. A large black pearl set in gold and surrounded by thirty small diamonds. He could hardly wait to see her face when he gave it to her at the party that night. She'd be impressed that he knew the pearl represented a thirty-year wedding anniversary. Actually, it was Jan who had told him that. The diamonds were the suggestion of the jeweler, and John loved the idea. Each year of their marriage had been a diamond.

Two hours after the plane landed, the customs inspector stamped Barbara's declaration form. "Thank you for your patience," he said in a worn-out, automatic tone pushing her open suitcases to the end of the inspection counter.

Patient was hardly what Barb considered herself at the moment. Exhausted by the sleepless all-night flight and emotionally spent worrying about her reaction to John, she just wanted to get past her initial meeting with him. She rearranged the contents of her suitcases, zippered them shut and lugged them through the door to the arrival area.

John stood just inside the entrance craning over the heads of the clamoring crowd. Tall, slender and even at this ungodly hour of the morning, he was as handsome as ever. She'd never stopped loving him, but would their love be allowed to continue?

Now that she was actually here and about to meet him, panic overwhelmed her. *Oh, God! What shall I do?* She was tempted to turn and run. But there was no escape now. He'd seen her and his face glowed with pleasure.

As the time had drawn closer for her to leave England, she'd wavered between making more excuses to stay, and facing John and telling him the truth. She'd finally convinced herself to come home and save her children the embarrassment of having to cancel the party.

She'd traveled all night wrapped in a blanket staring at the back of the seat in front of her, going over and over everything she'd learned. She still couldn't be sure she wasn't going home to her brother. And she wouldn't be certain until she got her parents' marriage certificate. Then she'd see if John's maternal grandfather and her own were the same man.

Please, let them be distinctly different men.

If she and John were brother and sister, what would she do? She couldn't go on living with him. It was too horrible to bear thinking about.

Now she had to face him. But harboring such conflicting thoughts, could she act naturally around him?

He'd want to make love!

Her pulse pounded in her ears. Her parched mouth wouldn't even produce enough saliva to let her swallow. All her life she'd heard and read about people's hearts breaking, but she never understood what that meant until now.

Her reluctant, slow steps took her closer to the man she'd loved for more than thirty years. Closer to her destiny.

He smiled his shy, lopsided smile and stretched his arms wide to fold her inside.

Hesitant steps brought her nearer and nearer.

"Hi, sweetheart. Welcome home." He bent to kiss her but she turned her cheek to him.

"Hi, John."

He dropped his arms and studied her face, a puzzled expression furrowing his brow. "Tough trip? You look beat. Come on home. You can get some rest before the big party tonight." He picked up her luggage and she followed him out to the parking lot.

The journey home in the car seemed interminable and more uncomfortable than she had expected. Her mind raced but she couldn't think what to say to him." Uh...how did the unveiling ceremony go?"

"Oh great! But I wish you had been there. I got an award for my design." He flashed her a smile then turned back to watch the road.

"That's wonderful! Congratulations!"

"Yeah, and a sizeable bonus too. I thought, since our trip to England got messed up, we could use the bonus money to take a cruise. How would you like that? Perhaps in the fall?"

"Sure." *Oh God, this is hard.*

"Barb, what's wrong, honey?" He glanced at her again.

"Nothing. I'm just tired." *Liar, liar. You're not too tired to keep thinking he's your brother.*

Somehow she made it through the journey to their home without totally breaking down. The car pulled into the garage and Tigger bounded up, barking excitedly. She stooped and hugged the dog, glad of the diversion but feeling guilty because she was giving the dog more of a greeting than she'd given to her husband. *Oh, poor John! He doesn't even know why he's being treated so coldly.* She released the dog and stood.

"I think I'll go straight to bed and shower when I get up."

"Good idea. You'll feel a whole lot better after some sleep." He carried her luggage to the bedroom and left her.

Later he came and tucked the blankets around her shoulders. She feigned sleep and heard the door click as he closed it behind him. Physical and emotional exhaustion finally overcame her. She closed her eyes.

"Barb, wake up, honey."

She smelled fresh coffee and forced her eyes open. John sat on the edge of the bed holding a steaming cup.

"Is that for me? Oh, thank you. What time is it?"

He told her. She'd been asleep for five hours.

She sipped the coffee and put the cup on the nightstand beside her. John reached for her and his mouth crushed her lips before she could stop him.

She struggled to free herself. "I need to get a shower and get something done to my hair before tonight." He looked so hurt she wished she'd stayed in England. One thing was for sure. She couldn't keep evading him much longer. If she could hold him off until after the party he'd go through the celebration ignorant. And her children wouldn't have to be embarrassed.

"Oh, I forgot to ask. Did you pick up the mail today?" Their mail wasn't delivered to their home so someone had to go to the post office each day and check the box.

"No, I forgot with all the excitement of you coming home. There's probably nothing but bills and junk anyway."

"Well, perhaps Donald could stop by on his way to the party and check. Would you call him and ask, please?"

"You expecting something important?"

"Yes, a certificate from England." *It could be the most important piece of mail of our lives.*

All day she managed to evade him, but she could tell John was becoming more and more resentful. He would never create a scene in public, so she was sure he'd control his anger until after the party. Then, she knew, she would have to confront him.

It was a relief to arrive at the hotel ballroom and find her children and grandchildren had already arrived. They rushed to greet her in a noisy, exuberant welcome home.

Barbara congratulated Janet on her new slim figure so soon after the baby's arrival, and admired Chris' new hairstyle. She hugged and kissed Jack and went from one grandchild to another fussing over them and remarking on how much they'd grown while she'd been away. It was all a ruse and she knew it. Pretending everything was normal and wonderful made her ashamed of herself.

She looked around. "Is Donald here? I haven't seen him." Donald was notorious for showing up to functions late and, true to form, hadn't arrived yet.

Little Laurie, in an aqua dress that matched her eyes, made Barbara's stomach lurch. This must have been what Lyn looked like as a child. The resemblance between her granddaughter and the photograph of her mother was uncanny. Outside the circle of family, John caught her gaze. He looked stricken and bewildered. *He doesn't understand why I've been dodging him all day.*

"Nanny, Nanny!" Her grandson grabbed her around the knees. "I've got a new puppy!"

Barbara welcomed the diversion. "Oh, Michael, how wonderful! What's his name?"

"It's a her and she doesn't have one yet. Will you come and see her tomorrow?"

She promised, and the little boy ran off to spread the news.

The three-piece band started warming up. The first guests drifted through the door and Barbara was relieved to have another diversion as she greeted friends. John shook hands and accepted congratulations on their thirty-year milestone.

Barbara wandered around greeting old friends and offering her cheek to be kissed as they wished her thirty more glorious years.

If they only knew.

"I love your dress," said one woman.

"Thank you." Barbara smiled. She knew the chiffon over silk was kind to her figure and the misty-blue color enhanced her eyes and her dark coppery hair.

Across the room, John, elegant in a dark blue suit, raised his glass to her in a salute. She raised hers in return. He smiled, the same lopsided smile she had loved the first time they'd met. She knew it so well, but tonight it tugged at her heart, and she could hardly breathe. She couldn't help it; brother or not, she adored him.

A couple dancing past called out a greeting. She waved to them and wandered toward the buffet. Janet had outdone herself with the array of food, and Chris' decorations and flower arrangements were beautiful. But her daughter-in-law would never turn out anything that wasn't first rate. She was so proud of her children for even thinking to put on such a celebration.

Two fat women that she knew from the local genealogical society were filling up their plates at the buffet table. Barbara stopped to thank them for coming to the party.

"Wouldn't have missed it for the world. It's a great party." The woman was large and had a voice to match.

"How was your vacation in England, Barb?" The second woman's voice was only a decibel lower.

"Great, thanks." Barbara turned to leave.

"Lucky you. I wish I could go to England and do research. You must have found a lot of good genealogy stuff you were gone so long."

The first woman had stuffed her mouth but managed to speak through the food. "I'll bet she found an old boyfriend," she cackled. "Isn't that right, Barb?"

John walked towards her and she could tell by his face that he'd heard. She wondered if that thought had already crossed his mind.

Oh, John, nothing could be further from the truth.

He came up beside her and stood with his arm around her waist.

"Ladies and gentlemen." Jack's clear, firm voice caught the crowd's attention. She turned to see her first born standing on the small stage at the end of the ballroom. The older he got the more he resembled John. He had the same bearing and quiet, commanding manner. "May I have your attention, please?"

He raised his glass and flashed a wonderful smile toward Barbara and John. "I'd like to propose a toast to my mom and dad, who have always exemplified what a real marriage should be." Everyone raised their glasses and made wonderful touching remarks.

Barbara's stomach churned. She tried to smile, but her face seemed like a block of wood and her muscles wouldn't cooperate to turn up the edges of her mouth. *Oh, my poor, dear children. And what will our friends say when they find out that John and I are brother and sister?*

"Mom." Donald startled her. "Hi, welcome home. Happy anniversary." He wrapped her in a bear hug. "I stopped and got your mail. I brought this over because it looked important." He handed her an official-looking envelope with stamps and stickers all over it. Across the top, it bore the printing *On Her Majesty's Service* and the return address of *The Registrar General, London.* Barbara's heart jumped.

"Excuse me." She grasped the envelope out of Donald's hand. The women and her son gaped at her, and John's eyes widened in a stunned expression. Barbara turned from them and ran.

She ducked into a side room and, with trembling hands, tore open the envelope.

Oh God, she prayed, *please let this be the answer. Let it be settled once and for all. Please, don't let John be my brother.*

Her breath came in short gasps as she fumbled with the paper until finally, she held her parents' marriage certificate in her palsied hands. She deliberately forced her eyes to the name of the bride's father. John C. Hayes. His occupation had been given as Master Tobacconist.

She closed her eyes and let out a long breath. Her whole body suddenly seemed to deflate. She leaned against the wall for support. Her knees turned to jelly.

The names didn't match.

John's maternal grandfather had been George Victor Hayes, a carpenter by occupation.

Carefully she folded the paper and returned it to the torn envelope, crushing it to her chest while she said a silent prayer of thanksgiving.

"Barb? Are you okay, honey?" John, gentle and caring as ever, came up behind her and gently placed his hands on her shoulders. He turned her to face him "What's wrong, Barb?" He showed no anger for her cold and erratic behavior, only love and concern.

She locked her arms around his neck. "Nothing is wrong. Everything is just fine. Oh, John, I do love you so much more than I can ever tell you." She kissed him with such passion he pulled away and gaped at her.

"Wow! I guess you are okay. More than okay! And may I say, you look absolutely gorgeous tonight, Mrs. M."

"Thank you, kind sir." She bobbed a little curtsey as she offered him the envelope. "Would you put this in your pocket for me?"

"What is it?"

She avoided answering by kissing him briefly on the cheek

He only glanced at the envelope before he tucked it away and reached into his other pocket. He pulled out the velvet box and handed it to her.

"Happy anniversary, my darling. I hope the years have been as happy for you as they have for me."

She opened the box and gasped.

John stepped behind her and fastened the necklace, then turned her to face him. "Hey, no! No tears. You'll spoil your make-up." He took out his handkerchief and dabbed away the puddles in the corners of her eyes.

"Happy anniversary, John, my love." She kissed him. "I didn't bring you a present nearly as wonderful as this gorgeous necklace."

"You brought me something better. Yourself." He hugged her to him and kissed her forehead.

She hooked her arm through his and they turned to rejoin to the celebration.

At the doorway to the ballroom, he suddenly stopped. "We sure have good-looking kids." He inclined his head in the direction of their three children posing for a photograph. "Jan reminds me so much of my mother."

"What? I thought you couldn't remember her?"

"I couldn't. But Jan is about the age I last saw my mum, and seeing her brings back the image of my mother. It was particularly evident tonight when she held Laurie. Jan's dark hair and Laurie's fiery red hair, reminded me of my mum holding Babs."

"Your mother had dark hair?" Barbara's mouth opened involuntarily. "You never told me that."

"Sure. I get my coloring from her."

"And your sister's hair was bright red, not dark like mine?"

"That's right."

Barbara gaped at her husband in utter astonishment. She'd been through hell and all the time he had the answers. What a fool she was not to confide in him right from the start.

As they entered the room arm in arm, loud applause broke out, and the band began playing the anniversary waltz. "Shall we?" John said.

"You're asking me to dance?" She grinned at him, incredulous.

"Sure, if you'll help me count in time to the music."

Seeing the familiar lopsided grin, she tossed her head at him. "I've heard that line before. You Yanks are all alike—sweet-talking—shower a girl with diamonds and pearls." She leaned towards him and whispered in his ear. "When all you really want is to get into her knickers."

He threw back is head and roared with laughter. "Yeah, but will you still fall for it?"

"That depends."

"On what? I've given you diamonds and pearls."

"How about a promise that you'll come with me the next time I go to England?"

"You're shameless." He grinned. "Still, I guess I'm safe since you said you didn't have plans for another vacation there. Okay, I promise."

"Great. Because I have to go back in a few months to testify in a murder trial."

"A what?" He stood completely still. "Geez, Barb. What the hell did you get involved in over there?"

"Murder was only part of it. Wait till you hear what else I have to tell you."

"As long as you weren't the murderer, can it wait until tomorrow? I sort of had other plans for us tonight after this bash." He tightened his arm around her waist.

His lopsided grin still had the same affect on her. Her feet touched the ballroom floor, but her spirit floated as light as dandelion fluff. "I had the same thoughts. Come on, Johnny-Boy, let's dance."

THE END